# THE LAST WIZARD

## SIMON HAWKE

D0451495

**WARNER BOOKS**

A Time Warner Company

WARNER BOOKS EDITION

Cover design by Don Puckey
Cover illustration by Donato

Aspect is a registered trademark of Warner Books, Inc.

Warner Books, Inc.
1271 Avenue of the Americas
New York, NY 10020

Visit our Web site at
http://warnerbooks.com

Ⓦ A Time Warner Company

Printed in the United States of America

First Warner Books Printing: October, 1997

10 9 8 7 6 5 4 3 2 1

# Prologue

The heat of the Sonoran Desert in July took him back over two thousand years. It brought back memories of a time when he stood in a white robe and feathered headdress, obsidian dagger poised over the heart of a sacrificial victim while worshipers numbering in the tens of thousands stood at the base of the pyramid, chanting his name. Well, one of his names, at any rate. He'd had more than a few.

The temperature in Tucson was over a hundred and ten degrees. Beladon felt it hit him like a blast from a furnace as soon as he stepped out of the air-conditioned airport building. Clearly, he was overdressed for this climate in his custom-tailored three-piece suit. He'd left New York in something of a hurry and there hadn't been even time to pack a bag, much less change his wardrobe. There was nothing like a BOT agent splattered on the sidewalk after a thirty-story fall to draw unwanted attention.

The Bureau of Thaumaturgy would be out for blood now, aided by the ITC, the FBI, and Interpol, as well as every local police agency from New York to Los Angeles. Still, they were the least of his concerns. The International Thaumaturgical Commission could be troublesome, for they employed some of the world's most powerful adepts, but the avatars remained the greatest danger. Calador and Delana had both made the mistake of underestimating them and they had paid for it with their lives.

Beladon relaxed in the back of the air-conditioned limo as it skimmed about two feet above the surface of the road. The driver had been waiting for someone else, but Beladon had commandeered him as soon as he'd spotted the long white vehicle. The human driver sat up front with no will of his own as he piloted the car, relying on a thaumaturgic battery charged with a spell of levitation and impulsion. When he returned, he would have no memory of anything that happened. He would feel strangely compelled to drive to a bar and proceed to drink himself into a stupor. He would probably lose his job as a result, but then he would retain his life and never know how close he came to losing it. Killing him would attract attention and Beladon wasn't ready for that yet.

They drove from the airport, headed west over the Tucson Mountains and then out into the desert, leaving behind the sprawling city in the valley. They passed several suburban developments, bedroom communities for the city of Tucson, then continued into the rural countryside, roughly forty miles from the Mexican border. The land here was mostly flat, with mountains rising in the distance. Thorny mesquite trees, blue-green palo verde, desert broom, yucca, and dry desert grass grew in profusion, interspersed with large agave plants and many different types of cacti—barrel, cholla, prickly pear, and the occasional majestic, multi-armed saguaro, some of which grew as tall as sixty feet and lived as long as 250 years. The bizarre-looking ocotillo plants, with their slender, multiple, spiny branches up to twenty feet long, made him think of squid with their heads buried in the ground and their tentacles reaching toward the sky. It was strange, alien-looking country, teeming with jackrabbits, deer, coyotes, turkey buzzards, javelina, scorpions, tarantulas, and rattlesnakes. It might almost have been another world.

He could soon see the site of the old Kitt Peak National Observatory as the limo approached Dragon Peak. Located roughly sixty miles from Tucson, the old observatory had been closed down and the mountain had been renamed when it passed into private ownership. As they reached the winding road that led to the summit, Beladon saw a large sign warning trespassers they were entering the grounds of the Dragon Peak Enclave at their own risk. If the sign was not sufficient to deter unwanted visitors, the huge walls built of thick, stuccoed concrete provided added emphasis. They were built not so much to keep people out as to keep something else in. Something large. As the limo passed through the gate, it skimmed over what appeared to be a wide steel cattle guard, except there was another sign warning visitors to remain in their vehicles, because it was electrified with very high voltage.

Halfway up the mountain, Beladon saw his first dragon. It was crossing the dirt road ahead of them and stopped to peer briefly at the approaching limo. Beladon leaned forward and touched the driver lightly on the shoulder, telling him to stop. As the limo hovered in place, Beladon gazed through the windshield at the creature on the road ahead of them.

It was about twenty-five feet long from its wedge-shaped head to the tip of its barbed tail, with thick stubby legs ending in large claws. Its skin was mottled black and red, pebbled-grained, and its leathery, batlike wings were folded back. The wings were nonfunctional, of course. They could never have lifted such a heavy creature off the ground. Its body was about the size of a large cow. The huge lizard flicked its long tongue out several times, then lost interest in the limo and disappeared into the scrub brush.

"Drive on," said Beladon, leaning back, and the limo glided forward once again.

The summit of the mountain had been leveled off many years earlier, when the observatory had been built. The old observatory buildings still stood within the walled enclave, but the astronomical equipment had long since been removed. The dilapidated housing originally built for the observatory staff had been renovated as residences for members of the enclave, some of whom could be seen tending the gardens and wandering about the grounds, dressed in simple white linen robes embroidered with southwestern patterns.

They were mostly young people, well-scrubbed bohemian types, though a few were older, in their late twenties and early thirties. The limo pulled up in front of a relatively new construction, an authentic-looking, baroque Spanish mission with thick, whitewashed adobe walls, towers, and a belfry. Beladon noted with some amusement the statues of Our Lady of Guadalupe and the missionary Padre Kino on either side of the arched, ornately carved front doors. Talon was not above a little sacrilege for the sake of appearances. But then, why should he care? After all, he predated Christianity.

He stepped out into the fierce heat, though it was somewhat cooler at this elevation, which afforded a panoramic view of the surrounding countryside. He dismissed the limo driver. As the long white Cadillac glided off, a pretty, dark-haired girl dressed in a white robe and sandals approached him. There was a small gold ring in her nose and another in her eyebrow. "May I help you, sir?" she asked.

"I am here to see Talon," he replied.

"Is Brother Talon expecting you?" she asked.

"Brother Talon?" He smiled. "Oh, I imagine he has been expecting me for quite some time."

"I see. Well, come this way, please."

She led him through the doors into the mission. The authenticity was carried through in the interior with wooden, Spanish-style pews arranged in rows beneath the vaulted ceiling of the cruciform structure. The baroque altar and pulpit were intricately carved. Wood statues of saints had been dressed in embroidered satin robes and placed in niches above stands for votive candles. A figure dressed in a long white hooded robe belted with a braided red cord stood with his back to them, at the altar. As Beladon came down the aisle with the girl, the figure turned and faced them. Beladon could not repress a smile. Talon always had a flair for the dramatic. He had known he was coming, of course. He would have felt it.

"Brother Talon," said Beladon with a slight touch of sarcasm. "How good to see you once again."

"Beladon," said Talon with a smile. "I have been expecting you. Thank you, Sister Maria. You may leave us."

The girl turned and left without a word.

"Should I genuflect?" asked Beladon wryly.

"Oh, we don't stand on that sort of formal ceremony here," said Talon offhandedly. "We are all brothers and sisters of the order."

"Indeed? And what order would that be?"

"The Order of Universal Spiritual Unity," said Talon, with a perfectly straight face.

Beladon raised his eyebrows. "Catholic?"

"Nonsectarian. We welcome all religious persuasions, so long as they are in accord with our designs, seek the peace of spiritual contemplation, and foster stewardship of our environment and the protection of our friends, the lesser creatures of the Earth."

Beladon chuckled. "Yes, I believe I saw one of those 'lesser creatures' on my way up here. It appeared in little need of protection."

"Ah, but that's where you're wrong, you see," Talon replied, coming toward him. "The dragons are an endangered species."

"You're joking."

"No, it's the truth."

Talon led him out a side door and through a garden courtyard to a white-stuccoed, Santa Fe–style house with red glazed tile trim. The courtyard was attractively laid with red brick in a crisscrossing pattern and a fountain burbled gently in the center. Shade was provided by two spreading acacia trees with stone benches placed beneath them. It was a comfortable and peaceful setting, very quiet and serene.

"Some years back, dragons were all the rage in this part of the country," Talon continued as they crossed the small courtyard. "A local thaumagenetics firm was turning them out, basing their designs on genetic material from chuckwallas, iguanas, gila monsters, and various other local species of lizard. People bought them by the score as cute little pets. The company had plans to market them nationally, but the plans fell through when it turned out their thaumagenetic engineering was a little sloppy. They were too mindful of the profit margin, apparently, and didn't hire the best people. Not a good idea when you're mixing magic with genetic engineering. The cute little creatures grew at a rather alarming rate, contrary to all expectations, and had a habit of consuming dogs and cats and the occasional small child."

"That could tend to raise problems with the neighbors," said Beladon.

"People started releasing them in the desert," Talon continued, "where they grew even larger and started to reproduce, which resulted in some rather serious charges being brought against the company that manufactured them. By law, thaumagenes are supposed to be incapable of reproduction. Only about ten percent of the dragons turned out to be fertile, but in the desert they thrived on jackrabbits, wild pigs, deer, and, as they grew larger, livestock. The ranchers were understandably upset, so they started organizing hunts with large-bore rifles. It takes at least a .375 to knock one of those beasts down. It was quite a popular sport for a while, until the environmentalists got wind of it. They demonstrated and lobbied to have the dragons protected as an endangered species. They eventually succeeded, but by then there were fewer than about a hundred dragons left. Once they reach their full maturity, they can't hide very well in this country and they make fairly easy targets."

"So you established a preserve for them," said Beladon, as they entered the house through a covered and tiled entrance portal.

"We have about fifty of them at present," Talon replied. "By now they're about all that's left. There may still be a few out in the wild, but if any of them are spotted, we'll receive a call to go out and pick them up. We use custom-made, high-powered tranquilizer darts, nets, specially designed forklifts, and a flatbed truck."

"No magic?" Beladon asked, raising his eyebrows.

"It would be easier," admitted Talon, "but then hiring adepts to do the work can be rather expensive. And I prefer to keep a low profile myself where that's concerned. No one knows that I am an adept. Periodically, we conduct guided tours, for which we charge a small fee to help maintain the preserve. We're also funded by several environmental groups and we're tax-exempt as a religious order. In the latter capacity, we do court-referred drug counseling and rehabilitation for young people with criminal records of violent behavior, for which we receive additional funding from various local and federal agencies. Sister Maria, for example, is a former prostitute with a record of over a dozen violent assaults and numerous counts of drug possession. All told, the funding we receive does not amount to a great deal of money, but it's enough to support our simple lifestyle."

Beladon looked around the interior of the house. It was designed on an open plan, making optimum use of space. The floors were handmade Mexican saltillo tile sealed with linseed oil, the walls were painted a light cream, and the fireplace was a beehive kiva style, with two built-in masonry ledges designed as shelves to hold an antique wooden crucifix and several votive candles. The furnishings were mission-style—a couch and several chairs, a table and two benches, bookshelves, some lamps made from ceramic jars. There were a couple of woven Navajo rugs on the floor and several plants in large ceramic pots. The heat outside was kept at bay by the thick walls and an evaporative cooler.

"Simple and austere," said Beladon, looking around. "An almost monastic existence, no pun intended. Have you gone human on me, Talon?"

"*I?*" said Talon, pulling back his hood to reveal thick, flaming red hair down to his shoulders; handsome, angular features; coppery skin; and bright, emerald green eyes. He grinned, displaying even, perfect teeth. "You're the one who's turned his hair dark and altered the color of his eyes."

"Contact lenses and hair dye," Beladon replied. "A necessary expedient. Somewhat uncomfortable, but not as energy-depleting as a spell. Nor as detectable to adepts. The authorities were on the watch for a tall man with red hair and green eyes."

"Yes, I heard," said Talon. "We are not so isolated that we fail to get the news here." He indicated a wooden cabinet containing a television set. "A rather messy business, the death of that BOT agent. I thought you would have been somewhat more restrained."

"I didn't kill him," Beladon replied. "It was a suicide. He threw himself out of a thirty-story window. He did it to escape me, but the fact remains that I was not directly responsible for his death. I wanted him alive. However, I doubt the Bureau would appreciate that fine distinction."

"And so you came to me," said Talon with a faint smile. He sat in one of the chairs and Beladon took the couch. "I trust you were careful and discreet."

"Of course. I must admit, however, that I had hoped to see you under somewhat different circumstances," Beladon replied.

"No doubt. You would have preferred coming as master rather than as supplicant. It must have stung your pride."

"Practical considerations prevailed," Beladon replied. "The avatars are strong. Much too strong for any one of us. In New York, we were three and still we failed, though I cannot entirely accept the blame for that. Calador and Delana shared a good part of the responsibility."

"I assume they're dead."

"Very."

"Pity. Had they listened to me, they might still be alive."

"And living in quiet seclusion on a mountaintop in the middle of the desert, supported by the charity of humans?" Beladon indicated their surroundings with a casual sweep of his hand. "After all those years of being imprisoned, I had a rather different vision of our return."

"Yes, I know," said Talon. "But times have changed. You cannot expect the humans to stay the same over a period of several thousand years."

"No. I realize they have evolved and become much more sophisticated. However, at heart they are still the same. They can still be ruled by fear."

"Not anymore," said Talon. "They can be made to feel fear, especially on an individual basis, but when enough of them grow frightened, they band together and become dangerously stubborn. And with the technology they have developed, coupled with their newfound use of magic, they can be far more efficient in their resistance than in the old days."

"Granted, but they are still inferior."

"They are *different*," Talon said. "Weaker, mortal, but not necessarily inferior. Not anymore. They have had over two thousand years to grow and change while we have remained the same."

Beladon gave a contemptuous snort. "I may have made a mistake in coming here. It seems you have given up and gone into hiding."

"As always, Beladon, you are much too quick to judge," said Talon. "In the old days, my opinions were frequently dismissed because I was the youngest, but if you can remember that far back, what did I say about the Old Ones who first spoke about the need for change?"

"I remember. You said they would unite and crush us if we resisted," Beladon replied dryly. "I concede that you were right about that. I can scarcely argue the point after being entombed for over two millennia. We had grown complacent. We were not prepared. We were not strong enough."

"Only because we did not try to unite our strength until it was too late," said Talon. "None of the others ever regarded the Council of the White as a serious threat. They were all too busy competing against one another. That was the essential difference between the Council and ourselves. They knew how to work together. We dismissed them as a bunch of Old Ones who had gone weak and sentimental with age. We were the Dark Ones, arrogant in our pride and obstinate in our adherence to the old ways. What we never understood, and what the Old Ones did, was the true nature of power. It is a force that feeds upon itself. The more you have, the more you need. It becomes a vicious circle from which there is only one path of escape. The path of discipline and moderation. The Old Ones realized that. We never did. In that sense, you are right. We were not strong enough."

"So how does all this fit into your enlightened realization?" asked Beladon as he glanced around him. "Hiding in a mountaintop retreat, playing at being a human monk with an environmental awareness and a social conscience. . . . Do you seriously hope to convince the avatars that you've reformed in the event they find you? Sooner or later, they will, you know. I did."

"Only because I let you," Talon replied. "Had I truly wished to hide, you never would have found me. There is rather more to this place than meets the eye. Observe . . ."

Talon made a languid pass with his hands and the floor began to open up. The hard saltillo tiles seemed to liquefy as they rippled and flowed, melting back to create a circular opening that grew wider and wider until it was at least eight feet across. Beladon glanced into the opening and saw a stone stairway leading down into the darkness.

Talon cocked his head and indicated the opening in the floor. "After you."

"You first," Beladon replied cautiously.

Talon smiled. "Don't you trust me?"

"Frankly, no."

"And yet, it was you who came to me," said Talon, gesturing from Beladon to himself.

"I had little choice. Alone against the avatars, I stand no chance. And neither do you. They shall hunt us down, relentlessly. They must, for they know that given the opportunity to grow strong enough, it is we who shall hunt them. We cannot afford our old rivalries, Talon. We must work together, as they do."

"But that is just what I have always said," Talon replied.

"In the old days, yes. But as you said, times have changed. And so have you, apparently. I find you in retreat upon a desert mountaintop, cloistered with the dregs of humanity and cloaked with their religious symbols. I remain committed to the old ways, however, and have yet to be convinced that does not make me a threat to you."

"Well, in that case, prepare to be convinced." Talon got up and descended the stone stairs. Beladon followed. Behind them, the floor sealed itself up once again and they were plunged into total darkness.

A moment later, torches blazed up in black iron sconces set into the rough, irregular rock walls. Their voices and footsteps echoed in the cool passageway as they moved down the long, curving stairs.

"Where does this lead?" asked Beladon. "Some sort of old government installation?"

"That would have been convenient, but there would have been a record of that somewhere and it would not have served my purposes," Talon replied as they continued down the narrow, spiraling passageway. "No, I excavated this tunnel myself."

"You?" Beladon was surprised. That would have required a considerable expenditure of energy. "Where did you gain the power?"

"From the people of the enclave," Talon said. "And to anticipate your next question, no, I did not kill any of them. That would have drawn suspicion. There would have been concerned inquiries from relatives, investigations by officers of the court, bureaucrats, police, and so forth. Killing humans can be rather complicated these days, as you have already discovered. Instead, I merely drained off some of their life force. It was fairly simple to make it look like a flu epidemic. They were sick for several weeks, but they all recovered. You might say I borrowed the methods of the Council from the old days. How did they put it . . . conserving the human resource? Within certain limitations, humans are not only more useful when their life energy is allowed to remain, they also develop a dependency. If they are kept in a slightly weakened state, they become much more docile and easier to manage."

"I see," said Beladon. "But then you are still faced with the same problem that led to our break with the Council all those years ago."

"True," said Talon. "Pure necromancy requires the complete consumption of life force. It is that last essential spark of life that provides the necessary energy to fuel the more ambitious spells and imbues the adept with greater strength. I have still not found any way around that. However, survival requires adaptation. That is something the humans have learned well. As I said, they have become a great deal more sophisticated, but that merely requires a variation of approach in dealing with them. If you try controlling them by fear, as we did in the old days, then eventually the point will come when they rebel. Yet for all the progress they have made, they still have a yearning for spiritual understanding.

They still want their gods, in other words, or God, as the case may be. And that desire can be exploited. Instead of controlling them with fear, I offer greater understanding."

"So then you have become a priest," said Beladon with a snort.

"Well, in a manner of speaking, I suppose I have," Talon replied. "A high priest. It is a role that we have played before. You must admit it has its uses. Humans were always fond of ritual. In that respect, they have not changed. However far they may fall from their spiritual traditions, those traditions still remain a part of their experience. It does not take much to bring them out once more."

"Brother Talon, shepherd to his flock of sheep," said Beladon dryly.

"Have your methods brought you further?" Talon countered.

"They would have, if Calador and Delana had done their part and followed my orders. And if those cursed avatars hadn't interfered."

"You knew about the avatars," said Talon. "And blaming others for the failure of your plans, whether the blame is justified or not, does not change the end result. You and the others were always too impatient, Beladon. However, I will grant you that you were not so narrow-minded as the rest. You, at least, had the wisdom to recognize that you required my help."

Before long, they came to the bottom of the flight of stairs, which opened out into a large cavern. Beladon stopped and stared. Thick stalagmites stood like sentinels, reaching high above his head, and stalactites of equal size hung from the ceiling, some of them joining the stalagmites below to form massive columns that tapered at the middle. Shimmering crystals veined the rock walls and the sound of an underground spring burbled gently as it emptied into a subterranean pool in the middle of the cavern.

However, what drew his gaze was the massive altar built

upon a natural stone outcropping just behind the pool. A ledge projected a short distance out over the water, providing a natural stage or pulpit. A stone arch spanning the pool functioned as a bridge to the altar, which was surmounted by a formation of large quartz crystals resembling organ pipes. It was beautiful, but at the same time, rather unsettling. It reminded Beladon too much of the underground cavern in the Euphrates Valley where they had been entombed by the Old Ones of the Council. But for a chance discovery by an archaeological expedition, they might still be there.

"This is a natural cavern, millions of years old, as you can tell by the formations," Talon said, apparently undisturbed by the similarity to their old place of confinement. "So far as I can tell, no one ever knew it was here. I detected it, tunneled down to it, and immediately realized its potential. The mission on the surface functions as the spiritual center for the general population of the enclave, but this is where I bring my select initiates."

"Initiates?" asked Beladon with a frown.

"Those who possess the latent ability for magic use," said Talon. "They don't all get spotted in the Bureau screening tests, you know. A lot of them wind up falling through the cracks of the system, particularly those from lower income groups who drop out of school early. Also, the Bureau's tests are not infallible, by any means. They usually reveal those with a strong latent potential, but not always, and borderline cases are often not spotted. And I hate to see potential go to waste."

"You mean to say you *teach* them necromancy?" Beladon said with disbelief.

"Why not?"

"Are you mad? They're humans!"

"Strictly speaking, the ones with the capability to use magic are not entirely human. They inherited that potential because somewhere in their distant past, one of us mated with one of their ancestors. For generations, that potential remained dormant in most of them, sometimes manifesting as what came to be called extrasensory perception or para-psychological abilities. In less enlightened times, it got many of them killed. It took a long time for their old fears to die. Granted, the strain became diluted over the years, so they will never grow as strong as we are, but breeding tells, as they say. It's a very dominant gene. Without us, there would have been no Bureau of Thaumaturgy or ITC. For that matter, there would have been no Merlin Ambrosius to return and usher in their age of magic."

"It's bad enough that Ambrosius taught them how to use white magic," Beladon said. "Now you propose to teach them necromancy? Give them even more power? They will only turn that knowledge against us!"

"Those are the old prejudices speaking," Talon replied. "We no longer have time for them. We are a dying race. And we have brought it on ourselves. Our rivalries resulted in a war that almost wiped us out and after the Council had imprisoned us, the humans proceeded to hunt down and exterminate the few survivors who remained. Once we ruled. Once we were their gods. Now we are little more than whispers in their folklore. Witches, demons, vampires, shape-shifters . . . that is what our legacy has become. We are the very last of our kind. And now they know about us, thanks largely to you. Perhaps the general human population doesn't know yet, but the ITC knows. And the Bureau knows. It will only be a matter of time before they all know. Now we have more than just the avatars to contend with. We have only three choices left. We can try to hide and pass as human, as many of the others tried to do before they were eventually wiped out. We can try facing them ourselves, against overwhelming odds. Or we can raise an army. An army of human necromancers. More powerful than the adepts they train and recruited from the ranks of human predators. What could be more ideal?"

"What makes you think they will remain loyal?" Beladon asked dubiously.

"Human nature," Talon replied with a smile. "Magic has made their lives much easier, but despite that, there are still many humans who distrust adepts. And those are adepts who use only the white magic that Ambrosius taught them. Imagine how they will react when confronted with true necromancy, magic that kills. My initiates will remain loyal because they will become addicted to their newfound power and want more. And because their fellow humans will hate and fear them for what they have become. The logic is simple. And the result is a new beginning. They will become our legacy. Our new acolytes. And we will not have to fight the avatars. They shall do it for us."

"There are a few things you have failed to consider," Beladon said. "For one thing, the avatars may be human, and therefore vulnerable, but they are possessed by the three runestones which hold the spirits of the Council. The avatars can be killed, but unless the runestones are also destroyed, they will merely find new hosts and new avatars will be created. Secondly, however strong your human necromancers may become, the avatars will always remain stronger, collectively and on an individual basis. It will take more than a mere handful of human acolytes to prevail against them, however well you train them. Especially since the avatars now have the backing of the Bureau and the ITC."

"Yes, and they would not have that backing now if it were not for your carelessness," said Talon. "By acting rashly, you and the others have made things a great deal more difficult than they had to be. Well, the others are all dead now. Which leaves only you and me."

"And you're going to need me if you hope to keep the avatars at bay while you train your human necromancers."

"Not necessarily," Talon replied offhandedly. Beladon tensed as he suddenly became aware of movement in the shadows of the cavern. Figures in hooded black robes appeared all around him, dozens of them. "You see, my plans are already well advanced. And while I do not really need you, I could certainly use your power."

Before he could react, Beladon was struck by a blinding beam of blue-white light that bathed him from head to toe and he found himself unable to move or utter a sound. The beam was coming from one of the large crystalline formations above the stone altar over the pool. The huge, faceted crystal was glowing brightly and as he watched, the crystals alongside it in the clustered formation also began to glow, becoming brighter and brighter as the thaumaturgic force beam held him in its grip. As the other crystals brightened, they became transparent and he could see dark forms within them. As the crystals grew brighter still, he could make out what those figures were and a chill ran through him.

"I see you recognize some of our old friends," said Talon, following his gaze toward the figures trapped inside the towering crystals. "As you can see, you were not the first to come and seek me out. But then, I was prepared for them, as I was prepared for you."

Talon had outsmarted him. He had the spell already prepared and instead of doing it himself, he had used his acolytes to trigger it. There had been no warning whatsoever.

"With Calador and Delana dead, and the others disposed of by the avatars, you were the last one left," said Talon. "Now we are all accounted for."

Beladon could see the expressions on their faces now as the light from the crystals filled the cavern. And he realized with horror that they were not dead. He recognized Vorstag, Adreia, Torvig, Zelena, Corvald, and the others who had managed to escape their tomb alive. Eight of them in all, not counting himself. All trapped inside the crystals, still alive, but barely . . . kept in a suspended state to feed Talon's power, which had grown greater than he could ever have anticipated.

"As I said, you and the others were always much too quick to judge," said Talon. "Too arrogant, too rash, and much too overconfident. You dismissed me all those years ago because I was the youngest and my opinions were not worthy of consideration. You were all older, stronger, more experienced. I was expected to keep my place. Well. How very embarrassing this must be for you."

Beladon tried his utmost to move, but he could not. He wanted to scream in rage and frustration, but he could not make a sound. Talon was drawing on the life force of the others trapped within the crystals to hold him absolutely immobile. There was nothing he could do. Nothing at all.

"Rather appropriate, don't you think, the way things have come full circle?" Talon said. "From a subterranean tomb inside a cavern in the Euphrates Valley to a tomb inside a cavern deep within a mountain in the Arizona desert. You have traveled from one side of the world to the other, only to wind up in the same place, figuratively speaking. I rather like the irony of that."

Fear struck Beladon as he realized there would be no escape. Not even in death. Talon would keep him imprisoned forever, just as the Old Ones of the Council had intended when they had entombed them deep within that underground pit all those centuries ago. He would be left with just enough life force to keep him alive, to enable Talon to draw upon his power, just as he was doing with the others even now. He would drain them almost to the very point of death, leaving them just enough strength to allow them to recover over a period of time, only to be drained again. And again, and again, and again. For centuries to come.

The beam of force lifted him off the ground and drew him, helpless, toward the crystal that was waiting for him. As he was drawn closer to the others, he could sense their mental cries of anguish as Talon drained them to empower the spell and further build up his own strength. The crystalline formation loomed before him and the beam inexorably pulled him in, to be trapped forever like a fly in amber, a renewable, living, tortured source of energy for Talon's spells. As he was pulled inside the crystal, he had a brief image of that BOT agent in New York, hurling himself out of a thirtieth-story window to escape him by plunging to his death. And Beladon envied him.

# **Chapter 1**

Sebastian Makepeace was not accustomed to traveling by limousine. He was even less accustomed to being accorded such VIP treatment by the ITC, whose official scrutiny he had always carefully avoided. The International Thaumaturgical Commission was the agency that administered and regulated magic use throughout the world and they employed the highest-ranking adepts in the profession, some of whom possessed among their talents the abilities of clairvoyance and clairsentience. It wasn't what they would see that used to worry Makepeace. It was what they wouldn't see. And in his case, they wouldn't see anything at all. And that would bother them. It would undoubtedly bother them enough to make them want to find out why.

Makepeace was used to people trying to dig into his past. His students did it all the time in attempts to prove that he was not, as he claimed to be, a fairy. Even in a time when magic had become commonplace, they still had difficulty accepting there was such a thing as a fairy outside the pages of the Brothers Grimm. Especially one that stood six feet six inches tall and weighed three hundred pounds. Once they stopped snickering at the idea, they usually set about trying to prove that Makepeace was as human as they were, albeit considerably more eccentric.

Makepeace did not discourage them. He liked to see his students developing their research skills and he enjoyed chuckling at their frustration when they discovered that while he held doctoral degrees in metaphysics and occult studies, as well as history and literature, there was no record of his ever having attended a graduate school of thaumaturgy. They were mystified when they could find no proof that he had ever formally studied magic anywhere, because he was as proficient at performing magic as any advanced-level adept.

Over the years, his past had become something of a *cause célèbre* among the students of New York University, and not only his students in the History and Metaphysics Departments. They would form byzantine research alliances with graduate students in the School of Thaumaturgy joining students in the Law School and the Department of Criminology in efforts to prove the colorful Professor Makepeace was merely an eccentric, amiable fraud. Except they couldn't. There was no proof that Makepeace was, in fact, a fairy. However, at the same time, there was no proof that he wasn't.

In a world where magic was not only alive, but afoot all over the damn place, they couldn't find a single documented instance of the existence of a fairy, whether it was a diminutive creature with gossamer wings or an apparently middle-aged man with shoulder-length white hair and the build of a linebacker. The general consensus among the students was that Makepeace was self-taught when it came to magic.

While officially discouraged, it was not illegal for people to study magic on their own. It was, however, rather dangerous, as public service announcements sponsored by the Bureau of Thaumaturgy on radio and television reminded people regularly. In some countries, the informal study of magic was a crime, but in the United States, with its constitutional traditions, freedom of information was a sword that cut two ways. The solution was not perfect, but it was typically American. One could study thaumaturgy without the benefit of a formal graduate program administered by licensed adepts, but one was also legally responsible for the potential consequences and it was illegal to practice it without a license. And while Makepeace could and did perform magic, he neither claimed to be an adept nor practiced the art professionally. Consequently, he had never fallen afoul of the Bureau of Thaumaturgy or the ITC.

However, while he found it amusing to have skeptical students trying to research his background and qualifications, having the ITC start looking into his past was something else entirely. Students could be very clever and persistent at doing research, but the ITC was downright scary. They had access to anything and everything. And there were certain things about his past that Makepeace did not want people looking into.

They were the kind of details that students, no matter how persistent, would never be able to unearth, but the ITC certainly could. Details such as his old connections with a certain secret government agency that had conducted the occasional assassination and toppled foreign governments every now and then. And then there were his connections with organized crime, which were rather tenuous at best, but nonetheless the sort of thing that could make academia extremely nervous and jeopardize his tenure.

And if the ITC really started digging, checking way back to his childhood on the Old Sod, there was a possibility they might even discover that Sebastian Makepeace was a name taken from a tombstone in a little country kirk in County Kerry, near St. Finan's Bay, the grave of a little Irish boy who had died about sixty years ago, at the age of four. And past that point, the trail would stop cold. And that would *really* bother them.

So Makepeace had always steered well clear of the ITC. A colorful and bombastic university professor who dressed like a stolen car, frequented the rebeat bars in the Village, and claimed to be a fairy was merely a charming and amusing old eccentric not to be taken very seriously. He was a prominent fixture on campus and in the Village arts and social scenes, but outside of those small and relatively insular worlds, no one had ever paid very much attention to him. Except now all that had changed and he was having a hard time getting used to it.

He was now on a first-name basis with the DA and the police commissioner. He could even get the attorney general or the director of the BOT on the phone. He had met the director of the FBI and the head of the NSA, as well as the chief of the Washington office of the ITC, and he had little doubt that by now his past had been researched about as thoroughly as possible. The curious thing was that it didn't seem to matter anymore, because now they had bigger things to worry about than a man whose paper trail ended at a tombstone.

The limo was passed through the security post at the gates of what used to be the United Nations complex overlooking the East River. It was now the New York headquarters of the International Thaumaturgical Commission. The tall glass Secretariat Building housed the offices of the ITC and the old General Assembly Building was where the Commission held its meetings. The car pulled up in front of the Secretariat Building and gently settled to the ground, then the driver came around to open the door for him.

Makepeace got some curious stares as he came through the revolving doors into the lobby. Though a few high-ranking adepts still wore traditional sorcerer's robes on occasion, most dressed rather conservatively these days. Retro pinstripes and power ties were the current vogue among the movers and shakers of the corporate world and Makepeace stood out among this crowd like a werewolf at the Vatican. His ankle-length black leather trench coat was open to reveal a suit of crushed black velvet with a black and orange paisley brocade vest, a white Oxford button-down shirt, a bright orange Flemish silk cravat, and a black beret. His rather large feet were shod in black retro All Stars high tops.

He paused as a marine noncom in full dress uniform approached him.

"Dr. Makepeace?" It was spoken as a question, but it wasn't. The guard knew who he was. "Good afternoon, sir. This way, please."

He was escorted to an elevator that differed from the others in the lobby in one significant respect. It had no call buttons. The guard spoke into his radio. "This is Sergeant McMullen, in the lobby. Dr. Makepeace has arrived."

The elevator doors opened.

"You may go up now, sir," the sergeant said.

"Thank you, Sergeant," Makepeace said. He stepped inside the elevator. There were no buttons on the inside, either. The doors closed and without any action on his part, the express elevator quickly took him to the penthouse, at one time the private residence of the UN secretary general. When the ITC took over, it was maintained as a temporary residence for visiting dignitaries. Recently, however, it had acquired new and permanent tenants.

The doors opened onto a small, carpeted lobby with several large plants in glazed ceramic containers on the floor. There were some tasteful abstract paintings hung on the beige-painted walls and the lobby was softly lit with indirect lighting. There was a brown leather upholstered sofa and several matching chairs, as well as a mahogany coffee table. It might have been the waiting room of a Park Avenue psychiatrist or a Fifth Avenue lawyer, except for the security desk with banks of monitors and four U.S. marines on duty in full dress uniform, complete with sidearms. Two of them were posted on either side of the double doors just beyond the security station, one stood by the elevator doors, and one was seated at the desk, behind the monitors. As soon as he saw them, Makepeace started to whistle "The Halls of Montezuma." The marines didn't smile.

"Good afternoon, Dr. Makepeace. We've been expecting you, sir. You can go right in."

"Aren't you going to search me, Master Sergeant?" Makepeace asked, checking the marine's insignia.

"No need, sir. You were x-rayed and T-scanned coming up in the elevator."

Makepeace frowned. "T-scanned?"

"Thaumaturgic trace scan, sir. Designed to check for trace emanations that would reveal magic."

"You don't say," said Makepeace. "And how did your T-scan read?"

"Off the scale, sir. We were warned to expect that in your case. Still, it was a bit unnerving."

"I didn't know a marine could be unnerved," said Makepeace, raising his eyebrows in mock surprise.

The master sergeant grinned. "You never heard it from me."

The marines by the double doors held them open for him as Makepeace entered the penthouse suite. He came into a small open foyer about ten feet wide. The spacious and airy living room was down three steps, with a kitchen and dining area to the right and bedrooms down a hallway to the left. The entire back wall of the living room was glass, probably bulletproof and spellwarded, with sliders opening out onto a rooftop patio garden. As Makepeace took it all in, an attractive, barefoot young brunette dressed in black jeans and a matching tank top came bounding toward him.

"Sebastian!" Kira said, as she gave him a big hug. "I'm so glad you came! How do you like our new place?"

"It's very nice," said Makepeace, "but a bit intimidating out there, with all those armed marines."

"You should see the gun emplacements on the rooftop," said John Angelo, formerly of the NYPD. Dark-haired and lean, with brown, sleepy-looking eyes, chiseled features, and a slightly drooping lip that gave the impression he was sneering, Angelo looked like a Brooklyn hood and dressed the part in handmade Italian loafers, silk socks, dark designer slacks and sport coat, and an open-necked black silk shirt revealing a gold crucifix on a chain around his neck.

"Gun emplacements?" Makepeace said. "You're joking."

"Four fifty-calibers, mounted in towers, one on each corner of the roof," said Angelo, handing him a cup of black coffee. "The air space is restricted over the entire complex. If a helicopter so much as breezes this joint, it gets shot down. These people are serious."

"I liked it a lot better when we were unofficial," Wyrdrune said, from his stretched-out position on the couch. He was dressed in his usual attire, faded jeans, a short brown warlock's cassock, white athletic socks, and red running shoes. His curly blond hair hung well below his slim shoulders and was held in place by a red bandana rolled up as a headband, which also served to conceal the emerald runestone embedded in the center of his forehead. "Can't even go out for pizza or a cappuccino anymore without a dozen bodyguards tagging along."

"Don't worry about it, kid," said Angelo. "People probably just think you're a rock star."

"Or maybe a major dope dealer," Kira said with a grin.

"Nah, a drug dealer would be better dressed," said Angelo.

"Yeah, like you," Wyrdrune replied.

"Hey, what's wrong with my clothes?" asked Angelo.

"Nothing, if you're a loan shark or a bookie," Wyrdrune replied.

"This from a guy who dresses like a walking thrift shop," Angelo said.

"I hate to interrupt this mutual admiration society," said Makepeace, "but can anyone tell me what was so important that I had to be pulled out of a class and brought here?"

"Your guess is as good as ours," said Kira. "We just got word this morning that a special briefing has been scheduled, but beyond that, we don't know anything. It's all very hush-hush."

"Where's Billy?" Makepeace asked.

"He went with the district chief to pick up Steve and Natasha," Kira said. "They should be back anytime. The briefing's scheduled for noon and it's about that now."

"You think perhaps Beladon has surfaced?" Makepeace asked.

"It's possible," said Wyrdrune. "If he has, things are going to get nasty real fast."

The memory of the last time they had encountered Beladon was all too fresh. Makepeace wasn't there when it began, but he knew all about it. The necromancer had managed to place a BOT agent under his spell and the possessed agent, along with his unsuspecting partner, had staged a massive raid on their penthouse in Sutton Place, only a few blocks away. Angelo, who had been working undercover for the DA's Organized Crime Task Force, had been commandeered for the raid while he was at the precinct checking through some case files. His role had been to provide a distraction while the SWAT team got into position. However, what neither Angelo nor any of the other cops who took part in the operation knew was that the raid was an elaborate cover for a necromantic hit.

They had been told the purpose of the raid was to take down a renegade adept named Michael Cornwall, who was holed up in the penthouse with his confederates. However, none of them had any way of knowing that "Michael Cornwall" was an alias for the immortal son of the legendary King Arthur and the sorceress Morgan le Fay.

By the time the smoke had cleared, two BOT agents were dead, Wyrdrune was in critical condition, and Angelo was in a coma, his life force almost completely drained. Things took an even stranger turn when Angelo abruptly and inexplicably recovered from his coma, walked right out of the hospital, and disappeared.

Confused and sharing fragments of both his own memories and Modred's from the runestone which had bonded with him, saving his life in the moments just after the attack, Angelo had been suffering from amnesia. He mistakenly believed his undercover identity from his work with the DA's special task force was real, but could not reconcile the thought of being a professional killer with his sense of ethics and morality. All the evidence he found—part of his elaborately constructed cover—kept pointing to his being a hit man for the mob. The crime family he had infiltrated as "Johnny Angel" knew there was a police informant in their midst . . . and they assigned the hit to "Johnny Angel." Meanwhile, Beladon was orchestrating a covert takeover of the mob, with an aim to distributing a lethal thaumagenetic drug known as Ambrosia to the city's population and then expanding nationally.

In time, the others found Angelo and helped him recover his memory completely, but not before Beladon had subverted yet another high-ranking Bureau agent and almost brought the city to its knees. It was only then that the authorities became aware of the threat that they were facing from a race of necromancers who had existed since the dawn of time.

Wyrdrune, Kira, and Billy Slade had up to that point been forced to wage their war against the Dark Ones without any support from the authorities, receiving help only from certain individuals in various police agencies throughout the world, such as Chief Inspector Michael Blood of Scotland Yard, Inspector Armand Renaud of the Paris police, and Captain Rebecca Farrell of the LAPD. Now, all that had changed. Instead of being hunted by the authorities, they were now aided by them. The ITC had provided them with top-security clearances and brand-new quarters in their New York headquarters, complete with around-the-clock protection.

"I know I probably should not complain," said Wyrdrune, "considering that when all this started, I was a down-and-out dropout from Thaumaturgy School without two cents to rub together, but sometimes I sure do wish that I could get my life back. It wasn't much . . . but at least it was mine."

"If you think we've got it tough, imagine what it must be like for Billy," Angelo said. "He's gone through a complete physical transformation as a result of merging with the life forces of Gorlois and Merlin. He's not even the same person anymore and probably never will be."

At that moment, the object of their conversation came walking through the door, accompanied by ITC district chief Bill McClellan, Police Commissioner Steve McGuire, and Natasha Ouspenskaya, better known as the Gypsy. Of the four, Billy and Natasha looked most striking. Billy Slade looked about nineteen and wore black leather pants with a metal-studded belt, snakeskin boots, and a white cotton shirt that laced up at the throat. He was an albino, with long, snow-white hair that hung down almost to the small of his back. He had not been born that way, however. He was an orphan from London's East End and had grown up in the streets, ignorant of his roots, which were clearly multi-ethnic. His complexion had been dark enough to give strong evidence of African ancestry, but his eyes looked Asian and there was probably some West Indian and Caucasian in there, too. It was the Caucasian part that proved the most significant, however, for he was descended from none other than the legendary Merlin Ambrosius, court wizard to King Arthur and father of the Second Thaumaturgic Age.

The flamboyant Natasha "Gypsy" Ouspenskaya rarely looked the same. On this occasion, her long hair was dyed black and silver and she wore a gray silk scarf around her head. Large gold hoops dangled from her ears and about a dozen amulets hung around her neck. She wore a red silk blouse with a black, silver-embroidered vest over it, a calf-length black cotton skirt, and high red leather boots with stacked heels. A profusion of bracelets jangled on her wrists and she wore rings on every finger save the thumbs.

By contrast, Steve McGuire and Bill McClellan looked

very sedate. The dark-haired police commissioner stood about five-ten and wore an off-the-rack dark suit, a white button-down shirt, a dark blue tie, and comfortable dress shoes. McClellan, the white-haired ITC district chief, stood over six feet tall and was dressed almost identically, except his suit was custom-made and his tie was a designer original, reminiscent of a painting by Picasso.

"Well, it looks as if everybody's here," said Billy as he entered. His accent still betrayed his Cockney roots, though there was a strong trace of Celtic in it, as well. He glanced at McClellan. "Now do we get to find out what this is all about?"

The bespectacled McClellan cleared his throat, but before he could reply, several things happened simultaneously. The doors behind them opened once again and several very serious-looking men in dark suits and headsets entered, quickly glancing all around the room. At the same time, any remarks McClellan might have made were drowned out by the loud, staccato clatter of helicopter blades as a military chopper landed on the roof. Moments later, the sliding doors leading out to the roof were opened by the Secret Service agents and the head of the National Security Agency came in, accompanied by several aides and the President of the United States.

As the whine of the helicopter motor outside on the roof diminished, the Secret Service agents took up position around the room, out of the way, but where they could see and cover everything and everyone. President O'Connor glanced around the room as Brian Wetterman, head of the NSA, performed the introductions. Makepeace and Billy had met Wetterman before, at a briefing arranged by the DA, who had gone to school with the attorney general. The director of the NSA stood six feet tall and weighed about two-fifty, but he was not an imposing-looking man. He wore glasses and his brown hair was cut short and neat. He looked like an engineer, or perhaps a computer technician. He had an amiable, casual manner that belied the importance of his position.

"My apologies for the rather sudden and clandestine nature of this briefing," he said, "but I'm sure you'll understand that since this is a matter of national security, we had to take special precautions. No one even knows the President is in New York. Officially, she is still conducting budget meetings at Camp David."

President Katherine O'Connor cordially shook hands with each of them and then settled down into a chair in a very businesslike manner. She crossed her slim, attractive legs and brushed a stray lock of her light brown hair back out of her face. "Please, everyone be seated," she said. "Before we get started, I believe I smell some fresh-brewed coffee. Do you suppose I could impose on you for a cup?"

"Broom!" said Wyrdrune.

"I'm coming, I'm coming, already! *Gevalt!* Such noise! You'd think this was Grand Central Station. If that *farshtinkener* helicopter landed on my petunias, somebody's going to hear about this, I'm telling you right now!"

"Oh, my goodness!" The President gaped as an ambulatory straw broom swept into the room, carrying a tray with coffee cups, a bowl of sugar, a creamer, and some spoons in its spindly, rubbery-looking arms. "What on earth is that?"

"A broom, Miss Hoity-Toity, what does it look like?" Broom replied. "And didn't your mother ever teach you that it was rude to stare?"

Wyrdrune groaned and rolled his eyes. "Broom . . . you're talking to the President."

"President, Director, Chairman, Doctor, Lawyer, District Chief . . . we've got more titles waltzing in and out of here lately than the public library," Broom replied, setting the tray down on the coffee table. "Use the coasters. President of what, if I may be so bold as to inquire?"

Wetterman cleared his throat slightly. "Of the United States," he said softly.

Broom turned toward him and seemed to notice the grim-faced Secret Service agents for the first time. Then it turned back toward the President, who was watching with a bemused smile. "*Oy!* Me and my big mouth! I really stuck my bristles into it this time. I meant no offense, Madame President, truly. Can you find it in your heart to forgive me?"

"Of course," the President replied. "No offense was taken. And I apologize for my inadvertent rudeness. You merely startled me, that's all."

"No, no, it was my fault entirely," Broom said. "I'm such a *putz,* you should excuse the expression. How do you take your coffee, Madame President?"

"Black with sugar, please."

"One lump or two?"

"Two."

"There you are. And would you like some halvah, maybe? A nice prune danish?"

"No, thank you, just the coffee will be fine."

"You're sure? I could whip you up a nice cheese omelet. Some raisin toast, a bran muffin, perhaps?"

"No, thank you, really, this is fine."

"You should eat something, really. Look at you, such a little thing, all skin and bones. Besides, you really shouldn't drink coffee on an empty stomach—"

"*Broom* . . ." said Wyrdrune.

"All right, all right, so sue me because I care!" the Broom said, shuffling out of the room. "If the President gets acid stomach, don't go blaming me!"

The President giggled. "I've never seen anything like that!" she said, delighted. "How does it talk?"

Wyrdrune sighed heavily. "I haven't the faintest idea. It was one of my first spells when I was an undergraduate and I don't recall exactly what I did. I animated it for my mother to help her around the house and being around her all the time resulted in Broom becoming imprinted with her personality. When she passed away, the lawyers brought it over and I've been stuck with it ever since."

"Well, I think it's rather charming," said the President. "However, we really should get down to business." Her demeanor became serious as she glanced at Wetterman. "The director has briefed me on the general situation, but it sounded so incredible I wanted to hear it from you for myself. And, under the circumstances, since we all agreed that there would be absolutely no files on this situation, I felt it was important that we meet in person." She looked from Wyrdrune to Kira to Billy. "I must admit, you three are not quite what I expected."

"You expected older, more experienced adepts," said Wyrdrune.

"Frankly, yes. You seem very young for the nature of the task you've undertaken."

"You make it sound as if we had a choice, Madame President," said Kira. "We didn't. We never chose the runestones. They chose us."

"Why don't you tell me about that?" asked the President.

"Well, I don't know how much Director Wetterman has told you—" Wyrdrune began.

"Assume he hasn't told me anything and start from the beginning," said the President. "I'd like to hear it in your own words."

Wyrdrune nodded. "Okay. But this could take a while."

"Take all the time you need."

Makepeace and the others listened quietly as they told the story of how it all began.

"I suppose it started for me when I was kicked out of the College of Sorcerers in Cambridge," Wyrdrune said.

"Isn't that where Merlin taught?" the President asked.

"Yes, he was my teacher," Wyrdrune replied. "I guess you could say it all really started with him. When he awoke from the spell Morgan le Fay had placed him under some two thousand years ago and brought back magic to the world, he also unintentionally brought back something else. Of course, he didn't know it at the time. Nobody did. But when magic once more started to proliferate throughout the world, it awoke the Dark Ones, who had been imprisoned in an underground cavern in the Euphrates Valley by the Council of the White. I'll have to back up a good deal at this point.

"You see, at one time," he continued, "long before recorded history began, there were two humanoid races—us and the Old Ones. At least, that's what we call them. They looked very much like us—that is, like the way we do now—and they were magic users. It was more than simply knowledge, however. The ability was natural in them. It was how they had evolved, apparently. Now, as to whether they evolved on earth or came here from someplace else, that's anybody's guess, but either way, at the height of their civilization, we were still Neanderthals. And they used us much in the same way we use cattle. That is, they didn't eat humans in the literal sense, but they did consume them. They had the ability to drain off human life force to empower their spells and to revitalize themselves."

"You mean . . . like vampires?" asked the President.

"A good analogy," said Wyrdrune, nodding. "They're probably what inspired our legends about vampires, demons, shapechangers, and so forth."

"Why hasn't there been any fossil record of their existence?" asked one of the President's aides.

"Because they're immortal," Wyrdrune said.

"You mean they can't die?" one of the other aides asked.

"No, they can be killed," said Wyrdrune, "but the wounds have to be immediately fatal, otherwise they will recover. They're apparently immune to all known diseases and they're capable of cellular regeneration, so effectively, they can live forever. In addition, they can extend their lives immeasurably or strengthen their powers by draining human life force. Or life force from each other. That's assuming they don't use it to empower their spells. As you probably know, a white adept uses his own life energy to empower his spells, which means there has to be a period of recovery—how long depends upon the spell. Cast enough high-energy-cost spells without allowing for sufficient time to recover and you inevitably shorten your life span. You could even age prematurely or die. A necromancer, on the other hand, uses someone else's energy or life force to empower his spells, at no direct cost of energy to himself. The result is that a necromancer can become stronger more quickly than a white adept. But I'm getting a bit ahead of myself.

"As we started to evolve," he continued, "the leaders of these Old Ones—they called themselves the Council of the White—came to realize that we were more than animalistic brutes and began to practice what they called 'conservation of the human resource.' In other words, they decided they would no longer drain humans to the point of death, but only use a portion of their life force, leaving them enough to allow for an eventual recovery. This marked the beginning of white magic. However, this didn't set well with all of them, because it effectively placed a limitation on the amount of energy they could acquire, which in turn limited the spells they could cast."

"Essentially, the principles of thaumaturgy or white magic and necromancy are the same," said Billy. "The difference is one kills and one doesn't. It's also a difference of degree. Necromantic spells can be much more powerful. And some of the Old Ones were very competitive and didn't want to give up that power. Or at least the ability to acquire it quickly. They rebelled against the Council and refused to abandon the practice of necromancy. They were called the Dark Ones."

"In time, this schism led to war," continued Wyrdrune. "A mage war. And it must have been really something. It wiped out most of them. It probably also accounts for why there isn't any fossil record of their existence. Blast someone with a bolt of thaumaturgic energy that's strong enough and you'll completely vaporize him. No remains to leave a record. Not even a molecule."

"Jesus," said one of the aides softly.

"In the end, the Dark Ones lost," said Wyrdrune, "and their leaders, those who had survived, were entombed in a deep pit in an underground cavern in what is now the Euphrates Valley, imprisoned by a spell that kept them in a sort of suspended animation. The keys to this spell were three enchanted runestones, an emerald, a sapphire, and a ruby, which were imbued with the life forces of the Council."

"You mean they sacrificed their lives to keep these Dark Ones prisoner?" asked the President.

"Well, in a manner of speaking," Wyrdrune replied. "The members of the Council were the most powerful adepts of their race. The magic we use today doesn't even begin to approach what they were capable of doing. But at the same time . . ." he paused. "Well, I suppose you could say that they were very spiritual, but that doesn't quite describe it. They had a very strict code of ethics and morality, to the point where it was almost like a religion to them. The war had terrible consequences. It almost wiped them all out and the Council felt responsible. I guess you could say that what they did was a punishment for the surviving Dark Ones and a penance for themselves. One that was supposed to last forever."

"Only it didn't," said Kira.

"Let's not get to that just yet," said Wyrdrune. "So the Council members infused their life forces into these three enchanted runestones, animating them so that they became living gems, each one containing the life forces of several Council members. Physically, they died. But their spirits lived on in the stones. That is, all except one of them. That was the youngest member of the Council and his name was Gorlois. It was his responsibility to put the stones in place and seal the spell, and then close off the cavern. Afterward, he went out to live among the humans, passing as one of them, as did the others who had survived the war, because now they were greatly outnumbered and their strongest adepts were dead. Their society had fallen apart and they were being hunted.

"Gorlois eventually made his way to what is now England, where he took a human wife and had a son with her. That son was Merlin. Part human, part immortal. But Merlin's mother was all human and all mortal. As she grew old, Gorlois left her and took another wife, with whom he had three daughters, also part human, part immortal. One of them, Morgana, became famous as the legendary sorceress, Morgan le Fay. Merlin never forgave his father for abandoning his mother, so he took revenge on him by helping a warlord named Uther Pendragon kill him. Uther took Gorlois' human wife and had a son with her who grew up to become King Arthur. But the cycle of revenge continued. Morgana wanted revenge for the murder of her father, but Uther was already dead, so she set her sights on his son, Arthur, her half-brother, and on Merlin."

"Are you kidding?" one of the presidential aides said. "This stuff is right out of the storybooks!"

"Be quiet, Daniel," said the President. She nodded to Wyrdrune. "Go on."

"It is right out of the storybooks," said Wyrdrune. "A lot of legends happen to be based on historical events. But in this one, the truth is stranger than the fiction. Morgana seduced Arthur and had a son with him whom she named Modred. Then she had one of her pupils, a girl named Nimue, seduce Merlin and slip him a mickey, after which Morgana placed Merlin under an enchantment, imprisoning him inside the trunk of an oak tree. Modred never really had a chance. He was raised to hate his father. You all probably know the story. According to the legend, they met on the field of battle and Arthur killed Modred, but was mortally wounded in the process. Except Modred didn't really die. If he had been an ordinary human, he probably would have died, but he recovered and lived a long life. A very long life."

"I'll take it from here," said Angelo, "since I'm the one who's got his memories." He sighed. "Boy, I'll tell you, this sure feels weird. It's almost as if I'm talking about myself. Except I'm not, exactly. The thing is, you could probably make a good case for Modred not being entirely sane. He'd dispute that, of course; that's simply my opinion and I'm no psychiatrist, but the fact is his mother had him so completely twisted around he didn't know what the hell he was. He figured it out eventually, though he didn't have the whole story, but imagine what it must've been like for him. He'd killed his own father and he'd sustained what should have been fatal wounds, except they healed. And he just kept on living. Never even got sick a day in his life. All around him, people lived out normal life spans, grew older, and eventually died, and he just kept on looking the same, aging at a fraction of the normal human rate.

"Anyway, I'll cut to the chase," Angelo said. "He survived for the next two thousand years, moving around a lot and using different names and becoming fabulously wealthy in the process. You can save up a lot of dough in that kind of time, even if you're not exactly thrifty. And Modred wasn't. He also wasn't very particular about how he made his money. Basically, he was a mercenary. He did a lot of other things, but he kept coming back to that. He was good at it. And he had a lot of hate stored up. And all that time, he had to keep ducking his mother, who was obsessed with finding him. He wanted no part of her, but she just wouldn't let go. And it went on for years. Centuries."

"Whatever became of her?" asked the President.

"She was killed by a necromancer," Wyrdrune replied.

"In the line of duty, I might add," said Angelo. "She was an ITC agent when she bought the farm."

"She worked for the Commission?" said McClellan with astonishment.

"As Special Agent Faye Morgan," Angelo replied.

"Faye Morgan," McClellan repeated. "Morgan le Fay." He snorted. "Incredible."

"I'll pick up from here," said Billy, "since this is where Merlin comes in. Cut to about seventy-five years ago. The height of the Collapse. Merlin wakes up from the spell Morgana put him under and the Second Thaumaturgic Age officially begins. You all know the story. He started in England, with a small college in the Midlands, and eventually his programs spread throughout the world, turning out adepts who in turn trained others. Eventually, he came to the States and founded the College of Sorcerers in Cambridge, Massachusetts, where Wyrdrune studied with him. But before that, his prize pupil was Rashid al' Hassan."

He saw everyone nod with recognition and continued. "He attained the rank of mage, one of only five people in the world to do so, and returned to his native country, where he sponsored archaeological research, using his abilities to discover many ancient treasures. One day, he detected unusual trace emanations in a certain location in the Euphrates Valley and he sponsored a dig under his personal supervision to investigate. You can guess what he found. He removed the runestones and became possessed by the Dark Ones, who were weakened from their long confinement and not yet strong enough to escape. But they were strong enough to seize control of his mind. However, while they were firming their hold on him, he lost control of the stones and they wound up being taken to New York, along with a lot of the other artifacts, to be auctioned off."

"And that's where we came in," said Kira. "At the time, I was making my living as a cat burglar."

The President raised her eyebrows.

"I suppose I could say I wasn't proud of it," continued Kira, "but the truth is that I was. I was pretty good, if I say so myself. I had things pretty well set up. I'd case a job, pull off the heist, and then have the goods fenced in a day or two, often before the owners even found out they were missing. I had my act down pat and I stuck to what I knew. Except this one time, when I read about the auction at Christie's and found out about the stones. I'd never tried pulling off a job like that before, a snatch-and-grab, it wasn't my style, but for some reason, I just had to have them. Only it seems somebody else had the same idea." She looked at Wyrdrune and smiled.

"My turn again," he said. "I was living in a small railroad flat on Fourth Street. I'd been kicked out of school for practicing magic without a license. There was a little accident . . . well, the details aren't important. But I'd come back to New York and I was kicking around, trying to figure out what to do with my life now that I'd thoroughly screwed it up. I read about the auction in the paper, too. And I didn't know why, but I became seized with an irresistible compulsion to steal the stones. Kira and I hit the auction at the same time and all hell broke loose, but we did manage to get away with the stones. We figured we'd fence them, split the take, and then dissolve the partnership, except things didn't work out that way."

"We fenced the stones several times," said Kira, "but they kept magically returning to us. And the people that we'd sold them to thought we'd pulled a fast one. One of them was pretty well connected and he put out a hit on us. And the guy who happened to pick up the contract was Modred."

"We had the police after us," Wyrdrune added, "as well as a bunch of hoods working for the fences who thought we'd burned them, and one of them called in some favors and imported this heavy-duty hit man from Europe—we didn't know it was Modred at the time, of course—and on top of that, somebody else was after us, as well. An adept. A necromancer who was working for Al' Hassan. We didn't know what the hell was going on. We just knew that we were in way over our heads. A lot of people were after us and most of them wanted us dead. All we wanted was to get rid of the damned stones. Except we couldn't. So as a last resort, I turned to my old teacher.

"Merlin was the first to figure out what the runestones were," Wyrdrune went on, "but before we could decide what to do next, Modred caught up to us. And that's when it happened. When the three of us were all together, the runestones bonded with us and we had this unbelievable moment of shared memory and experience that must have lasted only an instant, but felt like it took hours. It all came together and we found out who we really were. The three of us were all descended from Gorlois, through his three daughters, and that's why we were chosen by the runestones, which were still animated by the spirits of the Council. Together, we were able to effect the spell known as the Living Triangle, the most powerful weapon the Council had against the Dark Ones. It absorbs their life energy and kills them, which is what the Council should have done with the bastards in the first place. I don't know, maybe they weren't strong enough after the war. The spell consumes an incredible amount of energy. If it didn't absorb the life force of the Dark Ones it destroys, it would undoubtedly kill all three of us."

"But if that's the way it works," the President said, "then doesn't that make it necromancy?"

"Yes, I suppose it does," said Wyrdrune flatly. For a moment, no one spoke. Then Wyrdrune cleared his throat and continued. "Al' Hassan managed to release the Dark Ones before we could stop him. Merlin tried to hold them off until we got there, but we were too late and it cost him his life. Officially, he's supposed to have died when his mansion burned down in Boston's Beacon Hill, but just before the end, he managed to astral project and thereby preserve his life force, though it floated around disembodied for a while."

"Until he found me," said Billy. "Actually, he didn't find me so much as he was drawn to me, because I'm his descendant. He never knew he had a son with Nimue, much less a descendant in the present, so I was a complete surprise to him. As he was to me."

"You say his spirit was drawn to you," the President said. "How, exactly?"

"I really couldn't say," Billy replied. "It had to go some-where, I suppose, or else just keep drifting around on the as-tral plane, like some sort of ghost. I don't suppose he had any choice in the matter. Whatever it was, a psychic or ge-netic link or maybe both, it just sort of drew us together."

"What was it like?" the President asked.

"Well, at first I thought I was going crazy," Billy said. "Suddenly, out of nowhere, there seemed to be someone else inside my head. It's like looking in the mirror and having somebody else look back at you. It's your face, but there's someone else behind it. And then he started talking to me. It was like being possessed. And he wasn't too thrilled about it, either. Having his spirit trapped inside the body of an ado-lescent Cockney punk decked out in spiky hair and leathers wasn't exactly Merlin's cup of tea, if you know what I mean. And for that matter, I wasn't too keen on having some can-tankerous old geezer inside my head, telling me what to do, even if he was a wizard and gave me the ability to do magic. Actually, *he* had the ability, *I* didn't. We could only do magic when he was in the driver's seat. It was pretty weird, I can tell you. To say we didn't exactly get along at first would be a bloody understatement. We kept fighting each other for control. Eventually, we got things sorted out, after a fashion, but it wasn't easy, going around sharing con-sciousness with your own great-great-great-great-grandfa-ther."

"I think you left out a couple of greats," said Wyrdrune with a grin.

"Stuff it. Anyway, we all eventually joined up in London to battle a Dark One in Whitechapel, but there was still one more surprise in store for all of us. Me, in particular. Gorlois wasn't dead. That is, Uther had killed his physical form, but his spirit had survived. Just before he died, Gorlois infused his life force into a runestone that was mounted in a ring. A fire opal that passed down to Morgana and became the source of much of her power. She, in turn, gave it to her husband . . . that is, the one she married in the present time, an adept named Thanatos, who was working with her for the ITC. When he was killed helping us defeat a Dark One in Los Angeles, I got the ring and wound up becoming the repository of the life forces of both Merlin and Gorlois. And it just about put me around the bend, let me tell you. Merlin had helped Uther kill Gorlois and there was no love lost between them."

"You mean it's like having a split personality?" asked the President, fascinated.

"For a while, it was," said Billy. "But I'm integrated now."

"What exactly does that mean?"

"We've all blended into one personality," Billy replied. "That happened in Santa Fe, New Mexico, when I was nearly killed by one of the Dark Ones. And I would have died if Merlin and Gorlois hadn't both given up their life forces to revitalize mine. It resulted in a complete physical transformation where I took on aspects of both of them, in addition to my own. Gorlois was an albino, but Merlin wasn't, and I was a sort of melting pot of various minorities. I don't know what the bloody hell I am now. A bit of all three, I suppose. I've aged about ten years, but on the other hand, I'm part immortal now, so I guess I'll be living a lot longer. And I wasn't an adept before. Now I've got the powers of a mage."

"Hard to keep up without a scorecard, isn't it?" said Wyrdrune wryly.

"I'll say," replied the President, shaking her head with amazement. She glanced at Makepeace. "And just exactly how do you fit in, Dr. Makepeace?"

It was the question he had known was coming. He had

briefly debated giving the same answer that he always gave, but this time he knew it wouldn't be enough. He could tell by the way both McClellan and Wetterman were looking at him. They knew. And though the President wore a carefully neutral expression, she doubtless knew, as well. They knew about the Morpheus connection, the name under which Modred had functioned when he was a professional assassin. The best in all the world. They knew about the times he'd served as a middleman for Morpheus because on several occasions he had done it for the government, though never on American soil. They had dug down deep and no doubt found the tombstone in County Kerry where the paper trail ended. And beyond that, they knew nothing more. And that wasn't going to satisfy them.

"Sebastian is a vital part of our effort," Billy said. "He's an integral part of our support network, which includes—"

"No, Billy, I'm afraid that isn't going to do," said Makepeace, interrupting him. "They already know all that. What they want to know is who I really am. Or perhaps more to the point, *what* I really am. And I suspect that by now, Mr. Wetterman, at least, has already guessed the answer." He glanced at Wetterman.

The head of the NSA nodded. "You're one of them, aren't you?"

Wyrdrune frowned. "What are you talking about? One of whom?"

"There's no point to playing innocent anymore, Mr. Karpinski," Wetterman replied, addressing Wyrdrune by his true name. "As Dr. Makepeace said, we've already guessed the answer. He's one of the Old Ones."

# Chapter 2

"*What?*" said Wyrdrune, staring at Makepeace.

"You mean you really didn't know?" said Wetterman with some surprise.

"Sebastian?" Kira said, looking at him with a puzzled expression.

"It's true," admitted Makepeace. He looked at Wyrdrune. "You never really believed I was a fairy, did you? You thought what everybody else does, what I wanted them to think, that I was a rather dotty old academician, self-taught in magic, who cultivated an amusing eccentricity to seem a bit more colorful. Ironically enough, I really *am* a fairy. Though not in the way that you might think. Have you ever heard of the people of the *sidhe*?"

"The *shee*?" said Wyrdrune.

"It's spelled s-i-d-h-e," said Wetterman. "From the Gaelic *siod*, which means a barrow or a mound. The *aes sidhe*, the people of the mounds, were the legendary fairy race of Ireland, also known as the Tuatha De Danann."

Makepeace nodded. "I see you're a student of history, Mr. Wetterman. A doctorate, I presume?"

Wetterman nodded.

"Well, you're quite correct, of course," said Makepeace, "except in a few significant particulars for which you cannot really be faulted, since history does not report them. There was, indeed, a tribe known as the De Danann, who worshiped the pagan goddess Danu, or Diana in more modern terminology. They were conquered by the Milesians during the Bronze Age. Merlin's mother was a De Danann woman. She was human, as were most of the De Danann. But not all. When Gorlois first came to the British Isles, it was because he knew some of us had settled there to live among them and avoid the persecution we experienced after the war. Actually, persecution is not quite the proper term. Retribution would be much more accurate. The humans had little reason to love the Old Ones."

"But the De Danann accepted you?" asked Wetterman.

"They didn't know," Makepeace replied. "The world was a much larger place then and the islands of what is now Great Britain and Ireland were far removed from the Old Ones' sphere of influence. They had never lived among them, and they had never heard of them. The Old Ones became their wise men and their cunning women, their Druid priests. They lived together in peace and intermarried. When the De Danann were overrun, there were too few of us to help them. And our powers were not on the same level as those of the departed Council or the imprisoned Dark Ones. Many were killed. The rest scattered and became known as the fairy folk of legend."

"Exactly how old *are* you?" the President asked.

"I'm really not sure," Makepeace replied with a shrug. "I was a first-generation half-breed, like Merlin, one of the first of the true fairies. Half human, half immortal. My father was an immortal Druid priest, my mother a De Danann tribeswoman. They were both killed during the invasion. I was roughly in my teens then. I would estimate my age at somewhere around two thousand years, give or take a century or two. I'm afraid I never was quite sure when I was born, exactly. We didn't keep very careful track of such things back then."

"Two thousand years!" the President said with amazement. She shook her head with disbelief. "You don't look a day over sixty."

"Well, I *do* age," Makepeace replied, "albeit very slowly. I have no idea what my actual life expectancy is. I suppose I will die of old age someday, barring any unfortunate accident that may hasten my demise, but I have no idea when. Not for at least another thousand years or so, I should guess. Frankly, if I'd known I was going to live this long, I would have taken better care of myself."

"Why didn't you ever tell us?" Kira asked.

Makepeace shrugged. "Old habits die hard, I suppose. Those of us who had survived learned a long time ago to hide our true nature. Besides, you would have asked me many questions to which I had no answers."

"About the Council, you mean," Wyrdrune said.

"About the Council, the Dark Ones, and a lot of other things," said Makepeace. "In the past, quite long ago, there were a few people to whom I'd told the truth. It never worked out very well in the long run. I really do wish I had some answers for you. I wish I had them for myself. But the Council was before my time, you see. As were the Dark Ones. They were already gone by the time I was born and my father never mentioned anything about them. I learned the truth as you did, only recently. Mr. Wetterman was not quite correct, you see." He glanced at the NSA chief. "You were, in essence, but I'm not quite the same as the Council or the Dark Ones. I'm part human. And I'm not as old."

"But you're still one of them," said one of the presidential aides, staring at Makepeace with distrust.

"Only in a sense," Makepeace replied. "Natasha here is one of them, as well, in the same sense. She owes her psychic abilities to the fact that she, too, is descended from a mixed marriage between a human and an Old One, just as Wyrdrune, Kira, and Billy are. Just as every licensed adept is, even you, Mr. McClellan. The ability to use magic is the heritage of the Old Ones, passed on from generation to generation. It is diluted somewhat over time, but the genetic strain is strong. Adepts or those with the potential to become adepts live longer on the average than most people. Though I fear they will never live as long as me. The gene for longevity is not as persistent as the one for magic, I'm afraid. But humans who are descended from the Old Ones tend to be healthier, and they tend to be more sensitive, psychically speaking. It usually takes training to bring out the abilities, but not in all cases, right, Natasha?"

The Gypsy nodded. "I've had it since I was a little girl. I've always wondered why I couldn't really read you. I just figured you were one of those rare people who could shield."

"And you were right," said Makepeace with a smile. He turned to the President and Wetterman. "So, now you know the truth about me. And about the rest of this fascinating story. The question is, what are you going to do about it?"

"The question is, what *can* we do about it?" asked the President. "Legally, we can't have sorcerer vigilantes hunting down and killing necromancers. But at the same time, we can't exactly arrest them and hold them for trial, can we?"

"Not a chance," said Wyrdrune. "No jail ever built would hold them. And anyone trying to arrest them wouldn't live long enough to read them their rights. The only way to stop them is to kill them."

"How many of these Dark Ones are there?" asked the President.

"We don't know for certain," said Wyrdrune. "Some were killed before they managed to escape. Some we've taken out since then. And some remain at large. But there can't be very many of them."

"We'll know when the last of them is gone," said Billy suddenly.

"How?" asked Wetterman.

"Yeah, how?" asked Wyrdrune, puzzled.

Billy frowned. "I'm not sure. But Gorlois must've known, because I never knew that before. It must have been a memory fragment from him."

"That means the runestones must know, too," said Wyrdrune.

"But you don't?" the President asked.

Wyrdrune shook his head. "Consciously, we know only what they want us to know," he said. "It's difficult to explain. We can't really conduct a dialogue with the spirits of the stones. Or if we can, they don't want to for some reason. They give us strange dreams sometimes. They alert us if there's a Dark One nearby, or one of their acolytes."

"Acolytes?" asked the President.

"A human they've placed under their power," Kira said.

"I see. And that could be anybody?"

"Anyone they chose," said Wyrdrune.

"And is there a limit to how many people they could place under their power?" asked the President.

"Theoretically, no," said Wyrdrune. "It depends on how much energy they have. But it doesn't take much for them to possess someone."

"Great," said the President. "So we're looking at the potential for the terrorist group from hell."

"That's a good way of putting it," said Billy.

"Congress would go ballistic if they found out about this. And if they get wind of it, the press will know in a heartbeat." The President shook her head grimly. "Too many people know about this already. I don't see how we're going to keep the lid on."

"We're working on the assumption that we won't be able to," said Wetterman. "There are too many variables we can't control. But at least we have plausible deniability. Outside of a few trusted people in this administration, only a handful of people know about this, and they can all be counted on. And nobody except the people in this room knows this meeting is taking place. No one even knows you're in New York."

"What good is that going to do us?" asked the President. "For God's sake, there's a lot more at stake here than the next election, Brian."

"I couldn't agree more," said Wetterman, "but that isn't the point. The point is we've got to do everything we can to help these people, but legally, we can't. Specifically, *you* can't. If anything goes wrong, the office of the President can't be seen to be involved in something that circumvents our entire system of justice. Officially, you don't know about any of this. You can't."

"Okay, so I don't know about it," she said. "Where does that leave us?"

"It leaves the ITC holding the bag," said Wetterman. "Bill and I have already discussed this. A good case could be made for this being under their exclusive jurisdiction, since it involves magic crime on an international scale. But it's also a matter of national security, which means it comes under my purview, as well. Our story's going to be that I was the man in this administration contacted by the ITC as soon as they found out about it and I took it upon myself to classify this whole operation top secret. Officially, the buck stops at my desk. It never got to yours. And that's the way it has to be."

"So if it hits the fan, it's going to be your ass," the President said.

"I'm afraid so," Wetterman replied. "But I don't see any way around it."

The President nodded. "All right. Since you're the one putting it all on the line, it's only right that you should be in charge. As of right now, I want your deputy handling all other NSA matters while you give your full attention to this one."

Wetterman nodded. "She's up to it. We've already discussed it."

"I want a special task force formed immediately," the President continued, "comprised of FBI, BOT, and ITC personnel. The best people we've got."

"If I may make a suggestion, Madame President, I'd like to include some old CIA personnel on this, as well. They've got people with more experience in covert activities."

"Yes, I'm sure they do," the President replied with a wry grimace. "All right. But if we're going to turn the dogs loose, let's try to make sure none of them are rabid, okay? I don't want any wackos running loose on this one."

"Understood," Wetterman replied.

"I think the task force headquarters should be set up right here," the President continued. "Any objections, Mr. McClellan? Have you got the space?"

"No, ma'am. And yes, we do. We'll set aside the top floor of the Secretariat building for their exclusive use and then restrict access."

"Good. I also want a special hot line installed from here direct to the Oval Office, one in my bedroom at the White House, and a mobile unit to accompany me everywhere I go. Better make them all spellwarded and assign an ITC agent to carry the mobile unit, somebody with a low profile who won't stick out."

"Affirmative," said Wetterman, making notes on a small pad.

"Now, if I understand correctly, the first sign of activity by these Dark Ones is liable to show up as serial killing, is that right?"

"That's always been the pattern in the past, Madame President," said Wyrdrune. "And these killings always leave behind evidence of magic use."

"However, a series of necromantic murders may not necessarily be the first sign," said Angelo. "If they're smart, they'll start preying on elements of the population that won't easily be missed. We could look for patterns of disappearances or kidnappings."

"Well, that narrows it down," the President said sarcastically. She exhaled heavily. "Jesus, this is going to be a nightmare. Do whatever you have to do, Brian. You've got a blank check. Just get the job done."

"Oh, there's one more thing, Madame President," said McClellan. "I'd like to assign several adepts to your Secret Service detail. I hate to bring it up, but there's always a possibility the Dark Ones might come after you."

The President just stared at him for a moment, then nodded and said, "Right. Do it. Have we left anything out?"

"Transport," said Wyrdrune. "If any of the Dark Ones surface, we can teleport to the location, but that would use up a significant amount of energy."

"Good point," the President said. "Detail a military transport plane for twenty-four-hour standby duty. Something fast, piloted by SAC adepts. And have a support team standing by to accompany them, to set up a field command post and make sure we get cooperation from local authorities."

"We'll need a security designation for the operation," Wetterman said. "I suggest code name: 'Avatar.'" He indicated Wyrdrune, Kira, Billy, and Angelo in turn. "You'll be referred to as A-1, A-2, A-3, and A-4, respectively. Primary support personnel will carry a B designation, administrative support will carry the designation of C. Even though we'll be dealing with spellwarded lines of communication, we may not always be able to do so and so we don't want any names being used. And we don't ever want to refer to the Dark Ones. If any activity is reported, the code phrase will be, 'We've got a fire.' Any questions?"

"I've got one," the President said. She turned to Wyrdrune and the others. "I'd like to see these amazing runestones we've been talking about."

Wyrdrune removed his headband, revealing the emerald stone set into his forehead. Kira took off her fingerless black leather glove and held up her palm, displaying the sapphire stone bonded to her flesh. And Angelo unbuttoned his shirt, showing the President the ruby gem over his heart.

"There was a fourth stone," Wyrdrune explained, "the fire opal in Billy's ring, but it wasn't part of the spell used to contain the Dark Ones. It held the life force of Gorlois and was destroyed when he and Merlin fused their life forces with Billy's."

"They look so ordinary," said the President. "It's hard to believe they're actually alive. Or that they contain so much power. What does it feel like?"

"It doesn't really feel like anything," said Kira. "We're aware of them much in the same way you might be aware of having an earring, I suppose. We can feel them there, but when they exert their power, we sort of . . . go away. It's like blacking out, only when it's over, we remember everything that happened."

"The only other thing is that when there's a Dark One nearby, or someone possessed by their power, the stones glow. And if they're very close, we feel a tingling sensation," Wyrdrune said. "It's how they warn us."

"It's a bit frightening to think of that kind of power contained in something so small," the President said. "And you don't really control it, do you? I mean, it's the spirits of the Council in the stones that wield the power?"

"We have to be together to form the Living Triangle," Wyrdrune said. "But beyond that, the Council runs the show."

"I see," the President said thoughtfully. "So essentially, there's no check on their power whatsoever?"

For a moment, no one spoke. The uncomfortable silence stretched. "Not that we know of," Wyrdrune replied quietly.

"Then it's a lucky thing for us that they're the good guys," the President said. "Let's hope they stay that way." She got to her feet. "Well, I think we're finished. Mr. Wetterman and Mr. McClellan can take over from here. I probably won't be seeing you again, so I'll wish you the best of luck. Godspeed." She shook hands with all of them, then left. Moments later, the helicopter lifted off.

"Well, I'm not sure we're any better off now than we were before," said Wyrdrune, finally.

"What are you talking about?" asked Steve McGuire. "You've got the full resources of the government behind you now. The President gave you a blank check."

"She gave Wetterman a blank check," Wyrdrune corrected him. "And it's clear that he's going to be the one calling the shots. We had more freedom to act when we were on our own. You watch, the bureaucrats are going to try to take control of this whole thing. Besides, they're just as much afraid of us as the Dark Ones."

"That's absurd," McGuire said. "I think you're overreacting."

"No, he's not," the Gypsy said. "Those Secret Service agents had their hands on their weapons all the time they were here."

"Yeah, but that's their job," McGuire said.

"Okay, I'll grant you that," the Gypsy said, "but I could sense a great deal of apprehension in the President. And in Wetterman, as well. And you, Mr. McClellan."

McClellan smiled wryly. "I won't pretend I don't have certain concerns. But I think it's only natural, under the circumstances. The runestones are more powerful than any human adept. It's a bit unsettling to think of there being no control over all that power."

"Which begs the question of what they're going to do about us when all this is over," Wyrdrune said. "Assuming we survive, of course, what happens when the government decides we're too dangerous to be allowed to run around loose with 'all that power,' as you put it?"

McClellan pursed his lips and nodded thoughtfully. "That's a fair question. I suppose it depends on what happens, doesn't it? And on what the runestones decide to do."

"Perhaps now you'll begin to understand why I've kept

the truth about myself hidden," Makepeace said. "Because no matter how well-intentioned people may be, there is always going to be that element of distrust. And fear. When all this is over, I think Dr. Sebastian Makepeace, the outrageous university professor, is going to disappear. For good."

"That would be a pity," said McClellan. "The ITC could certainly use you."

"Yes, I have no doubt of that," said Makepeace. "Except, you see, I have a distinct aversion to being used."

"That wasn't how I meant it," said McClellan.

"Wasn't it? Well, perhaps not. At any rate, however, I think I had best be going. In the face of all these nightmarish concerns, I still have papers to grade and classes to prepare, which is something of a nightmare in itself, giving our current crop of undergraduates. If civilization is threatened, you know where to reach me."

"Sure," McClellan said. "Oh, and Makepeace?"

Sebastian paused by the door.

"Don't disappear on us just yet, okay?"

Makepeace raised his eyebrows. "Wouldn't think of it, dear boy. After all, we all still have a job to do, don't we?"

After a long series of bad breaks, Joey Medina had finally made a score. He had done it by walking in across the border from Sasabe, though he hadn't used the official port of entry coming in from Mexico. He had hiked in over open country, keeping a wary eye out for the Border Patrol, which had a distinct aversion to people sneaking into the United States. Though Joey took the same route many illegal aliens did coming into the United States in search of jobs, he was not a "wetback," an expression dating to the days when people swam the Rio Grande to get across the border into Texas. It still happened on occasion, but patrols and steel walls had cut down on a lot of traffic. Going overland was easier and the Arizona border was tougher to patrol.

Joey Medina wasn't an illegal alien, however. He was a

citizen, born and raised in East LA, whose family had moved to South Tucson to get away from all the earthquakes and the mudslides and the violence. His parents had wanted a quieter life for themselves and their kids, but Joey always had a knack of finding trouble anywhere he went. After he had been in and out of jail half a dozen times on various charges, his parents finally gave up on him and invited him to leave. At twenty-two, he had been on his own for the past six years, though some of that time had been spent living at the taxpayers' expense. Soon after he got out, he had made a trip across the border, and the reason for his rather circumspect entry back into the United States was the backpack full of cocaine he had returned with.

The hills of the Sonora Desert north of Sasabe were full of trails and old dirt roads where trucks could rendezvous with "mules" carrying in drugs. The undermanned Border Patrol, for all its earnest efforts, could not possibly cover them all. It was a gamble, but Joey knew the odds of making it were pretty good. He also knew that one more bust would send him away for a long time, so he was very careful, keeping to the brush as much as possible and watching out for choppers and the Border Patrol trucks.

He had met the transport and off-loaded the backpack, then hiked down to the highway and hitched back into town rather than risk being caught in a vehicle full of drugs. His cut of the deal had not amounted to a fortune, but it was enough for a nice stake to get him and his girlfriend to New Mexico, where he had a connection to a big-time dealer in Santa Fe. He had hopes of moving up in the world. Unfortunately, he had experienced a minor setback.

While he was away in jail, Maria had been busted. She'd been caught soliciting an undercover cop, something she should have been smart enough to avoid. It was not her first time, but Joey wasn't worried. It was no big deal. He had figured by the time he'd set up the score, gone into Mexico, picked up the drugs, and returned, she'd already be out and they could split. Except when he returned to Tucson, he found out the PD had pleaded her out into some kind of rehab center. So, he thought, no problem. Getting her out of a place like that would be a snap. Except this was some kind of different rehab center.

The place was in a walled enclave about sixty miles west of town, stuck on top of a mountain that was crawling with dragons. Dragons, for chrissake. It was some kind of preserve for the ugly beasts. Why anyone would want to preserve a bunch of giant lizards was beyond him. They weren't even natural, for cryin' out loud. Some thaumagenetics company screws up and instead of wiping out the damn mistake, a bunch of screwloose big-city Anglos decide to preserve it. Worse yet, the guy running the place was some kind of priest. Right there, Joey knew it was going to mean trouble.

Maria had this thing about priests. Like, she thought they were holy or something. She had lost her cherry when she was twelve and she'd been hooking since she was sixteen, but she couldn't even pass a church in the damned car without crossing herself. She always wore her little golden crucifix and her medallion of the Virgin and she went to Mass each Sunday. Always took confession. Joey used to wonder what she said in there.

"Bless me, Father, for I have sinned. It's been one week since my last confession, and I screwed six guys, performed thirty-seven blow jobs, and pulled a train for three salesmen from Yuma in the No-tel Motel."

No problem. Say a novena, push around a couple of beads, light a candle, pray for forgiveness, and the whole thing's a wash. See ya next week.

Joey never had any use for religion. The way he figured it, the priests had their hands out, just like everybody else. Except they didn't have to work for a living. It was just another racket. And a pretty good one, from what he could see. Maria hated it when he talked that way. She'd get really upset. She was one of the hardest chicks he'd ever met—

she'd stick a guy as soon as look at him—but when it came
to God and stuff like that, she just went all soft in the head.

Brother Talon. What the hell kind of a name was that?
Talon. Sounded like a bird's foot. He'd asked around and
found out that this Brother Talon was an Anglo and not really a priest. Some kind of monk or minister or something.
Young guy. Looked like a fuckin' rock star, too. Not good.
Bad enough Maria had this thing for priests, like they were
perfect, the only men who didn't sin or lust—yeah, right—
but on top of that, the guy has to be young and good-looking,
like some long-haired male stripper. Bad combination.
Guaranteed trouble.

He had tried to call her, but the woman who'd answered
the phone said there were no personal calls allowed to members of the enclave. She had agreed to take a message and
Joey left his name and phone number, but the woman said
the members of the enclave weren't allowed to make any
personal calls, either. He could write a letter or she could
pass on his message and give him an answer when he called
back. He said he wanted to see her. The woman told him visiting hours were from one to three on Saturdays.

He drove all the way out there the following Saturday,
keeping an eye out for those ugly dragons once he'd passed
through the gate and over that electrified cattle guard. They
didn't attack cars, but if he hit one, it could make a hell of a
mess. Maria met him in the courtyard, on a bench by a fountain in the shade of a eucalyptus tree. She had her hair down
and was dressed in a white robe and sandals. Even with the
stud in her nose and the ring in her eyebrow, she looked like
a goddamn angel. Well scrubbed, no makeup, you'd never
guess she worked the streets only a few short weeks ago.
He'd always hated that she hooked, and when he was
around, she didn't do it, but the problem was, he wasn't
around all the time. She was doing it when he met her and
as long as he kept her supplied with coke, she'd stay at

home, but when he was sent up, she was right back out again to keep the habit going.

Joey never used the stuff himself. Don't dip into the merchandise. First rule of the game. Lot of times, people you sold to wanted you to snort a line with them. That was okay. It was expected. But except for that, he didn't touch the stuff. That way, you wound up snorting all your profits. But Maria could snort Bolivia all by herself. She was one high-maintenance chick. Real pain in the ass sometimes, too. The trouble was, he loved her. Which made it all that much harder to take when she told him she didn't want to see him anymore.

She said it very nicely. About as nicely as anyone could say a thing like that. But she was firm about it. "I have a new life now," she had told him. "I have been cleansed and everything from my old life has been left behind. Everything, Joey. Even you. That's just the way it has to be."

"But what about Santa Fe?" he'd said. "I made the score. We can be married now!"

She shook her head. "I'm sorry, Joey. That's all part of my old life. I'm not the same person anymore."

"Bullshit! What, some guy gives you a white robe and sprinkles holy water over you and suddenly you're someone else? That Talon guy's not even a real priest, you know that? This whole thing is just a fuckin' racket, just another scam. C'mon, this is me, Joey, remember? Let's get in the car and blow this frickin' joint."

She shook her head again. "I'm sorry, Joey. I'm happy here. I've been reborn, and I've cast off my old life and all my old attachments."

"What, is this guy Talon getting into your pants, is that it?"

"It's not like that at all. I've found something much more powerful. You wouldn't understand, Joey. Go to Santa Fe. Forget about me."

"Like hell I will! I love you!"

"I'm sorry."

She got up to leave and he grabbed her by the arm, but suddenly half a dozen big guys in white robes were all around him and the next thing he knew, he was being politely, but firmly escorted out. He thought he recognized some of those guys, too. He'd seen them on the street. Couple of them he'd seen in the joint. Well, screw that, he thought.

This rehab center or enclave or whatever the hell it was supposed to be was clearly some kind of cult. He'd heard all about them. They took advantage of people who weren't too bright and filled their heads with all sorts of nonsense and turned them inside out. Next thing you know, Maria would be stringing beads or weaving Indian baskets out of yucca leaves to be sold in the tourist shops. Rehabilitative therapy, my ass, thought Joey. The whole thing was just one big con job.

He'd have to pull one of those interference things or whatever they were called. Snatch her out of there and take her away and sit on her until she got her head straight. But he knew he wouldn't be able to do it on his own. He'd called in a few favors and got some help. It had cut into his stake a bit, but he wasn't leaving town without Maria and there was no point in taking halfway measures. He'd gotten half a dozen local gangbangers, all strapped with iron. Brother Talon was about to find out that nobody screwed around with Joey Medina. Nobody.

They had boosted a van from a parking lot in the mall and headed out to Dragon Peak. It was late and the road was practically deserted. Didn't matter much if anyone remembered the van, anyway. They'd ditch it right after the job.

The boys had wanted to hit the place hard and hit it fast, but Joey told them to cool it. No heavy stuff until they got Maria. He got them all baseball bats and told them to use those to take down anyone who might get in their way, keep things quiet until he found out where Maria was. After that, they could rock 'n' roll.

They took the road up to the enclave with the lights out, going slow to make sure they didn't run into any dragons. The thaumaturgic battery allowed the van to glide a foot or so above the surface of the road without making any noise, so they'd be able to hit them without warning. Joey felt the butt of the 9mm tucked into his waistband and smiled. He was going to enjoy this.

As they rounded a curve, the van suddenly came to a halt, hovering silently. "Damn," said Ricky, the driver.

"What's wrong?" asked Rafe, one of the guys in back.

"Dragon on the road," said Joey from the front passenger seat as he looked through the windshield. In the moonlight, they could make out the bulk of the huge beast in the center of the road. It wasn't moving; it was just looking at them.

"Jesus, look at that son of a bitch," said Julio, moving up between the seats to look out the windshield. "Maybe we should back off a bit," he added nervously.

"Come on, let's get going," Rafe said impatiently.

"Can't," said Ricky. "That' lizard's blockin' the damn road."

"Well, run it the hell off, man!"

"Hey, I ain't about to piss off anything that big," said Ricky.

"Just drive, man," Rafe said. "It'll move."

"Yeah? And what if it doesn't?"

"What if it decides we're dinner?" Julio asked.

"Well, shoot the damn thing," said Rafe irritably. "I don't feel like sittin' here all night."

"No shooting," Joey said firmly. "Not until I give the word."

"Well, is it movin' or ain't it?" Rafe asked from the back.

"No, it's just standin' there," said Ricky.

"Well, shit, I ain't got all fuckin' night," said Rafe. They heard the sliding door open.

"Hey, wait a minute, man . . ." said Mike, sitting with the others in the back.

"*Rafe!*" said Joey. "Where the hell are you goin'?"

A moment later, they saw Rafe coming around the front of the van, holding a baseball bat. His shaved head gleamed darkly in the moonlight.

"That son of a bitch is crazy," Julio said.

Joey stuck his head out the side window. "Rafe! Are you nuts? Get back in here!"

Rafe did not reply. Holding the baseball bat before him, he slowly approached the dragon. It watched, flicking its long tongue out, as he came closer.

"Goddamn it, he's gonna screw up everything!" said Joey, racking the slide on the 9mm and getting out of the van.

The dragon flicked its long tongue out toward Rafe, but the big, muscular black man danced aside and brought the bat down with both hands in a powerful blow against the dragon's head. There was a loud crack, like a major leaguer connecting for a home run, and the bat splintered. Joey swore and brought the gun up, flicking off the safety, but the dragon gave a loud hiss and staggered, recoiling from the blow, then lumbered off unsteadily into the darkness.

Joey exhaled heavily, slipped the safety back on, and lowered the gun as Rafe discarded the broken bat and returned to the van. "You got some big fucking brass *cojones,* man," he said, shaking his head.

"Whatever," Rafe said. "C'mon, let's get this show on the road."

They got back into the van and continued up the road to the enclave without further incident. The gates were closed, but they weren't locked. Joey got out and opened them, then stood aside as the van went through. They parked in the courtyard and got out, carrying their baseball bats, except for Rafe, who had broken his. He pulled out his old Mac-10 and slapped a clip in.

"Remember, keep it cool until I find Maria," Joey said.

The place looked deserted, but it was late and everyone was probably in bed. The first thing they did was cut the phone lines; then they spread out and headed for the residence buildings. The first one they came to, everybody was asleep. That was what Joey had figured on. He'd planned on waking up a couple of them and scaring them shitless, making them tell him where Maria was, then tapping them out and getting her before turning the boys loose on the place to teach Brother Talon a lesson. The only trouble was, they couldn't wake anyone up.

"C'mon, get up!" said Rafe, shaking one of the sleepers hard. It was a guy of about nineteen. Rafe lifted him right off the bed, shaking him like a rag doll, but there was no response. It was the same with the next two. Rafe shook them and slapped them, but they would not wake up no matter what he did.

"What the hell is wrong with these people?" Mike asked, perplexed. "They keep 'em all drugged up or something?"

"I dunno," said Joey with a frown. "I didn't count on this."

"Well, if they're all like this, it'll make things a hell of a lot easier," said Esteban, one of the other toughs. "We'll just find your chick and carry her back to the van, then trash the place and split."

"I don't like this," Julio said. "It's fuckin' creepy, man."

"They've got 'em all doped up, that's all," said Rafe. "Probably put it in their food or somethin'."

And then they heard the chanting.

"What the hell is *that*?" said Julio, glancing around with alarm. He was getting jumpy.

Esteban moved to the window. "Hey, check this out," he said.

Joey came up beside him and the others crowded around. A line of figures in hooded black robes was moving across the courtyard from the buildings on the opposite side. They were headed toward the mission. As they walked, others similarly dressed moved up to join them, coming from the other buildings. Joey recognized Maria among them. Even in the robe, he knew it was her. He'd know that walk anywhere.

"What the hell is this?" asked Ricky. "Midnight mass?"

"Yeah, well, it's after midnight," Mike said, peering out the window. "This looks like some kinda cult shit to me."

"It figures," said Tony, Ricky's older brother. "They dope everybody else up so no one's awake to see them do their thing."

"This could be interesting," said Rafe.

"I told you, man, this is fuckin' creepy," Julio said. "I don't like this."

The robed figures were moving into the mission.

"Come on," said Joey. "Let's go."

"What do you mean, let's go?" asked Julio.

"We're goin' in there," said Joey. "This makes it easy. We get 'em all in the same place."

"Oh, jeez, man, I don't know," said Julio uneasily.

"What the hell are you afraid of?" asked Mike. "You've got a piece."

"Yeah, but that's a *church,* man."

"This don't look like no church service I've ever seen," Joey replied. "And I ain't payin' you for wussing out on me. You in on this or not?"

"Yeah, okay, okay, I'm in," said Julio reluctantly.

They waited until the last of the robed figures disappeared into the mission, then went outside and ran across the courtyard. But when they got into the mission, it was dark and empty.

"What the hell?" said Ricky, looking around. "Where'd they all go?"

"There's a door open over there," said Mike.

They went to the side door and entered the small walled courtyard between the mission and the house. Joey led the way. "They must've gone inside there," he said.

The others took their guns out.

They went through the door into the house. "What the fuck?" said Joey. There was a big hole in the center of the floor, with stairs leading down. They could see torchlight flickering in the passageway.

"Oh, that's it, man," Julio said, shaking his head. "I ain't goin' down there. Forget about it."

"Fine, stay here, you pussy," Joey said. "But you ain't gettin' a fuckin' dime for this job."

"Hey, c'mon, somebody's got to watch the van, don't they?" Julio protested.

"All right," said Joey, reconsidering. "You get half what we agreed. But you better be waitin' for us when we get back or I'll find you and waste your sorry ass."

"That's if I don't find you first," said Rafe.

"Okay, I get the picture," Julio said.

"Right, let's go," said Joey.

Julio watched them disappear down the stairs, then he was left alone. He hefted the big semiautomatic pistol in his hand and checked the safety. He looked around nervously. The house seemed deserted. He couldn't hear the chanting anymore. He didn't know which bothered him worse, the chanting or the silence.

He went over to the front window and looked out. From where he stood, he could easily see the van parked in the courtyard. No one was around. Still, he didn't like it. It was one thing to snatch a chick out of some rehab center and then shoot up the place a little, but nobody had told him this was some kind of religious cult on a preserve for dragons. If he'd known that, he wouldn't have gone for it. The money wasn't that good.

Things were liable to get out of hand. Joey was really wired and that Rafe was just plain crazy. Sure as shit people were going to wind up getting killed. It was going to be messy. It was one thing to off somebody on the street every now and then, but to waste a bunch of people in a church, cult or no cult, the cops were going to be all over this one. Man, I shouldn't've gone in on this, thought Julio as he watched out the window, glancing nervously around the deserted courtyard. Bunch of people lyin' around, all doped up to the gills, guys in hooded black robes chanting weird shit, desecrating a church . . . this was a bad deal all around.

He tucked the pistol into the waistband of his jeans and lit up a cigarette. He didn't like having to wait up here all alone, but he'd liked the idea of going down that hole even less. He didn't want to know what the hell they did down there. Some kind of Satanic shit, you could bet on that. Probably wouldn't be a bad idea if Joey and the others wasted the whole bunch. Maybe they would. Boy, wouldn't that be something? Then he could talk about the time he'd been in on this job that took out a whole Satanic cult. But things were going to be pretty hot around town for a while after that. Maybe the thing to do was take the money, skip across the border for a while, and just chill. Of course, now he wasn't going to get as much, because Joey was pissed he didn't go down there with the others. Still, could've been worse. He might've been cut out altogether. But there was no way he was going down that hole. He turned around and froze, the cigarette dropping from his lips.

The hole in the floor was gone.

He blinked and shook his head. "Son of a bitch. . . ."

Slowly, he walked over to where the hole had been in the center of the floor. Only now there was no hole. There was no sign of a door or anything. Tentatively, he felt the area where the hole had been with his foot. Julio swore softly in Spanish and got down on his hands and knees, feeling the ceramic tiles. Solid. No cracks or anything. He swore again.

Magic.

He swallowed hard and quickly crossed himself. This put a whole new slant on things. Joey never said anything about magic being involved. If they were going up against adepts . . .

From somewhere under the floor, Julio suddenly heard the muffled, distant sounds of gunfire. Just a couple of shots and what sounded like a brief burst from Rafe's Mac-10, then nothing. He put his ear down against the floor and listened. For a moment or two, he couldn't hear a thing. And then, just barely audible, he heard it.

The chanting.

"Fuck this . . ." he said, scrambling to his feet and pulling out his gun. He flicked off the safety and ran to the door, looked around, then dashed across the small walled courtyard back into the church. No sign of anybody. He ran through the church and went outside, turning this way and that, swinging his gun around to cover all directions. He made it to the van, got in, slammed the door, and turned the key. Screw this, he thought, I'm getting the hell outta here.

The van lifted off the ground and he slammed it into drive. He didn't even bother stopping to open the gates. He just crashed right through them. The van slewed sideways, but Julio got it straight and accelerated down the road, his high beams on, taking the curves as fast as he dared. The battery would only power the van up to about fifty miles per hour, but the curves were sharp and Julio had to watch his speed. He was halfway down the winding mountain road when he saw them up ahead, in the glare of his lights. Four dragons, standing in the center of the road, like cattle, blocking it. And several more moving up behind them.

"*Shit!*" Julio gritted his teeth and swerved off the road.

The van lurched as it plunged into the brush, unable to levitate more than about two feet above the ground. The thaumaturgic battery still had plenty of charge left in it, but it wasn't powerful enough to lift the van any higher. He heard the thumping on the undercarriage as the van plowed over the scrub brush and cactus, snapping off the brittle paddles of the prickly pear and breaking through the fragile cholla, but the van rocked and pitched as it ran over the tougher creosote bushes and young mesquite trees and rocks. Julio struggled for control as he tried to avoid the larger, multiple-trunked palo verde trees and the big mesquites. The van went sideways and smashed against a tree, rebounding and going sideways the other way as Julio tried desperately to straighten it out. The ground was steep and he was losing all control as the vehicle plunged down the side of the mountain, crashing through ocotillo plants and getting thoroughly banged up. He struck a glancing blow to a large saguaro cactus and the plant toppled in one direction while the van rolled in the other, striking the ground hard and caving the roof in, rolling over and over until it finally came to a halt against a stand of gnarled mesquite trees.

Julio wasn't wearing a seat belt and he got thrown around inside the van, striking the windshield with his head and getting bounced around as the vehicle rolled over and over. When it finally came to rest on its side, Julio was still conscious, but stunned and groggy. He tasted blood and felt it running down his face. He could feel no pain yet, but he knew he'd been hurt. The windshield was smashed and the van looked like a crumpled beer can.

He managed to drag himself out through the passenger side door, which was sprung and hanging open. The headlights were still on, sending the beams out at a crazy angle. Julio coughed and spat out blood. His chest hurt. He'd probably broken a few ribs.

Gotta get outta here, he thought. Get down to the highway, try to hitch a ride into town. There wasn't going to be much traffic on the road this time of night. And Tucson was a good sixty miles away. How far was he from the highway? It was dark and, though the moon provided some light, he couldn't see the road he had gone off of and couldn't get his bearings.

Then he heard something moving toward him through the brush. Something big. Shit, he thought, the dragons. He tried to put weight on his leg and felt a sharp stab of pain go through it. He swore. It wasn't broken, but it was cut up and he saw the dark dampness on his torn jeans from the blood. It looked pretty bad. He was starting to feel the pain now. *Which way was the goddamn road?*

He figured he couldn't go wrong if he headed downhill. The highway had to be down there somewhere. Hobbling painfully, he started down the slope, picking his way through the scrub brush. He stumbled and felt a sharp pain in his arm as he brushed up against a cholla cactus. Its segmented branches broke off at the slightest touch and were covered with a profusion of sharp spines. Several of the four-inch-long, sausagelike branches had detached and stuck to him. Instinctively, he tried to brush them away and got one stuck in his hand. Cursing and wincing with pain, he shook it off, but now he could hear heavy, thumping footsteps behind him, twigs snapping, and loud hisses punctuated by the snapping of large jaws. He reached for his gun. It wasn't there.

It must have fallen out back in the van. He couldn't go back for it now. There was no time to look for a weapon. He had to get the hell out of there. Ignoring the pain, he half limped, half stumbled down the slope, watching for cactus as best he could, but sticking himself a dozen times before he had covered twenty yards. The damn stuff grew all over the place. And behind him, the footsteps kept on coming. It sounded as if there were at least two or three of them. And they were after him. How fast could they move?

The ground was gradually starting to level off. The highway couldn't be much farther. Whimpering with pain, Julio redoubled his efforts, trying to put some distance between himself and the creatures behind him. He stumbled and fell, bruising himself and scratching his face on some yucca leaves, dragged himself to his feet, and kept on going. Where the hell was the damned road?

And then he stopped suddenly, and his stomach tightened up with fear. The fucking wall. He had forgotten about the wall. It stood about twenty feet in front of him, about twelve feet high and running as far as he could see in both directions. Behind him, he heard the snapping and rustling of brush as the dragons came closer. He could hear them hissing hungrily.

Panic struck. He lurched toward the wall and tried to climb it, but he couldn't find any purchase. Desperately, he clawed at it, ruining his fingers on the stuccoed concrete and sobbing as he tried to find a handhold without any success. His breaths came in sharp gasps as he tried to remember which way was the gate they had driven through. He had to pick a direction, any direction. But then he saw a huge form come lumbering through the darkness to his left. And another to his right. They had him boxed in.

"Oh, Jesus," Julio sobbed. "Oh, Jesus, Mary and Joseph. . . ."

He could see five of them moving in on him, flicking out their long tongues and hissing, reptilian eyes glaring at him, jaws snapping open and closed with a sickening sound. *Hhhhhhhhhh-uppp.* . . . *Hhhhhhhhhh-upp.* . . . They were only several feet away now. He felt a long, sticky tongue lash out and curl around his leg, tightening painfully.

Julio screamed.

# Chapter 3

Someone was sitting at his table in the back when Makepeace got to Lovecraft's Café on Friday evening, after classes. Lovecraft's was his regular place, a rebeat bar popular with students and artists and other Village counterculture types. The atmosphere was sort of "kitsch occult," with fake skulls on every table in which candles were inserted; black tablecloths; black walls with murals painted in white of graveyards and mausoleums, gargoyles and skeletons; sawdust on the floor; and macramé spiderwebs hanging in the corners. The wait staff all wore black, a retro beatnik look to which some added black eyeshadow, black lipstick, and black-painted fingernails. The look was not as important as the demeanor, however. Most rebeats were anti-fashion and anti-anything that smacked of any sort of enthusiasm. The rebeat style was to cultivate a disaffected, jaded boredom with everything, a world-weary cynicism immune to the blandishments of Madison Avenue ad agencies, image makers, trend-setters, and politicians.

Makepeace lived in an apartment several floors above the bar, which was located in the basement of the building. Some of his students worked here during the evenings and a number of his colleagues dropped in from time to time, notable among them the irrepressible Dr. Morrison Gonzago, the literary lion of the English Department.

Gonzago's main claim to fame, outside of his literary accomplishments, was that he was the only member of the faculty who was regarded as even more outrageous than Makepeace. An adept of considerable skill, he had degrees in English literature, occult studies, and creative writing, as well as a doctorate in thaumaturgy. He was a hopeless alcoholic who had won the Pulitzer prize for his first novel and had scarcely written anything since, save for the occasional scathing review in the *Village Voice* or controversial piece of academic criticism in the *English Journal.* If anyone was sitting at his regular table in the back, it was usually Gonzo, waiting patiently for his colleague to show up and stand him to a drink or two.

However, on this occasion, it wasn't Gonzago who was seated at his table. Makepeace didn't immediately recognize the stranger as he came in. The man had close-cropped white hair and was balding. He wore an old tweed jacket in a brown glen plaid and khaki trousers. An old tan raincoat was folded and hung neatly over the back of the chair beside him. Makepeace frowned.

"Elvira . . ." he said, stopping a waitress as she went past. "Who is that gentleman at my usual table?"

She shrugged. "He didn't give his name, Dad. Said he was an old friend of yours."

"Indeed? What is he drinking?"

"Mineral water with a slice of lime."

It clicked. "Well, bring him another, my dear, and I'll have my usual," said Makepeace. He made his way through the bar to the table in the back. As he came around the table, Makepeace looked down at the man seated there. He sat with his hands clasped in front of him, a cigarette hanging from his lips. He had a high forehead and a close-cropped beard that had once been sandy and was now almost completely white. He looked to be in his late fifties or early sixties, still fit and muscular, but slightly soft around the middle. He looked up and regarded Makepeace with gold-flecked, hazel-colored eyes staring through wire-rimmed glasses.

"Hello, Sebastian."

"Hello, Victor."

"Been a long time."

Makepeace nodded. "At least thirty years or more," he said, pulling out a chair and sitting down across from him. "I didn't even recognize you at first. It was the mineral water and lime that did it."

"Well, we all get older." Victor Simko regarded him steadily with his sleepy-looking hazel eyes. "Or at least most of us do. You're looking remarkably well for a man your age."

The waitress came over and set the drinks down before them. Makepeace thanked her and she left.

"We're both still creatures of habit, I see. Bushmills and black coffee, no whipped cream. Or Guinness in a pitcher, if it's the afternoon. You always could put it away. And you still dress like Oscar Wilde on acid."

"Whereas you look like a college professor," Makepeace replied with a faint smile. "Not quite the dapper fashion plate that I recall."

"Well, I had to give up on my tailor. And a few other things, besides. Retirement isn't all it's cracked up to be. Things have been a little lean the last few years. But they should be picking up now that I'm back on the company payroll."

Makepeace raised his eyebrows. "You've been reactivated? I thought the old department was disbanded."

Victor smiled. "Ever since they put us old warhorses out to pasture, there hasn't been much call for people with our particular talents. The young turks are all a bunch of bureaucrats. Oh, they still have a few bright field agents here and there, but they lack our *je ne sais quoi.*"

"That was a long time ago," said Makepeace, remembering.

"So what's thirty, forty years to a man who's lived to be two thousand?"

Makepeace pursed his lips and nodded. "I see you've been fully briefed. Wetterman?"

"The big man himself," said Simko. He smiled again. "He told me quite a story. Answered a lot of questions that've been troubling me over the years. It's funny. Wetterman was still in diapers the last time I was active, so of course he wouldn't remember. I'm just a file to him. But I make for some impressive reading."

"I have no doubt of that," said Makepeace. "But then, you're not as young as you used to be."

"No, but I'm still just as persistent. Maybe a little more so. Age has a way of giving you perspective. Makes you take things more in stride. But then, I guess you'd know all about that."

"It bothers you, doesn't it?" said Makepeace.

"That I've gotten old and you haven't?" Victor shrugged. "Yeah, I guess it does, a little. It's nothing personal. It's just that it's taken me a long time to get used to being on the downslide. Retirement didn't sit too well with me. And now I see you and you look just the same. Hair's a little longer, you've gained some weight, but otherwise you don't look a day older than the last time I saw you, thirty-five years ago. Makes me feel old."

"I'm sorry."

Simko shrugged and took a drag on his cigarette, then stubbed it out. "Not your fault. You can't help it. Just feels strange, that's all. But I'll get over it."

"I think we're about to have company," said Makepeace, as he glanced up and saw Gonzago coming toward them.

"I'll be heading out, then. I'll be in touch."

As Simko stood and picked up his coat, Gonzago came sweeping up to them, resplendent in his blue sorcerer's robes with little moons and crescents and cabalistic symbols on them. His long beard was wild and unkempt, as usual, and he was carrying a battered old leather briefcase.

"I'm not intruding, I trust?" he said.

"It's all right, I was leaving anyway," said Simko. He gave Gonzago a quick once-over, sizing him up with a glance.

"Not on my account, I hope?" Gonzago thrust out his hand. "Dr. Morrison Gonzago, at your service, sir."

Simko took his hand and shook it in a perfunctory manner. "Nice to meet you. Be seeing you, Sebastian."

Gonzago watched him leave, then turned to Makepeace with raised eyebrows. "Well, not exactly the outgoing sort, is he?"

Makepeace shook his head. "No. Not exactly."

"I don't believe I've seen him around before," said Gonzago, sitting in the chair Simko had vacated. "Friend of yours?"

"He's someone I used to know a long time ago."

"What does he do?"

Makepeace watched as Simko went through the bar toward the front door, attracting no attention whatsoever. He looked like a senior faculty member at the university, or perhaps an antiquarian book dealer.

"He works for the government."

The top floor of the ITC complex was bustling with activity. Additional security cameras and T-scan monitors had been installed, as well as dozens of hack-proof computers with thaumagenetically etched chips and spellwarded phone lines. The ITC had brought in their best and brightest to man the center around the clock and within days they were plugged in to every data bank and communications center in the country. Teams of analysts accessed and scanned financial statements, social security files, vehicle registrations, phone records, police computer files, real estate transactions, everything they could possibly think of in search of any patterns that might emerge to guide them in their investigation. Gypsy was heading up a special section of psychics to help analyze the data.

It was a massive undertaking, but they were aided in their efforts by the extensive resources of the National Security Agency, which had years of experience in accumulating and analyzing billions of pieces of data from every available medium. The thaumaturgically animated computers were capable of learning as they went along and aiding in the decision-making process that guided their analysis of all the data that kept flowing in to them. Telephone conversations throughout the country were being randomly monitored by programs designed to scan for certain key words and phrases. It was the greatest electronic manhunt ever assembled, except the quarry they were hunting wasn't human.

By contrast, the atmosphere up in the penthouse was far less frenetic. Wyrdrune, Kira, Angelo, and Billy had little else to do but wait and sit through briefings and go through condensed reports that were compiled for them every day. And it was driving them all to distraction. They welcomed the periodic visits from Steve McGuire or the Gypsy or Makepeace, which provided them with the only breaks in an otherwise dull and monotonous routine.

"I don't like it," McGuire was saying as he sat on the couch sipping an iced tea. "Bringing in people like Simko is asking for trouble. I tried to run a check on him, but I ran into a wall of security. I even invoked my clearance and it got me nowhere. I didn't need Natasha's crystal ball to tell me what kind of operative Simko was or who he worked for. But I don't like being stonewalled. I thought we were all supposed to be on the same team."

"We are," said Wetterman. "But Simko has been assigned to this operation as a senior field agent by my office. I cleared him for it personally. We didn't go through the regular channels, for reasons of security."

"I didn't think we used people like Simko anymore," McGuire said with a grimace of distaste.

"Well, we don't. That is to say, we haven't for quite a while. But this is a rather unusual situation and we've had to reactivate some operatives who had retired."

"I think you're making a mistake," McGuire said.

"Who is this guy?" asked Wyrdrune.

"Victor Simko was a covert operative for the CIA, specializing in what they called 'wetwork,'" Makepeace replied. "In other words, assassination. He was recruited out of the army in the period following the Collapse, when magic was only starting to spread throughout the world. There was a great deal of concern at the time about establishing regulatory agencies and so forth, and certain people in the government were alarmed about 'thaumaturgic proliferation,' as they called it. It was a confusing time and there was a great deal of paranoia. Not all of it unjustified. There were people in certain foreign governments—and some in ours, as well—who wanted to use magic in ways Merlin never intended."

"A lot of mistakes were made," Wetterman added, nodding. "It was before my time, of course. In those days, the NSA and Central Intelligence weren't always on the same wavelength."

"There were occasionally certain jobs the CIA was either unable or unwilling to handle directly," Makepeace said. "They had used freelance operatives in the past and it wasn't unusual procedure for them. Victor Simko specialized in setting up those kind of jobs and cleaning up after them, if any cleaning up was needed."

"So he was the agency's contract man for Morpheus?" said Wyrdrune, referring to Modred's onetime alias.

Makepeace nodded. "And I was the middleman. The two of them never actually met, but they knew about each other. Simko never knew who Modred really was, of course. The agency had used him on several jobs in the Mideast in the days before the ITC finally started getting things under control. And then they started using their own field agents. The BOT was formed and the CIA was downsized, rendered largely redundant. Simko was taken off active duty and retired. They didn't really need people like him anymore. Until now, apparently."

"You should have called me before running a check on him," Wetterman said to McGuire. "That may have created some problems for us. Nothing very significant, I hope. Officially, Simko is retired. I didn't want anyone to know he'd been reactivated."

"Then you should have told us about him first," said Makepeace. "I tried to get hold of you, but kept getting the runaround from your office. I called Steve because I didn't know what else to do. Simko said he'd been reactivated, but I wasn't about to take his word for it. With you being unavailable, I figured Steve's inquiries would eventually shake something loose. And apparently they did, because you're here."

"All right, so we have some kinks to iron out," said Wetterman. "I've been swamped trying to get us up and running and I admit I may have dropped the ball on this one, but from now on, I'll be available twenty-four hours a day. I've moved into my office downstairs and the hot lines are in place. From now on, if you have any questions about any aspect of the operation, you come straight to me."

"My only question at the moment is how this guy Simko fits in," said Wyrdrune. "And how many others have you got just like him?"

"It doesn't matter how many others there are," said Kira. "They won't be much use against the Dark Ones unless they happen to get real lucky."

"That isn't their intended purpose," Wetterman replied. "We've reactivated a dozen of our old covert operatives, including Simko. Their primary role is twofold. One, to work the field and provide first response to establish for certain what we're really dealing with. It would be counterproductive to have you running all over the country, responding to every report of possible necromantic activity. Two, to provide backup support and make sure nobody gets in your way if we do have to put out a fire."

"Put out a fire," Wyrdrune repeated. "That makes it sound so innocuous."

"That's the general idea," Wetterman said. "We want to avoid panic at all costs."

"So how are we supposed to know who these people are?" asked Billy. "Is there going to be some sort of code phrase or recognition signal?"

"Yes, there is," said Wetterman. "They will identify themselves to you by the phrase, 'I used to be a fireman, but things are warming up again.' The response is, 'Yes, things are getting hot.'"

Kira giggled. "God, that's so corny!"

"It's meant to serve a purpose, not provide scintillating repartee," said Wetterman dryly.

"All right, fine," said Wyrdrune. "Let's just hope we come up with something soon. I'm starting to get stir-crazy being cooped up in here."

Maria almost felt bad about Joey. After all, he had come back for her. Too bad he hadn't listened when she told him she didn't want to leave. In a way, she liked it that he had come back, because it meant he cared, but in another way, it made her angry because what she wanted didn't count for anything. So when it came right down to it, how much could he really care?

That was the way it always was with Joey. It was always what Joey wanted that mattered. Joey wanted to make a big score, so he blew it and he went to prison and then she had to go out on the streets again. She hadn't really minded that so much. It was an easy way of making money and it beat hell out of working. She could have made more money as a stripper, but she wasn't pretty enough and they didn't like her scars. The johns on the street weren't so particular. Men always wanted it and no matter what they said or how they acted, in the end it always came down to that one thing, so she had decided early on that she might as well get paid for it instead of giving it away and then getting treated lousy.

Joey hadn't wanted her to work the streets, so when he was around, she hadn't. She had stayed at home and watched TV, because he didn't want her going out, and she had started gaining weight. She was doing too much coke, she knew that, but what else was there to do? And then Joey got sent up and the money had started to run out and she went back to work again. But she had gotten sloppy. There were a lot of girls on the street, many of them younger and with better bodies, and the johns weren't hitting on her like they used to, so she had gotten desperate and dropped her guard and got busted by an undercover cop. It was the best thing that ever happened to her.

When the public defender set up the plea bargain with the rehab center, she had told herself it was exactly what she needed. Clean up, get straight, make a fresh start. She'd told herself that dozens of times before and each time she had thought she really meant it, but then she'd start climbing the walls and she'd have to score some coke, telling herself it was just to take the edge off, she'd try again tomorrow. Only tomorrow never came. Until she met Brother Talon, who had shown her an entire infinity of tomorrows.

He had told her he could make the craving go away and he had, just like that, with a mere touch. He had the power and he told her he could show her how to get it for herself, the power of true faith, not the watered-down version she'd been taught. Had it helped her? Had it given her what she wanted? Had it made her stronger? No, of course it hadn't, because there were secrets that she didn't know about, things they never taught you because they wanted to keep you under control.

At first she doubted him, as had all the others, but Talon had a way of making you believe. He had charisma. He had the power. He had shown it to her and he had made her want it, too. And now, for the first time, she was about to find out what it was really like.

It was ironic that Joey finally made his big score. Too bad. He should have just taken the money and gone to Santa Fe, like he had planned. There was nothing stopping him. She had given him the chance. But no. Joey had to have things *his* way, as always. If he had wanted to go to Santa Fe without her, he would've just split and probably not even said good-bye. What she would've wanted would have made no damn difference. Just like it made no difference this time. He didn't like the idea of anybody else having what was his. He didn't like the idea of her standing up for herself and what she really wanted. So he came with a bunch of tough guys to take her away by force and teach Talon a lesson. Only things had turned out different than he'd planned.

"Goddamn it, Maria, get me down from here!"

She stood before him, watching curiously as he struggled to move, without success. He was pressed up with his back against a large stalagmite, his arms over his head, looking as if he were nailed there. Except he wasn't. There were no nails holding him, even though he did look a bit like Jesus on the cross, Maria thought, with his long hair hanging down and his shirt ripped away, revealing his bare, slim, and practically hairless chest. There were no ropes binding him, nothing but power. And there was no way he could break free, no matter how he tried.

"Maria! For chrissake! Get me down!"

She cocked her head and stared at him, as if seeing him for the first time. In a way, she was. She was seeing him from a completely new perspective. This wasn't a Joey who could slap her around whenever she did something to displease him, or whenever he just happened to be in a shitty mood from something else that happened that had nothing to do with her at all. This wasn't a Joey she had to wait on hand and foot, bringing him and his friends beers while they were watching football, cooking for them, cleaning up after them. This wasn't a Joey who could tell her what to do. Not anymore.

"Maria! *Please!* For God's sake!"

Please. He had never used that word with her before. She smiled.

"Forget it, man," said Rafe, from the other side of the stalagmite, where he was similarly held immobile. "Bitch ain't listenin' to you. She's one of them."

"Maria . . ." Joey's tone became pleading. "Maria, honey, you gotta get me down from here. I came back for you, baby. For *you*. Maria, I love you, baby. . . ."

"Fascinating, isn't it?" said Talon, coming up behind her. "He had power over you once. Now he would grovel at your feet if he could. Because he knows that you are stronger now. So he will beg and plead and bargain with you, promise you the world, swear undying love and loyalty, say anything at all to save himself . . . and then kill you the moment you display the slightest sign of weakness."

"Maria, don't listen to him! He's lying! Baby, I love you! *Please.* . . . You gotta listen to me!"

"Do you think he sounds sincere?" asked Talon.

Maria looked at him questioningly.

"Well, perhaps he is, right at this moment of emotional duress," Talon said. "Perhaps he even believes he really loves you. But ask yourself this: If you were to release him now and go away with him, go back to the way things were—assuming that you could—what do you suppose it would be like? How do you suppose he'd feel, remembering this moment? Because he would, you know, for the remainder of his life. He would never be able to forget the power you have displayed. He would always know that it was there, because once you have acquired the power, it never goes away. The knowledge will remain with you always, as will the taste for it. He'd know that he would never again be able to exert dominance over you and, more significantly, he would know that you could always control him. There would be no possibility of equality, because he would always know that you were stronger, that you held the power. And that knowledge would eat away at him, whether he remained with you or not. He would always be a slave to his knowledge of his own weakness. His only path to freedom would lie in killing you."

"Maria . . . don't listen to him, baby! I could never hurt you, never!"

"But you've hurt me before," she said softly.

A look of fear came into Joey's eyes.

"You see?" said Talon. "The weak will always fear the strong. And that which people fear, they hate. That is the way of the world. He will always fear your power, envy it, and hate you for possessing it. But you can set him free. You can take away his fear, his pain, his anger, his uncertainty, his cares . . . his mortality."

"Maria, no, don't do it. . . ." said Joey, his voice cracking.

"He came back to impose his will on you," said Talon. "To claim what he thought was his. And to kill me, for giving you the power to choose. He does not want you to have it. But now that you have tasted it, can you ever give it up?"

"No," she said, breathing heavily. "No, I want it. I want more."

"Then take it. Choose to be strong, Maria. Take his power and make it yours."

She murmured a spell under her breath and her eyes began to glow.

"Maria!" Joey shouted. "*Don't!*"

His dying scream reverberated throughout the cavern.

Even before the echos had faded, Joey Medina's body went limp and then collapsed to the cavern floor as the glow faded from Maria's eyes. Talon watched her as she breathed heavily through parted lips, her chest heaving as she trembled with the delirious sensation of life force coursing through her. It was like no high she had ever experienced before.

"*God* . . ." she whispered, gasping and shuddering as she closed her eyes in ecstasy.

Talon smiled as she reached out for him. He took her hands, interlacing his fingers with hers as her grip tightened convulsively. It wasn't a gesture of affection, but of desperation. She needed something to hold on to, something to anchor her to reality. He knew what she was feeling. The sensation of feeding on life force was intoxicating beyond words, absolutely overwhelming. He had experienced it countless times, but there was nothing like the first time, and watching her discover it took him back over the span of centuries, remembering what it was like for him when he became awakened to the power.

It had changed everything for him forever. Beyond the irreversible step of taking a life, a step from which there could be no return, there was the consumption of it, which rendered every other sensation that could be experienced paltry and dull by comparison. He knew, afterward, that he would never eat food the same way again, because the taste of it, no matter how well it was prepared, would seem utterly bland. Besides, there would be no need to take nourishment the ordinary way, although he could, because he would never feel hunger. Not in the same way. Not when life essence could be absorbed directly in a manner that invigorated every fiber of his being.

Yes, he knew how she felt as she hung on to him, squeezing his fingers with surprising strength, trying to maintain some touch with reality in the face of the incredibly powerful force that was flowing through her like a tidal wave.

There would be a very different sort of hunger for Maria from now on. No amount of stimulation would ever be able to compare with this. From now on, she would be hooked on necromancy as no drug had ever addicted her before. And the addicted personality had been already in place when he had picked her out. He had sensed the hunger in her, not so much the hunger for her drug, though that had been the most immediate manifestation of her need, but the all-consuming, driving hunger for something, anything, that would make her feel alive. For Maria had been almost completely dead inside when she had come to him, with just a faint spark of vitality deep down inside that cried for sustenance and could find nothing in life on which to become sated. She was a user because she was used up, and without using something or someone, she would always feel useless. She was the perfect predator.

"Go and rest now," he told her, releasing her hands. "For a time, everything will feel strange to you. Your perceptions shall be clearer, sharper; your senses shall be more acute. Your thoughts shall race out of control. You will need time to become accustomed to your new strength. Return to your quarters and meditate as I have taught you. Find the stillness. I shall come for you in the morning."

As Maria left, Talon walked around to the other side of the stalagmite, where Rafe was held immobile by a spell. The others were all dead, their life energies consumed by acolytes Talon had selected, the first of his new necromancers. The big, muscular black man he had saved for last.

"So," he said, his gaze meeting Rafe's, "it now comes down to you."

Rafe met his gaze unflinchingly, defiantly. His dark eyes were cold and hard and filled with fury.

"What a look!" said Talon. "I do believe you would tear me apart with your bare hands if you could."

"Just turn me loose and see, muthafucker," Rafe replied through gritted teeth.

"Very well," said Talon. "Show me."

He made a brief, languid pass with his hand and Rafe suddenly felt the force holding him against the rock disappear. Immediately, he lunged at the necromancer with a snarl, seizing him around the throat. Talon didn't even move. His eyes flared with blue light that completely obscured the whites and the pupils and Rafe felt icy tendrils wrapping themselves around his mind, filling his head with a numbing cold fog.

All the strength suddenly seemed to leave his hands and fingers; he barely felt aware of them. Gritting his teeth and grunting, he fought against the relentless numbness that swept over him. His shoulder muscles bunched with the strain, but the chilling numbness was inexorably spreading up his arms and through his body. He refused to submit, fighting it with every ounce of will that he possessed, but it was useless.

It was as if he were anesthetized, detached, unable to control his body or his mind as the freezing cold permeated his entire being. He became dizzy, and though he tried to fight it, he felt as if he were falling, spinning away into some dark abyss. Inwardly, he screamed with rage and frustration, but outwardly he couldn't make a sound as his lips pulled back from his teeth and he trembled violently with the effort he was making, all to no avail. His numbed hands slipped from Talon's throat and he collapsed to the floor of the cavern, still conscious, but unable to move.

"Such primal rage!" said Talon as the glow faded from his eyes. "I am impressed. Your will is unusually strong. I knew you were different from the others. It would be a shame not to exploit such excellent potential."

Rafe heard him through a fog of numbness. He felt trapped in his own unresponsive body, yet a glimmer of hope suddenly flared within him as he realized that he was not about to die, after all. At least, not yet.

"You are a man who understands power," Talon said, looking down at him, "but until now, you have only understood brute strength. Now you begin to see what true power can do. It can take your life effortlessly, or it can bring you rewards beyond your imagination. Both are within my control. Meditate on that while you regain your strength. We shall speak again tomorrow."

# Chapter 4

"I think we may have something," Wetterman said as he referred to a report. None of the others bothered looking at them anymore. The summarized printouts that arrived each morning and afternoon made for boring reading and had quickly palled on them. Wetterman realized that and took it upon himself to condense the process even further in a daily briefing over a late breakfast.

He knew the isolation and the inactivity was wearing on them. He had encouraged them to become more actively involved with the daily activities of the task force, spending more time with the analysts and conducting briefings about what they should look for, as well as working out with trainers each day in the gym to keep themselves fit. He had arranged for them to take martial arts classes and weapons training, which they seemed to enjoy, and he had also tried setting up lectures by NSA instructors in such subjects as data analysis, security and surveillance techniques, but those seemed to bore them as much as the reports. He finally gave up on the idea of trying to turn them into field agents when Wyrdrune pointedly reminded him that they didn't work for him and unless something broke real soon, they were all going to take a walk. And Wetterman knew he couldn't really stop them. What would be the point? Legally, perhaps, he might have plenty of grounds, as the situation concerned national security, but realistically he needed them and if they chose not to cooperate, things could get real sticky.

"What is it this time?" Kira asked wearily. None of the possible leads so far had panned out and there had been no reported cases of death by necromancy anywhere. The tension was getting to everyone. "We've come up with a rehabilitation center for substance abuse and juvenile offenders near Tucson, Arizona, run by some sort of religious group calling itself the Order of Universal Spiritual Unity."

"Never heard of it," said Angelo.

"It's largely funded by a nonprofit foundation operated by a minister named Armitage, James P., who was ordained through the mail. Nothing illegal about that, though, and on the surface, at least, they seem to have all their ducks lined up in a row."

"But?" said Billy.

"But when you look closer, things start to get a bit more interesting," said Wetterman. "They've basically dotted every 'i' and crossed every 't,' and they haven't had any trouble, not even the slightest irregularity. The center is located on a mountain called Dragon Peak, the site of the old Kitt Peak National Observatory. The land is owned by a foundation chaired by Armitage, the same foundation which administers the center. It also functions as a natural preserve. For dragons, no less."

"*Dragons?*" Wyrdrune said.

"Thaumagenes." Wetterman gave them a brief rundown on how the preserve had been established. "The Armitage Foundation contributes heavily to a number of environmental groups," he continued, "as well as to the political campaigns of some significant incumbents, among them the governor of Arizona and several congressmen and senators, as well as local elected officials. The environmental groups, in turn, help support the preserve and the politicians grease the bureaucratic wheels for the center."

"So they're run by a rich and well-connected philanthropist who knows how to play the game," Angelo said with a shrug. "Doesn't necessarily mean anything."

"Except this particular philanthropist used to be a small-time drug dealer and loan shark known as Jimmy 'the Arm' Parker, who managed to plea-bargain several felonies down to misdemeanors and skated on about a dozen other charges due to various technicalities and witnesses suddenly changing their stories or refusing to testify."

"That *is* interesting," said Wyrdrune. "So where did Armitage or Parker get the money to start up his foundation?"

"Are you ready for this?" asked Wetterman. "He won the lottery."

"You're kidding," Angelo said.

"Biggest pot in the history of the state," said Wetterman. "Over a hundred million dollars. It just kept turning over and over until he won the whole thing by buying one five-dollar ticket."

Kira whistled. "Wow. What are the odds of that?"

"You want to know? Right here," said Wetterman, showing her the figure on the report. She whistled again.

"So a guy like this suddenly decides to turn over a new leaf and become a good samaritan?" said Angelo. He shook his head. "I suppose it's possible, but I don't buy it."

"Neither do I," said Billy.

"It gets better," Wetterman said. "Parker has some sort of religious experience, changes his name to James P. Armitage, gets himself ordained a minister, then starts the Order of Spiritual Unity, counseling drug offenders, hookers, and juvenile delinquents. He sets up the Armitage Foundation with the help of a team of lawyers and accountants, starts doing good works and cultivating relationships with various politicians, all very low-key and apparently well-intentioned, then sets up the Dragon Peak Enclave as a spiritual retreat, counseling center, and ecological preserve. But he doesn't hire a single trained substance abuse counselor from either the Tucson or Phoenix areas, or anywhere else so far as we can tell, nor a single qualified therapist. A number of people in the area expressed interest in working for the center, but all of them were told politely that applications were not being accepted. The center uses only peer counselors, and whatever training they receive, if any, they receive at Dragon Peak. And there's nothing on record about how the center functions, either. We don't know anything about the specific nature of the treatment or the counseling."

"What kind of results have they had?" asked Kira.

"They've been very successful," Wetterman replied. "Remarkably so. Not a single case of a reported relapse. And among the court-referred cases of various offenders who went through treatment and counseling at the center, not one has ever had any trouble with the law since being discharged from treatment. In fact, some of the worst offenders chose to stay on at the center as either peer counselors or members of the enclave. Their success rate seems to be a hundred percent."

"That's impossible," said Angelo.

"Well, unlikely, maybe, but not impossible," said Wyrdrune. "Have they got any adepts on their staff?"

"Not unless they're using unlicensed adepts," said Wetterman. "And that would leave them wide open to civil lawsuits, not to mention criminal charges."

"Yeah. Why take the risk when you can simply hire licensed adepts?" Angelo said.

"My point exactly," Wetterman replied. "There's no shortage and it's not as if they can't afford it. The center is technically a separate entity from the Armitage Foundation and receives state and private funding in addition to its foundation backing. Their finances and affairs are managed expertly, by top people. In the few years they've been operating, they've acquired an excellent reputation. Jimmy the Arm has come a very long way. He seems to have been a street-smart operator, but not smart enough to do all this on his own. He had to have a lot of help."

"How would a street hustler like that know who to go to?" Billy asked.

"Well, with the kind of money he fell into," Angelo said, "he could easily hire a bright lawyer to find the right people for him. He'd certainly have known who the top lawyers in town were. But I'm wondering if he had any help winning that lottery in the first place."

"Yeah, I was wondering about that, too," said Kira. "Only how do you rig a state lottery?"

"On the surface, it doesn't seem as if you can, even using magic," Wetterman replied. "There's simply too much of a random element involved. A lot of the numbers are computer-generated, while others are picked at random by the ticket buyers. I don't see how you can influence anything like that on a state level. It does seem impossible."

"There's that word again," said Wyrdrune. He frowned, thinking. "Nothing is impossible. Especially when it comes to the Dark Ones. If the ticket companies are generating the numbers, then the obvious way to rig that would be to control the computers."

"But what about the numbers picked at random by the ticket buyers?" Wetterman asked. "You know how people are. Some of them play their birth dates for luck, or the birth dates of their kids, social security numbers, anniversary dates, any sort of combination that might have some sort of personal significance. You can't possibly influence every individual who buys a ticket. And that's pretty much what you'd have to do. You'd have to cast a spell capable of covering an entire state. Nobody has that kind of power. I just don't see how it could be done."

"You've got a point there," Angelo agreed. "It does seem impossible."

"Maybe not," said Wyrdrune thoughtfully. "We have to look for common factors. What's the one common factor among everyone who enters the lottery?"

"Tickets!" said Kira.

"Influence the *tickets*?" Angelo said.

"Or the paper they're printed on," said Wyrdrune. "The job is probably contracted out to one place that provides the paper for the machines and the entry forms the customer fills out. Cast a spell on the paper and you can influence both the machines and the customers. Then all you have to do is control the choice of the winning number by casting a spell on the machine that pops the balls out. That reduces the whole thing to controlling just two elements."

"Boy, that's good," said Angelo.

"How come you never thought of this before, when we were broke?" asked Kira wryly.

Wyrdrune shrugged. "Never occurred to me, I guess. Besides, back then I wouldn't have had the skill to pull it off."

"Yeah, I remember how you kept screwing up your spells," said Kira. "It's a miracle you didn't get us killed."

"Well, if that's how it was done," said Wetterman, "then we couldn't check the tickets, because too much time has passed. They're all gone by now, thrown out and recycled, but the machine that picks the winning number might still have some trace emanations on it. Unless they've changed it. But it's worth checking out."

"We're forgetting one thing," said Kira. "Armitage or Parker or whatever his name is might have gotten some adept to rig the lottery, but there's still no indication that any of the Dark Ones are involved. Wherever they turn up, people wind up dying."

"I was getting to that," said Wetterman. "We still don't have any authenticated reports of necromancy, but we have established a possible connection in several reported disappearances." He consulted the documents in front of him. "Joseph Medina, a recently released repeat felony offender, failed to report to his parole officer and has apparently disappeared. A warrant has been issued for his arrest. Several known associates of his, all with records, have also disappeared." He briefly went over their names and prior offenses. "They were all last seen together at a bar in South Tucson two weeks ago. A day after they were spotted in the bar, a van was stolen from the parking lot of a shopping mall in Tucson. That same van was found wrecked at the side of the road on Ajo Highway, about forty miles west of town. The van had numerous dents and scratches on it, along with pieces of brush stuck in the undercarriage. It had been rolled several times, though there was no trace of an accident where it was found by the side of the road, nor were there any traces of damage to the brush in the vicinity. Medina's fingerprints were discovered in the van, as well as the prints of several of the other men who disappeared. There was a fully loaded 9mm semiautomatic found lodged under the passenger seat rails. It had been reported stolen a year earlier and the fingerprints of Julio Rodriguez, one of the missing men, were on the gun."

"Not exactly pros, were they?" Angelo said. "But where's the connection?"

"Ajo Highway is the road leading out to Dragon Peak," said Wetterman. "And Medina had a girlfriend named Maria Sanchez, an addict with a number of arrests for possession and prostitution. Her last arrest was dated shortly before Medina was released and her attorney plea-bargained her out into the drug rehabilitation program at Dragon Peak."

"So Medina gets out, decides he wants his girlfriend back, and gets some friends together to help bust her out of rehab," Angelo said. "And the next thing you know, the van they stole for the job is discovered out in the desert, wrecked and with a gun inside it. And no trace of the suspects. I could believe they walked away, but I don't believe they picked up the van and moved it. And guys like that wouldn't leave a perfectly good gun behind."

"Were there any trace emanations on the van?" asked Billy.

"Plenty," Wetterman replied. "The sheriff's department ran a T-scan as soon as they realized the vehicle had been moved and it was in no shape to be driven. The battery had been cracked in the accident."

"I think we need to take a trip out to Arizona," Wyrdrune said.

"Maybe, but not just yet," said Wetterman. "I'm going to ask you to sit tight for a while longer." He raised his hands to forestall their reaction. "Look, I know this isn't very easy for you all. But before we go off half-cocked, I want to make sure we've really got a fire to put out. We know magic was involved somehow, but we don't know for sure that it was necromancy."

"Yes, but *we* will," said Wyrdrune. "The runestones react to the emanations."

"But suppose it's a false alarm and while you're off in Arizona, we get a real one somewhere else," said Wetterman. "We'll lose valuable time and that could result in more people being killed. I know you're used to doing this on your own, but you've got a lot more resources backing you up now. Let's use them to full advantage. That way, we minimize the chances of making any mistakes."

"He's got a point," said Angelo.

"But suppose while we're waiting here for confirmation, it all suddenly blows up in Tucson and a lot of people die," said Wyrdrune.

"I'm prepared to take that responsibility," said Wetterman. "It's a calculated risk, but I have to make decisions like that every day."

"Not like this, you don't," said Wyrdrune. "If time's a factor, and it is, we could teleport to Tucson without depleting any of our energy by having a team of ITC adepts combine to cast the spell."

"And if you need to get back in a hurry, how do you get back without using up a lot of energy?" Wetterman countered. He shook his head. "Besides, it's much too risky teleporting over that kind of distance. All I'm asking you to do is wait until we get some more hard data. I'm putting Simko on it. And according to the CIA, he's one of the best there is."

Wyrdrune shook his head. "I don't care how good he is; if he runs into a necromancer, he'll be way out of his league."

"Then if he fails to report in as scheduled, we'll know what we need to know, won't we?" Wetterman replied.

The buzzer sounded in Makepeace's apartment. Without getting up from his desk, he reached back over his shoulder and jabbed a finger into the air. The talk button on the buzzer by the door, clear on the other side of the apartment, was pushed in. "Who is it?" Makepeace yelled.

"Simko."

Makepeace sighed, jabbed at the air again and buzzed him in. He leaned back in his chair and stared at the pile of papers he had yet to grade. Not tonight, apparently. "Oh, well," he said to himself.

He swiveled his chair around and made a beckoning gesture toward the small kitchen at the front of the apartment. One of the cabinet doors over the counter opened and a glass drifted out and down onto the counter. Makepeace gestured once again and the cabinet door closed, then the one next to it opened. A chromed martini shaker drifted out and down, setting itself on the counter by the glass. A pitcher followed it.

Another spare gesture and a bottle of vermouth placed back against the wall atop the counter slid out, the cap unscrewed itself, and the bottle floated up and poured a dash into the shaker, then capped itself back up again and returned to its proper place. Next, the freezer door opened and a tray of ice cubes slid out to hover in midair. Makepeace inverted his hand, from palm up to palm down, and the tray flipped over. He wrinkled his nose and the ice cubes cracked out of the tray and, instead of falling to the floor, drifted gracefully across the kitchen to clink into the shaker.

The empty ice cube tray slid back into the freezer and a bottle of Stolichnaya slid out and poured a generous amount into the shaker, then floated back into the freezer. The freezer door closed, the shaker capped itself, rose up into the air, and at a signal from Makepeace, proceeded to shake itself. It then poured the martini into the glass pitcher and the pitcher poured a drink just as a soft knock came at the door. The latch on the deadbolt clicked back.

"Come in, Victor, it's open," Makepeace called.

As Simko entered, the glass rose up into the air and met him, hovering before him. Simko smiled and plucked it from the air. "How thoughtful," he said. "Stoli?"

"But of course," said Makepeace. "I figured you'd be dropping in at some point. And I know you only drink things that are clear. Martinis, mineral water, 7-Up . . . as neutral and colorless as you are."

Simko grinned and came through the kitchen into the living room where Makepeace sat. He was still dressed the same way as when Makepeace last saw him in the bar. He set the glass down on the coffee table, removed his shabby raincoat and dropped it on the couch, then sat down beside it and picked up the glass, taking a sip.

"Ahh . . . perfect. Like an early morning mist in winter. Here's to better times." He raised his glass and drank again.

"You should have stayed retired, Victor," Makepeace said with a sigh.

"And enjoy my princely pension, you mean?" Simko drank again. "A dollar doesn't go as far as it used to. And they give me so very few of them. I deserve better, don't you think so?"

"I'm sure you do. But this job is one you don't deserve, believe me. Even a wicked man like you, with all you've done."

"But they're paying me very well," said Simko, raising his eyebrows. "I insisted on much better terms this time. I figured I had nothing to lose."

"You don't seem to have spent any of it on clothes," said Makepeace with a smile.

"No, I'm being rather more thrifty this time around. I don't know how long this job will last and I'm not deluding myself that there will be another one to follow. This will be my last hurrah, I fear."

"And then?"

Simko shrugged. "I was thinking Mexico. Maybe Jamaica. Someplace warm, where I can sit on a beach with a good book while young dark-skinned girls in thong bikinis bring me good cigars and ice-cold drinks with little umbrellas in them."

"Sounds very pleasant."

Simko grunted. "Beats hell out of sitting in the park feeding the pigeons."

"Why don't you just leave now?" asked Makepeace.

"Well, there's the small matter of the money," Simko said.

"Suppose I wrote you a check right now."

Simko raised his eyebrows.

"How much would you need?" asked Makepeace. "A hundred thousand? Two hundred? Three?"

"Are you serious?"

"Name a sum."

"Half a mil."

Makepeace swiveled his chair around and opened a drawer in his desk. He took out a checkbook with a dark red leather cover embossed with silver runes.

"You keep a checkbook for an account with that kind of money in it in your desk drawer?" asked Simko.

"It's spellwarded," Makepeace said, indicating the runes. "Assuming anyone managed to get past the wards protecting this apartment, then even if they got the drawer open, they still wouldn't see it."

"I can see it."

"That's because I'm holding it," said Makepeace. He put

it down on the desktop. The checkbook promptly disappeared.

"Nice touch. What bank would it be drawn on?"

"The Bank of New York," said Makepeace, reaching for a pen. "It's my petty cash fund. I'll call the bank president and let him know you're coming. It will all be handled quite discreetly."

"Sebastian . . . wait."

Makepeace paused with pen in hand and looked up.

"I don't doubt you have that kind of money," Simko said. "But why? You don't owe me anything."

"Let's just say it's for old times' sake," Makepeace replied. "I'd like to see you live long enough to enjoy your tanned girls, good cigars, and ice-cold drinks. You can buy yourself a brand-new wardrobe and leave first thing in the morning."

"Afraid I can't do that," Simko said. "I'm on a flight for Phoenix in two hours."

Makepeace frowned. "Phoenix?"

"Then a connecting flight to Tucson. We may have a fire. I'm supposed to check it out."

Makepeace put down his pen. "Jamaica's much nicer at this time of year."

Simko shook his head. "No can do, old friend. I already took the job. Can't take a job and then not do it in this line of work. It's not good for a man's reputation. And mine is about all I have left. It's worth a lot more to me than half a million dollars."

"I see," said Makepeace. "Well, I won't insult you by trying to put a dollar value on it. Something like that would never be for sale, not with a man like you."

"I appreciate that," said Simko. "Even more than I appreciate the offer, believe me."

Makepeace nodded and put away the checkbook. "Well, in that case, I'd better start packing."

"For what?"

"I'm going with you."

"Wetterman wouldn't like that."

"I don't much care what Wetterman likes or doesn't like," said Makepeace. "I don't work for him." He gestured toward his bedroom and a battered leather suitcase slid out from underneath the bed, floated up onto the mattress, and opened up. Another gesture and the bureau drawers slid open, disgorging clothing that started floating neatly into the open suitcase.

"You always were a lazy bastard," Simko said. "Seriously, Sebastian, I don't think you should go."

"Nonsense. You didn't come here just to say good-bye before you left. That never was your style."

Simko smiled. "Am I that transparent?"

"No, not really. I just know you."

"I could handle this myself, you know."

"I'm sure you think you can," said Makepeace. "I was hoping I could talk you out of this, but seeing as how you've got your pride all tangled up in it, I'm not even going to try. This isn't really about money, Victor, is it?"

Simko pursed his lips and stared at him over the top of his martini glass. "No, I suppose not."

"This isn't going to make you young again, you know."

"Oh, I know that," Simko said. "But it might keep me from feeling old. It'll be like old times, Sebastian. I miss those days. Don't you?"

"To be perfectly honest with you, no," Makepeace replied. "Believe it or not, I like my life right now."

"Teaching a bunch of snot-nosed kids and grading papers? What kind of a life is that, Sebastian, after where you've been and what you've done?"

"It actually has much to recommend it," Makepeace said. "Being a teacher has rewards you couldn't begin to understand unless you'd tried it."

"What does it do, satisfy some frustrated parental urge or something?"

"No, it's not like being a parent; you don't have the same responsibilities," Makepeace replied. "The focus is much narrower, more clear. You are responsible for the development of young minds. They come to you intellectually unformed, not really trained to think yet. Even starting college, most of them aren't thinking, just reacting. A few have started to develop, showing that first spark of real intellectual curiosity, and those can be particularly enjoyable to watch and guide along, because they already have the eagerness and the desire to learn. But most of them are merely there because they think they have to be.

"They think they're there to get good grades," he continued, "so they can get their degrees, which will help them get good jobs, careers. Most of them don't really understand what the purpose of a college education is. And it has only one purpose . . . to teach them how to think. It doesn't matter what they want to do. If they want to become lawyers, they need to learn to *think* like lawyers. Or if they want to become doctors, or adepts, or engineers, they need to know how to *think* like doctors, adepts, and engineers, how to think logically and systematically. Even creatively. Natural creativity cannot be taught, of course, but even if you possess it, you still need to learn how to organize your thoughts and how to communicate them effectively. Of course," he added with a smile, "they all believe they know how to do that already. After all, they're young adults. It's great fun to watch them realize they're wrong. And then become motivated because they don't like being wrong. Or because they've suddenly discovered that learning how to think is fun and stimulating. Or both. It's very rewarding to see them grow intellectually and realize you've had something to do with that. It's a form of satisfaction you really can't find anywhere else."

Simko smiled. "I'll bet you're a pretty good teacher."

"I happen to be an excellent teacher."

"But you're coming with me anyway."

Makepeace shrugged. "Well, when the fate of the civilized world is at stake, lecturing and grading papers doesn't seem quite as important, somehow."

Simko chuckled. "What about your classes?"

"Finals are coming up in a couple of weeks," said Makepeace. "My friend Gonzago can cover for me."

"That Merlin wannabe I met down in the bar?" asked Simko.

"Don't sell him short," said Makepeace. "He's a brilliant intellect, a gifted writer, and a very talented adept."

"He looked like a rummy to me," said Simko.

"Alas, he is that, also."

"You certainly know some strange people," Simko said.

"Present company included. But Gonzo is a good man, Victor. Not an evil son of a bitch like you."

Simko raised his glass. "*Touché.*"

Makepeace glanced over his shoulder. "Well, I appear to be all packed. If you hurry up and finish your drink, we've still got time for a quick lunch before we make our flight."

"Except you haven't made flight reservations," Simko said.

"I made them this morning," Makepeace said.

Simko frowned. "You knew?"

"Billy called me after the morning briefing, when he found out you were being sent to Tucson. He asked me to go along, to make sure you don't mess up."

"Cute," said Simko with a grimace. "I'm glad they have such a high opinion of my capabilities."

"They don't really know much about your capabilities," said Makepeace. "But they do know what the Dark Ones are capable of. As do I."

"Yeah, I guess you would." Simko drained his glass. "Well, let's see if a couple of old men still have what it takes to save the world."

"After lunch," said Makepeace.

"By all means," said Simko. "After lunch."

# Chapter 5

Talon was fascinated by the big, muscular black human. He was different. Not because he was black, but because unlike any other human he had ever encountered, regardless of race, nationality, or gender, he had a will of iron. It was disconcerting. Humans had always been easy to subjugate and control. This one, however, resisted to the last extremity. Talon could break him down. That was not the problem. The problem was that Rafe resisted with such a stubborn rage that the effort completely exhausted both his body and his mind. When Talon finally prevailed, as he did each time, of course, the man was absolutely useless, reduced to such a weakened state that he could barely even move or cogitate.

Each time Talon came to him down in the cavern, thinking that this time he would finally surrender, Rafe somehow always found the strength to fight him and it was necessary to beat him down again, reduce him to a sweating, trembling hulk lying on the floor, barely conscious and breathing raggedly. Much more of this, thought Talon, and his mind would be destroyed. And that would be a shame. With such immense strength of will, what a necromancer he would make! This brute, uneducated and barely civilized as he was, had the makings of a mage. Incredible that such outstanding potential could be wasted. Talon simply could not allow it to happen.

"Good evening, Rafe," he said, as he approached the stalagmite on which his captive hung, magically pressed up against the rock. "How do you feel tonight?"

"Like rippin' your fuckin' head off and pissin' down your fuckin' throat."

"A colorful image, if rather crude," said Talon with a faint smile. "Why must you continue to resist me? You are only making things harder on yourself. You haven't eaten for days. You must be starving. Wouldn't you like a nice, thick, juicy steak with all the trimmings?"

"Sure. Gimme a knife, bend over, and I'll cut myself a slice."

Talon chuckled. "I must admit, I have never met any human quite like you before. I literally hold the power of life and death over you and yet you refuse to submit with a dogged stubbornness that defies all comprehension. Why, when I have so much to offer you?"

"Nobody tells me what to do. Not you, not anybody. I don't care who the fuck they are. Or what."

"Indeed? Shall we test the limits of your commitment to that philosophy?" asked Talon. "We have barely even scratched the surface of what could be done to lower your resistance."

"Go for it. I don't give a shit."

Talon stared at Rafe thoughtfully. "You really don't, do you?" he said. "The paucity of your idiom notwithstanding, I begin to understand that you truly do not care. Whether you live or die, I mean. I find that fascinating. The strongest drive in humans has always been the instinct for survival. Yet you seem to lack that instinct. Does your life mean so little to you?"

Rafe simply shrugged. There was no point in trying to keep Talon talking. That would postpone the inevitable torture, but it would be only a postponement and nothing more. Sooner or later, Talon would try to break him down again. The bastard was relentless. And Rafe also knew that, sooner or later, he would probably succeed. Assuming Rafe survived. But Talon seemed intent on that. He didn't want him dead. If he had, Rafe knew he would be dead already.

The son of a bitch was *strong*. He could do things with his mind, things Rafe couldn't even begin to understand. Rafe knew about adepts. He didn't like them. He understood what magic was. But this was something else. This was like no magic he had ever encountered before. Talon kept talking about power. Yeah, it sure as hell was that, Rafe thought. He understood power real well. He could bench-press four hundred and fifty pounds. When he hit somebody, they stayed hit. But Talon had a whole other way of hitting.

He kept talking about humans as if he weren't one. So then what in the fucking hell was he? Somebody from outer space? He looked human enough, but maybe that was only a disguise. Magic could do things like that, if you were good enough and really knew your stuff. But hardly anybody believed that "beings from outer space" stuff anymore. Nobody had ever seen one. Nobody who had his head screwed on straight, anyway. Still, that didn't mean it was impossible.

Maybe he was a demon. Rafe didn't know much about that, but he'd heard stories about how some adepts experimenting with spells even mages should have known to leave well enough alone had summoned up some kind of nasty shit. Things that didn't like being summoned from wherever the hell they'd been summoned from. Wherever the *hell*. Maybe all that shit they taught you when you were a kid was true, after all. Who knew? Those stories always ended with the adepts becoming lunch in various unpleasant ways and Rafe had never really believed any of it. Until now.

If this guy Talon was an adept who'd crossed over the line and started playing around with black magic, he might have summoned up something that took him over. That could explain why he kept talking about humans as if he weren't one. Maybe the body was human, but whatever was inside was something else. Or maybe Talon was just insane, a skilled adept who had gone around the bend. In either case, Rafe figured, he was screwed no matter what he did. So why give the bastard the satisfaction of crawling at his feet?

Talon had been watching him curiously, studying him with a bemused expression on his face, like a little kid looking at some new kind of bug, Rafe thought. Well, fuck him. He didn't care if Talon was a space alien, a demon, or just some sorcerer who'd gone completely out of his gourd; it made no difference. If he could get loose, he'd kill the son of a bitch. And if he was going to die, then he'd go spitting in the motherfucker's face.

"I am intrigued by your defiance," said Talon. "I could do things to you that would drive most men insane. I could destroy your mind and turn you into a living automaton that would do my slightest bidding. It would be child's play. But I don't want that. No, that would be a waste. I do not want your destruction. You are the only one who seeks that. I want your submission."

"You got a long wait, man," said Rafe.

Talon smiled. "I am used to waiting. I have a great deal of patience. Besides, in a perverse sort of way, I am beginning to enjoy this little contest. Any other human in your situation would have long since submitted to me, or at the very least attempted to make the pretense. Not you. The rest of them submitted willingly, eagerly, when they understood what I was offering them. But not you. None of the others understood power the way you do. Yet even though I offer you more power than any ordinary human could possess, you still reject it. Because you reject me. I am not accustomed to being rejected. I find it an . . . interesting experience."

"Get used to it," said Rafe.

Talon chuckled. "You know, I'm growing rather fond of you. I could overwhelm you easily, but that would destroy the part of you I value most. I could cause you infinite pain, inflict horrors upon you beyond your imagination, and you would submit. You would. But I don't want you that way."

*I don't want you that way.* Rafe felt a wave of disgust. It sounded sexual. In a way, maybe it was. The guy was a control freak. Rafe understood that real well. It took one to know one. He was the same way with women. There were always women who had wanted him, because they were turned on by his body or his hard looks or else his reputation or, if they were white women, by the fact that he was black and dangerous-looking, but it was the ones who didn't want him that had always attracted him the most. Especially the racist white bitches who couldn't possibly imagine being with a black man. Those were the ones who really turned him on. He wasn't into rape. He wanted to *make* them want him. And it was so great when they turned. It was always worth whatever effort he put into it.

First there was that moment of discovery when they realized they wanted him. He could always see it in their eyes. Like they couldn't believe what they were thinking. And the more they thought about it, the more it turned them on until, eventually, they had to have him. And then he'd play with them. You want some nigger cock, bitch? Work for it, baby. Work for it. And when the anticipation had built up and they finally got down to it, it was always great, because they'd fucking well explode. And even though he liked the sex, that wasn't what it was all really about.

*I don't want you that way.*

So that's the game, you perverted son of a bitch, thought Rafe. All right, so it wasn't really about sex. But it was close enough. And in a lot of ways, it was even worse. The guy was fucking with his mind, with his goddamn soul.

"You'll have to kill me first," said Rafe.

Talon raised his eyebrows slightly, and then a look of comprehension came over his face. "You think my motivation is desire?" He shook his head. "No, you misunderstand."

"Do I?"

"I want you not for what you are, but for what you are capable of becoming," Talon said. "It is not a matter of desire so much as . . . aesthetics. It is easy to destroy something. But it is much more rewarding to create. And what I am creating is something unique. Something beautiful in its own way. The ultimate human predator. And when it comes to that, you possess far more potential than any of the others. You shall be my masterpiece, the closest thing to one of us that a human is capable of becoming."

"You think I want to be like you?" said Rafe. He snorted with derision. "Yeah, right."

"You do not have even the faintest conception of what it would be like to be like me," said Talon. "To live forever. To wield such power as to make others look upon you like a god. The others are only now beginning to understand."

"Your little cult members?" Rafe said scornfully. "So you give 'em black robes and teach 'em a few magic tricks. Big fucking deal. It's still the same old con game. How much do they kick in?"

"Kick in?" said Talon with a puzzled frown.

"Yeah, what's your cut of the action? They sign over all their worldly goods or what?"

"You think this is all about materialistic gain?" asked Talon. "If that is what you believe, then you have understood nothing I have said. I had thought you were more intelligent than that."

"Yeah, well, excuse me for being stupid," Rafe replied sarcastically. "So why don't you explain it to me, then? You give them all this power that you're talking about and, in return, what do they do for you?"

Talon raised his eyebrows. "They kill," he said simply.

"Kill who?"

"Why, anyone they like," said Talon, as offhandedly as if they were discussing the weather. "Of course, there are a few specific individuals who need to be removed, to make a greater impact and eliminate those who might be particularly troublesome. But otherwise they are free to choose.

Many of those you saw when you had first arrived have already left the enclave and gone out to feed . . . and to grow stronger. And then to feed some more. And then grow stronger still. That is the nature of power, you see. You have to feed it if you want it to grow. And the strong always feed upon the weak."

"You are one sick muthafucker," Rafe said.

"And you are a stubborn fool," Talon replied. "I am superior to you in every way. You cannot prevail. It would be like a gnat trying to take on an elephant."

"Yeah, but if that little gnat sticks to it and keeps buzzin' around, he can drive that big elephant plumb crazy," Rafe said.

"I wouldn't count on it," Talon said. "Each day, you grow weaker. Each day, my will encroaches further on your own. I could wipe out your resistance in an eyeblink, but that stubborn perseverance of yours would be destroyed and I could make good use of it. Very good use of it, indeed. So we shall take it in small steps, you and I. In a day or two at most, you will surrender and accept me. And then you will realize just how foolish you have been."

"Like you said, I wouldn't count on it," said Rafe. And then he jerked as he felt the icy tendrils of Talon's will insinuate themselves into his mind, like freezing tentacles.

His entire body went completely rigid, not from the effects of Talon's invasion of his mind, but from Rafe's efforts to resist it. Crucified as he was upon the huge stalagmite, he could barely move, but every muscle stood out in corded relief as he tensed, trying to find some way to fight it. Only there was no way. Brute force was something that Rafe understood, but no amount of physical force could overcome what was happening to him. He screamed with rage and frustration as the cold spread inexorably throughout his mind, like the roots of some parasitic plant invading his cortex, numbing everything they touched. His vision blurred as sweat poured off him and although he could not hear Talon's voice, he sensed his presence permeate his brain, aloof, confident, and mocking, willing him to submit.

There was no pain, just the numbing, freezing cold that continued to spread through him, slowly overwhelming his will, and the complete lack of pain somehow made it even worse. It was like fighting anesthesia, only this was like a living drug, sentient and ruthlessly determined. And Rafe knew that there was no way he could win the battle. He was slowly freezing from the inside out and he felt his mind become a brittle thing, capable of being shattered by a mere thought. He felt himself receding *from* himself, fading away into the cold that slowly froze his soul. He became a small thing within himself, shrinking down into a pinprick, on the verge of dark oblivion. And something else within him grew . . . unaccustomed, yet not completely unfamiliar; rigidly controlled, yet now uncontrollable; denied for years, and now made undeniable. And as Rafe felt himself falling away into nothingness, he felt despair, because he knew that he had lost.

Talon pulled back at the last instant. Another second, and Rafe would have been gone. He had pushed a little further every time, each time afraid that he would go too far and lose him and be left with nothing more than a mindless body to control, a zombie that would do his will, but have no will of its own. He had no need of that. There was no shortage of those whom he could use that way. In Rafe, he wanted something different, something more. And as he gazed at the massive, sweat-covered, and powerfully muscled body, watching it trembling like a whimpering, newborn child, he exhaled with relief.

It had taken every ounce of control that he possessed to force Rafe to the very edge of oblivion and then bring him back, undamaged and intact. Well, perhaps not entirely undamaged, he thought. It was like splitting a perfect diamond and leaving it with a tiny, almost imperceptible flaw. But it was a flaw he needed.

"Well," he said softly, "so you *are* human, after all. I knew that you could not possibly be completely fearless. Somewhere in the deep recesses of your mind, it had to be there." He nodded to himself. "An iron will, indeed. You had pushed it down so far, it took almost killing you to find it. Your one fear. The fear of fear itself. How very logical, all things considered. And there was no need to exploit it. All it took was showing it to you. You want to see it again?"

Rafe hung limp on the stalagmite, breathing raggedly, barely conscious, but he still managed to shake his head weakly. A small moan escaped his throat.

Talon smiled. "I know you now. And you belong to me."

He made a languid pass with his right hand and Rafe's body collapsed to the floor of the cavern as the spell binding him to the rock was canceled. He fell in a trembling heap, unable to move.

"Rest," said Talon. "When you awake, you will be strong again, stronger than you ever were before, stronger than you ever thought you could be. But never again strong enough to defy me. Wherever you go, whatever you do, a part of me shall be there with you, close to the one thing you had buried and kept hidden for so long. I *am* your fear now, Rafe. I can always bring it out and show it to you. Always. But you will find that is only a small price to pay for what I shall make of you."

He turned and left the big black man lying there, looking like a very large, discarded rag doll. There had never been any question in Talon's mind that he would prevail. No human had ever successfully resisted him. But none had ever put up so hard a struggle. Now it was over. Talon felt, at the same time, both smugly satisfied and strangely disappointed.

Maria didn't like Washington, D.C. It was cooler than Tucson, but it was much more humid, which made the heat of late summer feel sticky and unpleasant. She missed the comfortable dryness of southern Arizona and the familiar desert landscape. In the West, they had a saying that the distance got into your eye. She missed the open spaces, the tranquil vistas of the Sonora Desert where one could see for miles. Even the sky looked different here. The sunsets merely marked the end of day in a perfectly mundane and unremarkable manner, nothing like the spectacular washes of red, purple, pink, and orange that flooded the Arizona sky at twilight.

Maria had never been to the East Coast before. She had never even been out of Tucson before, except for that one trip to Vegas before she had met Joey. She had once entertained a dream of going to Vegas and making some big money, but she had quickly realized that the girls in Vegas were way out of her league. She just could not compete. She had returned to Tucson, where her dreams, such as they were, became anesthetized with drugs and she had settled into a comfortable and familiar, if slowly life-destroying, routine. Now, however, things were different.

The power had changed her. Her skin, which had never been very good to begin with and had been even further ravaged by her drug use, was now clear and glowed with vibrant health. Her dark eyes were bright and sparkling and her muscle tone had improved significantly. Her scars were gone and her black hair was long and lustrous, not limp and dried out from too much hair spray and too poor a diet. As a young girl, she had been pretty, but her prettiness had gradually faded after she started working the streets, replaced by a hard and trashy, vulgar sort of sex appeal that had still attracted a certain type of man, even though her looks continued to decay as her drug use had increased and her self-esteem was worn away. Now she looked like an entirely different person.

If Joey Medina could have seen her now, he wouldn't even have tried to make a move, because he would have thought that she was unattainable for someone in his station.

She was not only beautiful now, but she looked proud and classy and her new wardrobe reflected her image, one carefully chosen for her by Talon before he had sent her out to take the plane for Washington.

She had wanted to pick out her own clothes, but Talon vetoed all her choices as being crude and tasteless. And now, after she had learned a few things about how to act and dress, she knew he had been right. Before, even when she had money to spend on clothes instead of drugs, she had dressed like a cheap hooker. Now she thought she looked like a lady. Her dress was elegant, simple, and understated, but it flattered her figure, hugging her lush curves, and displayed an ample amount of leg without seeming too obvious. Her silk stockings made her legs look even better than they were, and they had always been her best feature. And her matching pumps had heels that were just high enough to give a flattering look without saying "come and get me." She noticed a lot of male heads turn in her direction when she walked into the restaurant and sat down at the bar.

The bartender glanced at her appreciatively as he took her order and treated her with a deference she liked. Her new sense of power gave her poise and confidence. It wasn't long before a man approached her. A good-looking man, well-dressed and obviously successful. He smiled warmly as he sat down next to her.

"I haven't seen you here before," he said. "New in town?"

She smiled, friendly, but just short of inviting, and nodded.

"You have the look," he said, smiling again. "A little overwhelmed. I felt like that when I first moved here. Are you a student?"

She shook her head. "Receptionist," she said. "Well, as soon as I can find a job, that is."

"Been going out on interviews?"

She nodded once again, then sighed. "Yes, but nothing definite so far."

He nodded sympathetically. "This can be a tough town to get work in if you don't have connections."

"Yes, that's what I hear," she replied. She glanced at her watch. "I was actually supposed to meet someone here who said he might know of an opening, but he's late and I'm beginning to think he's not going to show up."

"I find it hard to believe that someone would stand you up," the man said.

"That's kind of you to say."

"My name's Bill Robinson. May I buy you a drink?"

He offered his hand and she took it, holding it a second longer than necessary. "Maria Santoro," she said, improvising a new last name on the spot. "Thanks, I'd like that. It's been a long day of pounding the pavement. I'm thirsty and my feet are killing me."

Robinson signaled the bartender, who responded promptly. "You know," said Robinson, "I haven't had dinner yet and it's not much fun to eat alone. I don't mean to be too forward or anything, but would you like to join me? I'd be grateful for the company. And who knows, maybe we could brainstorm a little over food and figure out if I know anyone who might have a job for you. I've got a few connections in this town. I'm sure we could probably come up with something."

"That's very nice of you. I appreciate that. I'd love to."

After dinner, they lingered over drinks and then went back to his apartment. By then she had found out quite a lot about him. He was a businessman, single, upwardly mobile and on the fast track. She found out who he knew, which friends of his were influential, which ones were in business, which ones in politics. It was ridiculously easy. She didn't even have to say much, just act as if she found everything he said utterly fascinating. He kept up a steady stream of conversation, obviously trying to impress her. He tried, unsuccessfully, to hide his eagerness when she agreed to go back with him to his apartment. But once they were inside, he became eagerness personified and was all over her.

Five minutes later, he was dead. And Maria felt her power grow.

They had been in Tucson for over a week and Makepeace was growing restive. They took a comfortable suite at a hotel near the airport, not one of the best hotels in town, but well in the upper midrange, and the official cover story they agreed upon was that they were vacationing university professors.

"In your case, it's more or less the truth, isn't it?" Simko said when he suggested it.

"I have no objection," Makepeace replied, "but I hardly see the point. Why should we be so clandestine about this? All we need do is identify ourselves to the local authorities and we'll be able to get whatever cooperation we require."

"You've been away from this stuff for a while, Sebastian," Simko replied. "No offense, old friend, but you're not thinking it through. If we really do have a fire out here, how do we know none of the local officials are involved? It's happened before."

"Well, yes, I suppose that's true," Makepeace admitted. "But why do we even need to involve ourselves with the authorities here? It should be a simple matter to go out to the enclave and look around. After all, it's supposed to be open to the public, more or less. They schedule tours and have visiting hours, don't they?"

"No point in doing that until we've done our homework," Simko said. "We don't want to take any unnecessary chances, do we?"

Makepeace made a face. "No, you're right, of course. I'm not thinking. I haven't done this sort of thing in a long time, you know. For that matter, neither have you."

"All the more reason not to go jumping into anything," said Simko. "The deal is, we don't trust anybody until we know we can. We stay away from the local authorities completely for the time being. The enclave is politically connected in this town. Even if nobody's been suborned by magic, money always talks and chances are someone will drop a dime on us and let them know a couple of federal agents are in town asking around. Besides, we probably wouldn't get much more from the local bureaucrats than we've already got through the database. We already know everything there is to know about the enclave, officially. It's what the bureaucrats don't know that we're interested in."

"So what's the plan?" asked Makepeace.

"Well, they're running a rehab center up there, with court referral, right? So let's find out what the people on the street have to say about it. We already know what the bureaucrats think. Let's see what the junkies and the hookers have to say."

"What makes you think they'll talk to us?"

"We'll spread around some money. Neither one of us looks like a cop and for a few bills, we'll have no problem getting folks to talk to us. You're a worried father, desperate to find his little girl who ran away from home after she fell in with some fast company, and I'm the private eye you hired to help you find her. We're from New York City, where you're a successful gallery owner. Anybody can bullshit about art and the kind of people we'll be talking to won't know the difference, anyway. So we're looking for some spoiled little rich girl who got in over her head after she got involved with drugs. Just follow my lead and you'll do fine."

"What is my errant daughter's name?" asked Makepeace.

"I don't know. Pick one."

"Heather. I've always liked the name Heather."

"Okay. She's Heather Makepeace. Might as well use our real names. No reason not to and it'll make things easier."

"How old is little Heather?"

Simko shrugged. "Let's say she's sixteen. That way, anyone who would have been involved with her was playing around with jailbait and that might make some folks inclined to be cooperative."

"What does she look like?" Makepeace asked. "Shouldn't we have a photograph to show?"

"We'll get one. We'll just go down to the mall and pick up a cheap camera, then pay some kid a few bucks to get her picture taken. Tell her we're just testing out the camera. Main thing is to see what kind of scuttlebutt we can pick up about this rehab place. Though if you ask me, I think it's probably a false alarm."

"If it is, then it's all the more reason to check it out quickly and get back, in case there's a real one," said Makepeace.

"You know, for someone who's been around as long as you have, you ought to have more patience. Let's do this thing right, by the numbers. That way there's less of a chance of screwing up."

For the next week, they canvassed the streets, checking out the transient neighborhoods and the youth hangouts, flashing a photograph of a girl whose picture they had taken at the mall. Only once did someone seem to recognize the picture, and that was when a young girl in a coffeehouse thought it looked just like a friend of hers from school, but other than remarking on the strong resemblance, she had nothing of interest to offer. However, on the pretext of asking about drug rehabilitation centers the fictional Heather Makepeace might have been sent to, they did manage to pick up some information from several people who had heard about the enclave or known people who had gone there.

The general feeling on the street was that the place was some kind of religious cult, because people who had gone there never again went back to their old haunts or their old friends. They either got religion and stayed there or else they changed their lives around completely and usually left town.

By the end of the week, the two men actually managed to find someone who knew someone who had been sent there by the court and still resided in Tucson. When they tracked her down, they found the girl was living with her parents, who had nothing but praise for Brother Talon, who apparently ran the center.

The girl in question closely fit the profile they had designed for the fictional Heather. She was from a well-to-do family where both parents had careers that left them little time to spend with their children. Jane, the girl in question, was introduced to them and she seemed extremely well-mannered, happy, and well-adjusted. When Simko commented on that as they were leaving, her mother merely shook her head.

"It's amazing. You should have seen her before," she said. "We simply didn't know what to do with her. Janey was completely out of control. She was running around with a really bad crowd, getting involved with older boys who took advantage of her, using drugs, getting into fights. . . . We tried everything and nothing seemed to work. She dressed like something from a horror movie, was verbally and physically abusive to us both, and when we threatened to send her away to a boarding school in Prescott, she ran away from home and was missing for over a month. We were simply frantic with worry. For all we knew, she could have been dead, so it was actually a relief when we learned she had been arrested for possession."

"And the court sent her to the rehab center at Dragon Peak?" said Simko.

"We hired a good lawyer and it was her first serious offense, so it was made part of a plea bargain. Since she's a minor, her record would be sealed, and if she straightened out, it would eventually be expunged. To be honest, we didn't hold out much hope, but they worked miracles up at that clinic. You see what Janey's like now. She's clean, she's happy, she's like a completely different person, a normal little girl who goes to school and gets good grades and even attends church regularly. Every day, I thank God for Brother Talon."

"That's an unusual name," said Simko. "Sounds Native American or something. What sort of man is he? Have you met him?"

"Only briefly, when we went to pick her up. I'm sure he's not an Indian, though. He's got rather dark skin, but I think it's just a deep tan. He has red hair and most Indians are dark-haired. And he has the most incredible eyes. They're magnetic, a really bright emerald green. He's really quite handsome and he's got a lot of charisma. I can see why he's so successful with the troubled young people they send him. He looks very young himself, not like a clergyman at all. More like a rock star with that long hair of his. He has a real presence, one of those people who just seem naturally compelling. You can tell he's an intensely spiritual man."

"Sounds like a man I'd like to meet," said Simko. "Maybe he's heard something about Heather. We know she came to Tucson and she's had some trouble with drugs, too. We're just looking for any leads we can find."

"I really hope you find your daughter," the woman said to Makepeace sincerely. "I'm sorry I couldn't have been more help."

"Well, we appreciate your time, just the same," said Makepeace. "Thank you very much."

"Good luck," the woman said. "My prayers are with you."

As they were heading back to their rental car, Makepeace turned to Simko. "Red hair, dark skin, bright green eyes, a strong presence . . . That describes a Dark One to a T."

"Maybe. Or it could be a coincidence," said Simko with a shrug. "Could be he's just Irish. We need to be sure before we go sending up the balloon."

"Victor . . . you're not entertaining thoughts of handling this yourself, are you?"

"I must admit it crossed my mind," Simko replied. "But

advancing age tends to give one a sense of self-preservation. I've got no intention of playing hero on this one, Sebastian. But at the same time, I don't want to fuck up. And there's a few things about this situation that just don't seem to fit. If Talon really is a necromancer, then where's the evidence of necromancy? There just isn't any."

"There are those men who've disappeared."

"Yeah, but we don't know for sure they're dead. No *corpus delicti*. From everything we've learned so far, this place sounds like exactly what it appears to be on the surface, a rehab center that functions from a strong spiritual basis, sort of like AA. A little cultish, maybe, but they do seem to turn people around. Cults generally take people in, but they don't cut them loose."

"Maybe he's purposely cut some people loose, as you put it, just to keep up appearances," Makepeace suggested as they got into their car. "If no one ever came back from the enclave, it would certainly look suspicious."

"That's a good point, but from everything you've told me, these necromancers need to feed their power regularly and they've got pretty big appetites. But we don't have a single documented instance of murder in this town involving magic. Just a few small-time ex-cons who disappeared after boosting a van. Sounds to me like nothing more than a drug deal that went bad. Chances are their bodies will turn up in the desert somewhere, with nothing more exotic than bullet holes in them."

"So what's our next step?" Makepeace asked.

"I think it's time to check out Dragon Peak," said Simko as he drove. "But first I'm dropping you off at the hotel."

"What do you mean? I'm going with you."

Simko shook his head. "Not this time. I think we're barking up the wrong tree, but just in case we're not, I don't want to take any chances that this guy Talon can make you as an immortal. Or an agent. I'm going to go up there myself, using the Heather cover story, and see what I can learn. But personally, I think this was a wasted trip."

"I'm not so sure," said Makepeace. "I don't like it. Suppose something happens."

Simko shrugged. "Then that'll tell you what you need to know, won't it?"

"Just keep thinking about that beach and those girls in the thong bikinis," Makepeace said. "Don't take any foolish chances, Victor."

"Who me? Hey, I'm a pro, remember?" He glanced at Makepeace and smiled. "I'm touched by your concern. Really. Don't worry, Sebastian. It'll be fine. We'll probably be on a plane back to New York in the morning."

# Chapter 6

The smell was what made the neighbors summon the police. When they got there, they immediately knew what they would find. Before they went into the townhouse, they all started pulling out handkerchiefs and lighting up cigars and cigarettes to help overcome the odor. They couldn't overcome it, of course, but it always seemed to help a little.

Ron Parker was a well-known lobbyist on Capitol Hill. He was forty-six years old, stocky, and slightly balding. A big man, physically fit, with the body of a onetime college football player, which he once was. He had been dead for several days, at least. The trouble was, they couldn't figure out what killed him. He was lying on his living room floor, fully dressed, as if he had just returned from being out for the evening. But when they turned him over, they found his shirt open and runes carved into his chest.

"What do you think?" one of the detectives asked the deputy coroner.

"Offhand, I'd say it looks like a heart attack," the coroner replied. "The cuts appear only superficial. Certainly not deep enough to be lethal, but we won't know for sure until the autopsy."

"Hey, Marty, check this out," one of the detectives said. He indicated two glasses sitting on the wet bar. There was a bottle of expensive single-malt scotch on the floor, unopened. The glasses were both about one-quarter filled with water from melted ice. "Looks like he was entertaining. He was just about to pour the drinks when it happened."

Detective Marty Massoglia frowned. "So, what, he has a heart attack and the person he's with decides to cut him up a little, then just splits?"

"Maybe she was married," his partner said with a smirk. "And a kink."

Marty shook his head. "No, something smells bad around here, and it's not just the stiff. Those look like runes carved into his chest." He turned to the lab man. "I want this whole place gone over for prints. And Doc, I want that coroner's report a.s.a.p." He turned back to the corpse. "Look at the expression on his face. Doc, do heart attack victims ever look like that?"

The deputy coroner shook her head. "Not usually, no."

"I didn't think so," Massoglia replied. "If you ask me, it looks like he was scared to death." He recalled a memo that had recently come down from the chief's office. "I'd like a T-scan on this body, Doc."

"You think it was magic?" the coroner said.

"What do you think?"

She shook her head. "I don't know. I suppose it's possible. I've never seen anyone killed by magic before. We don't have a T-scanner, but I can have the Bureau send over an adept."

"Do it," Massoglia said. "And get back to me right away."

"You want the other one done as well?"

"What other one?"

"We had a body come in yesterday, male, similar circumstances. Neighbors smelled the odor of decomposition. He'd been dead for several days, maybe as long as a week or more. It looked like a heart attack to me. We haven't gotten around to the autopsy yet. We're a bit stacked up." She chuckled at her own pun.

"If it was magic, would there still be T-emanations after all that time?"

She shook her head. "I have no idea. It's not my field of expertise."

"Well, then let's *get* an expert on it," Massoglia said. "And as soon as you find out, I want to know about it right away."

"You're thinking about that memo from the chief?" said Detective Bard, his partner.

Massoglia nodded and pursed his lips thoughtfully. "Yeah. I was wondering what that was all about. I think somebody knows something we don't. But if we've got a serial killer using magic to dispatch his victims, then the shit's really going to hit the fan."

Kira couldn't sleep. She stood out on the rooftop patio, dressed in a short robe. She would have liked to feel the coolness of the late summer air against her bare skin, but this was New York City, after all, home of the long-range apartment telescope, and besides, there were the guards up in the gun towers and the security cameras mounted on the outside of the building. She felt as if she were living in a fishbowl.

She didn't want to sleep and worry kept her awake, anyway. She was tired of being cooped up, waiting for something to happen; tired of the boring day-to-day routine they had fallen into ever since they had been moved into the penthouse; tired of the dreams. She didn't remember any of them, but she knew she had them every night. They were the sort of dreams that were deeply unsettling, that she was aware of while she had them, but then she would wake up and, for a fraction of a second, she would recall what she had dreamt and then it would be gone, like a screen being suddenly erased. And she could not remember what she'd dreamed. She wasn't sure she wanted to.

The pressure was getting to them all. But it was more than just the waiting. It was the wondering. Wondering what the runestones would do. What her runestone would do to her.

So far, she was the only one who had remained unchanged. What had happened to them since it all began had turned their lives upside down and changed them all, but the others had gone through changes that were much more profound than anything she had experienced.

It began with Billy, who was just a kid when they had met, a streetwise little Cockney boy who packed a knife and knew how to use it. Young, but by no means innocent. The changes had begun for him when Merlin's spirit reluctantly possessed him, drawn to him because of their blood tie. Then Gorlois' ring came into his possession and with it, the bond with Gorlois' spirit. Billy became three people—himself, an ancient mage, and an even more ancient immortal, the last of the Council of the White. It had been difficult enough for her to grow accustomed to Billy shifting personalities like a multiple, so she could only imagine what it must have been like for him.

And then the physical transformations had begun. At moments of extremity, Gorlois would manifest and suddenly Billy would simply disappear and in his place would stand a fully armored knight over six feet tall, complete with sword and shield. They never saw his face and Gorlois had never spoken when he manifested. He did his talking with his deadly blade. Billy, at those times, was . . . somewhere else, totally submerged.

Then, when she thought that they had lost him, Gorlois and Merlin had both committed the supreme sacrifice to save him—with neither knowing what the other had intended. As Billy lay dying, both mages had simultaneously fused their life forces with his, effecting yet another transformation, resulting in the Billy she now knew. He was no longer the same person. He had changed physically, grown years older in the moment of the merging, and his personality had altered. He no longer even spoke or acted quite the same way. Kira often wondered what would happen if a change like that came over her.

It could. She had seen it happen to Wyrdrune. He, too, had gone through a series of changes which had affected him deeply, though not in any way that was physically obvious. When Modred died—or when his body had died—the rune- stone he had been bonded with absorbed his life force and chose Wyrdrune, so that for a time he had carried two rune- stones in his flesh. She still recalled how it had shocked her when she discovered that Wyrdrune could physically meta- morphose into Modred. She had never known for sure which one she would be with in bed. Both of them, she supposed, even though sometimes it was physically Wyrdrune and sometimes it was Modred. She loved them both, in different ways and for different reasons, but it was bizarre to have two lovers in one body—a body that could change suddenly and without warning.

Now the runestone that was Modred's and then Wyr- drune's had bonded with John Angelo, a man she lived with but still scarcely knew. A part of her would always regard John as a cop—and as a former burglar, she had never been fond of cops. But John carried Modred's life force. Only Modred—or what was left of him—was damaged and she did not know if he could ever be the same. She no longer saw him. And Angelo could not provide the answers to her questions. He still had many questions of his own.

On the surface, he was flip and cocky, friendly, outgoing, giving the impression of always being in control. But he had a lot of shields, not just the gold one he once carried as a cop. She knew that he had been in therapy, still went regu- larly, and she wondered what he told his shrink, who had top-security clearance and probably didn't sleep too well at night, either.

"Having dreams again?"

She turned and saw Wyrdrune standing in the open slid- ing glass doorway. He had thrown on a blue terry-cloth robe. She shook her head. "Couldn't sleep."

"Couldn't or wouldn't?"

She gave a slight snort and smiled wanly. "Both, I guess."

"You want to talk? Or would you rather be alone?"

"Talk," she said. "We don't seem to do much of that anymore."

He frowned. "We talk. Don't we?"

"Not the way we used to."

He nodded. "Ah. The heavy, introspective stuff, you mean."

She gave him a sharp glance. "Are you making fun of me?"

He held up his hands. "No, no, not me. Just trying to lighten up the mood."

"I don't want to lighten up the mood."

"Okay."

"You've changed, you know."

He nodded. "I know. I couldn't help it. It's as if Modred left a part of himself behind in me. I don't think he did, literally, but he's had a strong influence. Guess I just don't think the same way anymore. Does that bother you?"

"I don't know. In some ways. I guess it does, but not the way you think." She looked out over the city and felt the wind blow through her hair. "I'm wondering about me. What will happen when it's my turn. If it will be my turn. I just don't know. I don't want to change."

"We all change."

She shook her head. "Not like that. You get the dreams, too. I know. I wake up in the middle of the night sometimes from your tossing and turning. You mumble to yourself."

He raised his eyebrows. "What do I say?"

"I don't know. It's unintelligible. Sometimes you sort of whimper in a small voice. I put my arms around you and you stop."

"Hmm. I didn't know that."

"You don't remember the dreams, either, do you?"

He shook his head. "No, not really. Little snatches of them, sometimes. Voices murmuring. Chanting. I can't really understand them. I don't know if it's the language or if it's just indistinct."

Kira sighed. "Why don't they ever talk to us? Why don't they ever *tell* us anything?"

He knew she meant the stones. "Maybe they can't."

"You don't really believe that."

"No, I guess not. Maybe they're just trying to protect us."

"From what?"

"From knowing too much."

She snorted. "As if we could do anything about it if we did."

"Yeah, I know what you mean. It would be nice to have a life again, someday."

"You think we ever will?"

He remained silent for a moment. "I don't know," he said at last. "I hope so."

"I want it to be over."

"So do I. So does everybody."

"But at the same time, I'm afraid to find out what will happen when it's over. What will they do? Will they leave us or will they stay? And will we still be the same? As we are now, I mean." She shook her head. "I don't know if we can ever go back to being the way we were."

"Would you want to?"

"In some ways, yes. I like the way it was in the beginning."

He smiled. "In the beginning, you couldn't stand me. I don't think I'd like it if we went back to that."

"That isn't true, you know. I always liked you. Right from the first."

"You thought I was a *putz.*"

"Well . . . you were. But I liked you anyway, in spite of that."

"You sure as hell had me fooled."

"That was the general idea."

"Ah. I'm glad you cleared that up."

She moistened her lips. "What would you do, if it was over? I mean, if it was up to you?"

"Depends what happens to us, I guess. Offhand, I think I'd like to get certified officially. Maybe go back to school, get my grad degree, and teach."

"Teach? *You?*"

"Why not?"

She shrugged. "I just have a hard time picturing you as a college professor. I don't know if I can see you fitting in with the schoolies."

"Why?"

"None of them have ever done anything. Most of them don't know anything about the real world. I don't know how you could be happy in a classroom after all you've seen and done."

"Merlin was."

"Well, you're not Merlin."

"No, Billy is. Sort of."

"That's another thing. What about Billy?"

"What about him?"

"What's he going to do? We've all been together, like a family. It would be strange not having him around."

"Who says he's not going to be around? Why, has he said anything?"

She shook her head. "No. I haven't talked to him about any of this. Like I said, we never talk. Not anymore. Not about what will happen . . . after. It's as if we're all afraid to talk about it. And then there's John. In some ways I feel close to him, and in others, I feel as if we're living with a stranger."

"I imagine he probably feels the same way."

"How do you feel about him?"

"He's one of the good guys," Wyrdrune said. "Modred wasn't, though. I think that bothers him. I think it bothers him a lot. John's a straight-ahead sort of guy. With him, what you see is pretty much what you get. Modred was considerably more complex. I don't think John is very comfortable with being complex. He tends to like things black and white."

"That's because he's a cop."

"No, he's just John. McGuire's a cop, too, and they're not very much alike at all."

"That's because McGuire never worked the streets," said Kira. "He never really got his hands dirty. John knows all about that. And he also knows just how dirty Modred's hands were. You can pick up a lot of dirt in several thousand years. And now that's all a part of him."

"It didn't seem to bother you when it was Modred."

"That's because it didn't bother Modred. Modred accepted what he was. Angelo can't deal with it. That's why he's in therapy."

"I see. So, let me get this straight . . . it's okay for a man to be a professional killer when he accepts himself for what he is, but if it bothers him, you've got a problem with it?"

"That isn't what I meant and you know it."

"Do I? Sounds to me like you're the one who's having trouble dealing with it," Wyrdrune said. "John didn't ask for any of this."

"Oh, like we did?"

"No, but you and I have been there from the start. He's still playing catch-up. And for a while there, he really lost himself. None of us had to go through anything like that. Maybe you should try cutting him a little slack."

"That's unfair. I haven't been giving him a hard time."

"No, but you haven't exactly been his friend, either. You were right about our being like a family. We share a bond that nobody else will ever truly understand. Even we don't fully understand it. But you've been acting as if John is some kind of outside interloper. On the surface, you act friendly enough, but you don't really include him. There's a wall. You think he's not aware of it?"

"Why, what has he said?"

Wyrdrune grimaced. "He hasn't said a thing about it. He's not that kind of guy. He holds a lot of stuff inside. And don't say it's because he was a cop. It's because that's just the way he is. The funny thing is, he reminds me a lot of you."

"Of *me?*"

"The way you were in the beginning. You say you liked me, or were attracted to me or whatever, but you bent over backwards not to show it. I didn't have a clue. I thought you couldn't wait to get rid of me. You just didn't want me to know how you really felt because you thought it might make you vulnerable. Lot of wisecracks on the surface, that tough 'I-grew-up-on-the-streets' act, but it masked the fact that you were scared. Scared of what was happening to us and between us. We used to talk about how maybe it was the runestone that brought us together, but now you're telling me you liked me from the start. Well, okay, I was attracted to you, too. So why couldn't we just tell each other?"

"Well, it might've had something to do with the fact that there were people trying very hard to kill us at the time," she replied dryly. "There *were* other priorities. Such as survival."

"Yeah, but when things like that go down, it usually brings people closer," Wyrdrune said. "You kept pushing me away. At least until you finally figured out I wasn't going to hurt you. And now you're doing the same thing with John."

"It's not the same thing at all."

"I think it is, only the reason's different. You always had a thing for Modred. I understood that. Modred was handsome, suave, intelligent, and dangerous, like a superhero with a dark side. Part human, part immortal, with incredible charisma. What woman could resist all that? And yet you did, because of me, and I loved you for it, because I knew how much you were attracted to him. Hell, if I were a woman, I would have been attracted to him, too. As a straight male, I responded to him with admiration, even knowing what he was. He had done things I found absolutely reprehensible, but at the same time, I recognized his good qualities. He was both nobility and evil embodied in one package. After his spirit bonded with me, I thought you would enjoy having your cake and eating it, too. You could be his lover without cheating on me. It was something we both wanted to do—me and Modred, I mean—because we both cared for you. It was kind of kinky, in a way, but I enjoyed it. It was like being someone else and making love to you. Like doing it and watching it at the same time. Having my own feelings and yet sharing his. But now Modred's part of Angelo and you can't have him anymore. It's as if John took him away from you and you're jealous. But he never meant to do it, Kira. It's not his fault. I never begrudged you having Modred. Why do you begrudge John?"

She swallowed hard and bit her lower lip. "Is that what I'm doing?"

"You're the only one who can really answer that."

Kira looked down. "What's going to happen to us?" she asked. "All of us?"

"I don't know, love. We've gone through things no other human being has ever experienced before. It's no big surprise we're having trouble coping." He paused. "You know, it's funny . . . when I was a kid, reading comic books, I used to dream of being a superhero, just like every other kid, I guess. Except unlike other kids, I actually got to be one. And I found out it's not all it's cracked up to be. Superheroes have problems, too. But hey, at least we don't have to worry about costumes."

She smiled. "I love you, you know that?"

"Yeah, I know."

"Aren't you going to say it back?"

"Well, you know, us men have trouble with that sort of thing. We're just a bundle of conflicting emotions and testosterone."

"Up yours."

"I love you, too."

"I never doubted it. But it's nice to hear it, just the same. Now be a good boy and leave me alone for a while. Go back to bed. I need to think about some things."

"I'll see you in the morning. Which should be about a couple of hours from now. I think I'll just go read or watch the boob tube for a while and put on a fresh pot of coffee."

He went back inside and closed the sliding door. And smelled fresh coffee already brewing.

"Seems like the only one getting any sleep around here lately is the Broom," Billy said from the kitchen. "I dunno, does the bloody thing sleep or just go dormant or something?"

"Good question," Wyrdrune said. "Damned if I know. I think it sleeps. Sort of. Did we wake you?"

"Nah. Couldn't sleep. Tired of having all them bloody voices in me head."

Wyrdrune grinned. "You're sounding more like your old Cockney self."

"I *am* still me old Cockney self. I've just picked up a couple of extra selves along the way. Here you go, mate." He handed Wyrdrune a mug of coffee and then poured one for himself. "You want to take one out to Kira?"

"No, it can wait a bit. Let's leave her alone for a while. She needs a little space."

"Don't we all."

"Seems like nobody's getting much sleep lately. Except for John, I guess."

"Nah, he's awake as well. Went out for a walk about an hour ago."

Wyrdrune frowned. "He went out? Alone?"

"Well, there's not much chance of that, now, is there?" Billy said, tossing his long white hair out of the way. "There's sure to be at least half a dozen bloody marines on his tail, all dressed in civilian clothes and armed to the bloomin' teeth beneath their macks."

"Is he all right?" asked Wyrdrune.

"Oh, Johnny's okay. A bit wound tight, is all. He's still having a hard time getting used to all this rot."

"Yeah, I know. I wish there was something we could do to make it easier on him."

"If you figure something out, let me know what it is. I'd kinda like to try it on meself."

"I thought if any of us had a chance at getting some answers, it would be you," said Wyrdrune.

Billy shook his head. "Gorlois never did any talking when he was a discrete entity. And now he's just not there anymore. He gave me his life force and a few fragments of his memory—and some of his looks, besides—but if I know anything the Council did, I can't seem to get at it. And believe me, I've tried so hard, it's given me splitting headaches."

"I'm worried about Sebastian," Wyrdrune said. "I sent him out to Tucson with that guy Simko, just in case. I don't care what Wetterman says about him, if Simko runs into one of the Dark Ones, he won't be able to handle it. I wanted to make sure Sebastian was there to keep him from blowing it, but now I'm worried about him, too. We should've gone ourselves."

"Yeah, I've been thinking about that," Billy said, "but Wetterman's right, you know. If Tucson proves to be a wild goose chase and the real thing comes up while we're gone, we could lose precious time. And we can't go spreading ourselves thin. You three need to be together to form the Living Triangle, which leaves me as your backup just in case something should go wrong. Splitting up is out of the question."

"You're right, of course," said Wyrdrune with a sigh. "It's just that I hate the thought that people have to die for us to get the go-ahead."

"You can't hunt a murderer until you've got a murder," Billy said. "But I know what you mean. It stinks."

"In some ways, it was better when we were on our own, without all this infrastructure to support us," Wyrdrune said.

"I just feel weighted down by it all. And half the time I wind up feeling like a prisoner in here."

"You can go out, you know."

Wyrdrune shook his head. "It's not the same. I liked it better when we were calling our own shots."

"Yeah? And when was that? When did any of us get to call our own shots since we got involved in this?" Billy reached out and tapped the runestone in Wyrdrune's forehead. "*That's* been calling the shots ever since you boosted it from that auction at Christie's."

"You've got a point," said Wyrdrune wryly. He sipped his coffee. "You know, it occurs to me that the stress may not be the only reason why we're all having trouble sleeping lately. What you said about the voices in your head . . . the dreams none of us can quite remember . . . we've all had that sort of thing before, but never to this extent. It's as if something is slowly coming to a boil."

"What?"

Wyrdrune shook his head. "I don't know. I used to be a pretty sound sleeper, but now if Kira so much as burps quietly, I hear it, even if I'm not fully awake. No matter how quietly she moves, I can tell if she gets out of bed in the middle of the night. It's as if I'm becoming hypersensitive to her, much more so than occurs normally in a relationship."

Billy nodded. "I knew when John went out, even though I was in bed with the door closed and he was quiet leaving his own room. I knew you two were awake, as well."

"You haven't got a runestone," Wyrdrune said, "but Gorlois became a part of you and Gorlois was a member of the Council. Something's going on. It feels as if we're building up to something. Only what? Why don't the damn stones ever *tell* us anything?"

He suddenly noticed that Billy was staring past him intently, his mouth slightly open, his hand frozen in the act of bringing the coffee mug up to his lips. Wyrdrune followed his gaze toward the sliding glass doors and saw Kira standing outside on the roof patio, looking out over the city. Only it wasn't Kira.

In Kira's place stood a woman with long, thick, waist-length coppery red hair held in place by a thin circlet of hammered gold. She was barefoot and dressed in a long, flowing white robe that billowed slightly in the evening breeze.

*"What the bloody hell?"* said Billy softly.

As if she heard him, the woman turned, but suddenly it was Kira once again, the transformation occurring so quickly that they didn't even see it. She saw them looking at her and smiled.

"Oh, boy . . ." said Wyrdrune.

It was hard for four men to follow someone down an almost deserted city street at night without being noticed, especially when the man they were tailing was a New York City cop. Angelo knew they were there, of course. They weren't trying to hide the fact that they were tailing him, but at the same time, they were doing their best not to be too obvious about it. Two of them were walking about half a block behind him while the other two were roughly parallel with him on the opposite side of the street. They were all approximately the same height and build, they all had very short haircuts, and they were all wearing identical dark raincoats. Even the most inept mugger would have spotted them. But it wasn't muggers they were worried about.

Angelo wasn't annoyed at his escort. He knew they were only doing their jobs and he felt a little guilty about making them leave their comfortable security post to follow him out into the streets at night, but he just *had* to get out. He felt a pressure building up inside and he had to walk it off, feel some open space around him, get away where he could think.

As a cop, he'd always thought best walking around the city. He knew Manhattan like the back of his hand. He'd walked it all, the whole damn island. And parts of Brooklyn, too. For the average citizen, it wasn't exactly the safest thing to do, particularly at night, when Angelo thought best, but then the average citizen didn't vent steam by going out and looking for trouble. Angelo did. Or at least, he used to.

He had made a number of high-profile felony arrests while off duty. Twice he had prevented rapes this way. A number of times he had caught muggers, armed robbers, and once even a cop killer, all without any backup. He didn't do it for the glory. He had done it to stay sane. He had been a cop twenty-four hours a day, unable to turn it off. He came from a long line of cops; he had grown up in the profession. Ever since he was a little boy growing up in Brooklyn, he'd wanted to catch the bad guys. He had worked some of the toughest jobs in the department. Vice. Narcotics. Undercover for the Organized Crime Task Force. He saw the worst parts of human nature every day. And somehow it had never made him callous, although he affected the manner.

He still recalled one incident on the subway that always reminded him of why he had become a cop. There was a young kid obviously stoned, sick from whatever it was he had taken. It wasn't an overdose, it was just bad shit. The kid was in bad shape, puking all over himself, collapsing on the floor of the subway car. Angelo tried to help him. He was in civilian clothes. The other people on the car were either ignoring the whole thing or looking on with distaste. One middle-aged woman watched with open disgust as he knelt over the kid, looking as if she were about to puke herself. Finally she said, "How can you bear to touch that disgusting animal?" He had looked up at her, met her gaze, and said, "Lady, I'm a New York City cop, and this 'disgusting animal' could easily be your son."

She had grimaced and looked away, but then a moment later, he felt a hand on his shoulder and looked up to see an elderly man, not terribly well-dressed, somebody just struggling to get by on social security and maybe a small pension. And the man said, "How can I help, Officer?"

That one old man made everything worthwhile. That one old man was hope for the city. And who knew, maybe even that middle-aged lady thought twice about the whole thing later. Then again, maybe not.

It was all different now. He was still after the bad guys, but this time the bad guys weren't even human. And they gave "bad" a whole new meaning. But now he wasn't a cop anymore. Not exactly. He was officially "on leave" from the department and attached to the ITC, but for all the resources and manpower on "the project," as the support staff tended to refer to it, there was nothing official about it whatsoever. Officially, it didn't exist. And neither did he.

That last point was one to ponder. In a very real sense, the John Angelo he was before didn't exist anymore, either. There was a blood-red ruby magically embedded in his chest and it had dumped another person, or whatever had remained of him, into his psyche and he was still trying to sort the whole thing out. John Angelo, working-class cop. Modred Pendragon, multibillionaire hit man. Make sense of that, why dontcha? The shrink was helping, even though he never did like shrinks. This one was different. She looked like someone's grandmother, but she was one sharp lady. Tough. Smart. Opened him up like a can of tomatoes and proceeded to make sauce. Not like the other shrinks at all, with all their "well, how does that make you feel?" crap. This one zeroed in and started boring like an auger.

He liked that. He appreciated somebody who didn't waste time with any bullshit. And she helped. She helped a lot. Helped with lots of things. Helped him understand why he'd never been able to maintain a relationship. Why he took the kind of chances he did. Why he got such a charge out of "working the edge," as he called it. And why it bugged him so much to have Modred in there somewhere. It wasn't so much that it bothered him to have a professional killer sud-

denly become a part of him. It was that a part of him liked
it. He just wasn't sure which part. And that was what *really*
bothered him.

He felt the reassuring weight of the 10mm semiauto in his
shoulder holster. He had always carried a high-capacity nine
in a belt slide and a .380 in an ankle rig. He had never carried a 10mm before. It was a fucking cannon. It was
Modred's gun. Serious ass hardware, with custom bullets
designed for maximum expansion. He'd test fired the thing
into ballistic gelatin and the expended rounds came out
looking like fucking ashtrays. He'd gotten a compact 9mm
for the ankle rig. Scarcely bigger than the old .380, but it
seemed redundant now. That big stainless semiauto would
stop a charging elephant. And he was filled with confidence
that he wouldn't miss. That part was Modred. He'd never
been much of a marksman before. He'd always qualified,
but he wouldn't win any department sharpshooting matches.
Now, he felt . . . no, he *knew* . . . he could take on world
champions and win. Strange. Very, very strange.

He felt like a cocked pistol, ready to go off. Except there
was no one to shoot at. The stress was building up. And the
dreams, the goddamn dreams. . . . Why couldn't he ever remember any of them? He'd wake up suddenly, shaking,
feeling like he'd been off in some other world, and for a
fraction of a second, he'd almost grasp it . . . and then it
would be gone. It was making him crazy.

Crazy. Yeah. Like it was normal to walk around with an
enchanted runestone in your chest, one that was alive and
contained the souls of several immortal sorcerers, not to
mention King fucking Arthur's son, whom they'd dumped
into his head for safekeeping. Sure. That was real sane.
Jesus. He should've put on his running shoes. He was walking so fast, he was practically jogging. He felt like he could
go all night, work some of this crap off. He hoped none of
the marines had new shoes on.

He slowed his pace and glanced over across the street at

his escort moving roughly even with him on the other side, and that was when it happened. The runestone in his chest suddenly tingled, sending what felt like a small electric current through him. There was a flash of brilliant blue light and the side of the building just in front of him exploded in a shower of concrete dust and chips. He was down and rolling, without thinking, smoothly drawing the 10mm from its holster as he came up in a crouch.

The marines were already firing. The ones behind him were coming up fast, their coats open and flapping, their short-barreled, caseless assault rifles in their hands. The ones across the street were shooting, their weapons on full auto making a sound like pneumatic wrenches going full bore. More flashes of blue light, like a laser show, crisscrossing the street. The two marines on the other side were briefly wreathed in a blue halo and then they disappeared. Angelo swung his weapon around, looking for targets. And then he saw them.

They were wearing black coats with hoods. Three of them. No, four. The big semiauto cracked sharply and one of them went down across the street, hurled right off his feet by the impact of the bullet. He changed his point of aim and fired again and another one went down, and then another flash of blue light lanced out toward him from another direction and he was tackled by one of the marines as it passed over his head and slammed into the building behind him.

*"Get down!"*

There was a scream and the other marine bought it, leaving only the one who'd tackled him. They scrambled to take shelter behind parked cars.

"Stay *down,* for Chrissake!" the last marine said, firing his weapon with one hand while clawing for his radio with the other.

Several bolts of energy slammed into the car they were

hiding behind and it rocked as it exploded into flame, throwing them backward.

"Fuck that," said Angelo, coming up and firing as he ran. He saw another black-clad figure running across the street and dropped him, then plunged down a subway entrance, flying down the stairs. A wino huddled up against the wall didn't even flinch as he ran past with his gun drawn, sprinting underneath the street to get to the stairs leading up to the other side. Fortunately, it was very late and there weren't any people. It was a residential neighborhood. He reached the stairs on the other side and ran up, keeping close to the wall, listening intently. Silence.

He peeked around the wall. The street was empty. No lights were on in any windows. New Yorkers had sense enough to keep their windows dark and closed when they heard gunfire in the streets, especially automatic weapons. Angelo came out cautiously and looked around, holding his weapon ready. Nothing. He heard the distant sound of sirens approaching fast. No sign of the remaining marine.

"*Shit,*" he said through gritted teeth.

He ran across the street. The last marine was lying on the sidewalk, alive but bleeding badly from several lacerations he'd sustained when the car exploded. He looked shaky, but had managed to hold on to his gun. The radio was lying beside him on the sidewalk, broken.

"You okay?" said Angelo, crouching beside him.

"Yeah," the marine replied. "You?"

Angelo nodded. "Yeah. Thanks."

The marine grimaced. "Man, what a mess. We really blew it."

"You didn't know anything, soldier. I did. I got three of your guys killed."

"Hell, you didn't do it."

"I may as well have. If I'd stayed put, they'd still be alive."

"Yeah, and we wouldn't know the balloon's gone up,"

the marine replied, as several vehicles came up with flashing lights and sirens blaring. "Guess the waiting's over, huh?"

"Yeah," said Angelo grimly. "Guess so."

# Chapter 7

**W**ithin an hour after the attack, they had the three deceased assailants identified. They all had records, drug possession, dealing, burglary, theft, assault and battery . . . and they were all from Arizona. What was more, each of them had previously been remanded to the drug rehabilitation center at the Dragon Peak Enclave near Tucson.

"That's it," said Billy. "We've got to get to Tucson right away. Simko and Sebastian are going to need a lot of help."

"Not so fast," said Wetterman.

"What the hell do you mean, not so fast?" said Wyrdrune. "What more proof do you need?"

"Suddenly proof isn't something that we lack," said Wetterman grimly. He held up a sheaf of printouts. "It's been coming in since last night. We've now got documented cases of necromantic murders in Chicago, Los Angeles, Denver, Detroit, and Washington, D.C. Not to mention the attempt on Angelo early this morning. And at least one of those perpetrators is still at large."

"Jesus," Kira said.

"A well-coordinated murder campaign, breaking out in several areas at once," said Billy. "They know we can't split up. And we can't be in all those places at the same time."

"Hell, how many of them *are* there?" Wyrdrune asked. "I thought we'd accounted for most of them by now, except for Beladon and maybe a couple of others."

"Wait a minute," Angelo said. "You guys are forgetting something."

"What?" said Kira.

"Those guys who tried to put the hit on me were all small-time criminals—druggies, mostly. Where do they get off suddenly becoming necromancers? I thought you had to go to school for that. College and then graduate programs in thaumaturgy, right? Nobody gets that powerful from any home study course, and judging by their sheets, those guys would've been lucky to have-gotten out of high school. And I wouldn't take any bets they did."

"He's right," said Wyrdrune. "In all the excitement, I never even thought of that!"

"So then how come they were throwing bolts of energy like full-fledged mages?" Angelo asked.

"Good question," Wetterman replied. "I can run a check on them, but I think it's a safe bet none of them ever graduated from any thaumaturgy school, much less became certified. Not with those kinds of records."

"So then . . . how?" Wyrdrune asked.

"They were conduits," a new, mellifluous voice said. They stared with astonishment at the stranger who had suddenly appeared sitting in their midst.

"She's back," said Billy softly.

Kira had once again become transformed. It had taken place so quickly that none of them had seen it happen. One moment she was sitting there on the couch, and the next she had disappeared and in her place sat a woman with long, thick, coppery red hair and skin that was a light shade of reddish mocha, almost golden. Her eyes were an unusually bright and startling shade of green, so intense they seemed to glow, and her features were delicate, yet sharply chiseled, like those of some ethereal Aztec princess. She was barefoot and wore a long, sheer white gown covered by a matching, open robe that draped gracefully over her slim form. A slim chain of gold hung around her waist as a girdle and a thin band of hammered gold was worn as a circlet around her head. It was set with a single gem . . . a sapphire.

"What the hell!" Wetterman exclaimed, jumping to his feet. He snatched a small handheld radio from his belt. *"Security!"*

The doors opened immediately and the marines on duty outside came running in, sidearms drawn.

*"Wait!"* said Billy, holding his arms out and moving quickly to stand between them and the woman.

"There is no need for alarm," the woman said calmly. "I am not here to harm anyone. And you cannot harm me. You can only destroy Kira."

"Hold it," Wetterman said, extending a hand out toward the marines, who stood in combat shooting stance, pistols aimed with safeties off and held rock steady.

"She was here before, Brian," Wyrdrune said. "Billy and I saw her appear briefly last night. It's a metamorphosis, like I used to exchange with Modred and Billy with Gorlois."

"Who are you?" Wetterman asked.

"I am called Alira, one of the spirits of the runestone," she replied. "I cannot maintain this form for long or it will deplete our store of energy. Listen carefully, for you now face the greatest threat of all."

Wetterman waved his hand, indicating for the marines to lower their sidearms.

Alira turned to Angelo. "The assassins whom you faced were acolytes acting as conduits of power for one necromancer. They are now necromancers in their own right and will grow stronger each time they absorb more life force. However, with each large expenditure of power, such as was necessitated by their attack on you, they must replenish themselves or grow weak, age rapidly, and die. By themselves, they do not possess the skills of genuine adepts. Whatever knowledge they possess can be only rudimentary at best and depends upon their psychic link with their master. In effect, they act as conduits for his power, though they are capable of replenishing that power for themselves, aided by their link with him. Or her."

"Who is it?" Wyrdrune asked. "Beladon?"

"It is possible, but there is no way to know for certain," Alira replied. "There are still nine Dark Ones who remain unaccounted for. They are Vorstag, Adreia, Torvig, Zelena, Corvald, Darok, Sigrid, Talon, and Beladon. Of them all, Talon and Beladon have always been the strongest. Talon has the vigor and vitality of youth on his side, Beladon has the experience and strength of age. Both have always been ruthlessly ambitious. For one necromancer to control so many acolytes and use them as conduits of power, it is necessary for him to have achieved bond mastery over others, so that he could draw upon their power to revitalize his own and multiply it many times."

"You mean he had to kill the others?" Wyrdrune asked.

Alira shook her head. "No. That would not be bond mastery, but murder. And it would not provide continual reserves of power for him to draw upon as his own energy became depleted. For one necromancer to achieve bond mastery over another, the bond slave must be held in stasis, alive to recover life force energy naturally over time, but held restrained, unable to act or exercise free will."

"The way you once held the Dark Ones prisoner?" asked Billy.

Alira nodded. "The spell is both difficult and demanding. It consumes a great deal of energy. Whichever of the Dark Ones controls the acolytes, he must have subdued several of the others and placed them in spell bondage to control such power. Perhaps he has even subdued them all, which means that only one remains. We were able to effect our spell of bondage only by placing ourselves in stasis, surrendering organic form, so that only the spirit remained. The alternative would have been to become that which we had fought, killing constantly to keep the life force energy replenished.

That is what one of them is doing now, through his acolytes."

"So as they kill, he takes the power?" Wyrdrune asked.

"He allows them to retain enough to replenish themselves, and perhaps gain a bit more strength, but the rest he draws back into himself, through the link he has effected between them. And that, in turn, is reinforced by the life forces of the necromancers whom he holds in spell bondage. The more the acolytes kill, the more life force their master can draw back into himself and the more he can allow his acolytes to retain, thereby becoming stronger in their own right."

"But they still need him to work their magic?" Wetterman asked.

Alira nodded. "Without him, they are merely humans."

Wetterman gave a slight snort. "Right."

"Forgive me. I meant no offense. I meant only that if the necromancer is destroyed, the acolytes lose all their power."

"Well, that simplifies things," Wyrdrune said. "We're going to Arizona."

"But in the meantime, what about these acolytes?" said Wetterman.

"You've put this big juggernaut of a task force together— use it," Wyrdrune said. "The President promised us the full resources of the ITC, the Bureau, and whatever federal agencies were required. You're the man in charge. The acolytes will have to be your responsibility while we go after the necromancer who controls them. Simko and Sebastian need our help and they're going to need it fast. I want to be on that plane to Tucson within the hour."

"Suits me," said Angelo. "I can be packed in ten minutes."

"Packed?" said Kira. Alira was gone and in her place Kira stood, frowning slightly with puzzlement. "We going somewhere? What's going on?"

Wyrdrune and Billy exchanged glances. "I'll tell you all about it on the plane," said Wyrdrune.

Simko was escorted into an office inside the mission church. As he came in, the man behind the carved wooden desk got up to greet him.

"Mr. Simko, is it? How do you do? I am Brother Talon. Please, sit down."

Simko took the chair across from the desk as Talon examined his business card. "You're a private investigator from New York?"

"That's right," said Simko, crossing his legs and leaning back comfortably. He casually glanced around.

"How may I help you?" Talon asked.

Simko reached into his jacket pocket and pulled out the photograph they had been using. "I'm looking for this girl," he said. "Her name is Heather Makepeace, but she's a runaway, so she may be using another name. I've been hired by her father to find her. The girl's a minor who fell in with a bad crowd and got involved with drugs, took up with an older man, and ran away from home . . . well, I'm sure you've heard it all before."

Talon took the photograph and studied it. "Yes, unfortunately. So many of these stories are alike. By the time they get to us, those of them who do, so much damage has already been done. . . ." He shook his head. "It's a tragic thing. We do our best for those whom we can reach, but there are so very many of them. . . ." He allowed his voice to trail off as he continued to study the photograph. After a moment, he glanced up and handed it back. "She's not one of ours, I fear."

"Are you sure?" said Simko. "I mean, you get a lot of people coming through here and she may have altered her appearance since this was taken . . . cut her hair, dyed it, maybe lost some weight?"

"Well . . . here, let me see it again," said Talon, reaching for the photo. Simko handed it back to him. Talon studied it again for a moment or two, then handed it back and shook his head. "No, I'm quite sure I've never seen this girl before."

"You see all the people who come through here?" Simko asked.

"Every one," said Talon. "I am personally in charge of our addiction program. The nature of the counseling we do here is rather intense and very personal. The interaction between the patients and the therapists is prolonged, dramatic, and psychologically very intimate. And I become personally involved in every case. It can become quite stressful for both the patients and the therapists, but it's the main reason for our high success rate. If she had been here, I'm sure I would have remembered."

"Well, it was worth a shot," said Simko, getting up. "But keep my card, just in case. We know she came to Tucson, we've traced her that far. It's not exactly a small town, but you never know, she might show up here. If she does—"

"I'll be sure to let you know at once," said Talon, holding up Simko's card.

"Thanks. I appreciate your time."

"It was no trouble at all, Mr. Simko. I hope you find her. And if at any point we can be of any assistance with our program, we'll be happy to help in any way we can. We do not charge for out services, as we are a nonprofit institution, but private and tax-deductible donations are always appreciated."

"I'll pass on your offer to my client," Simko said. "And once again, I appreciate your taking the time to see me."

"As I said, Mr. Simko, it was no trouble at all. It is our ministry to serve as best we can."

"Well, you've got quite an impressive place here. I was admiring your gardens on the way in. It's all very quiet and peaceful, and the views are just spectacular."

"Yes, it's beautiful country," Talon agreed.

"Nothing like New York City, that's for sure," said Simko. "A fella could get used to this. It's real pretty out here. Mind if I look around on my own a bit before I head back to town? Or would that interfere with your activities?"

"Not at all," said Talon. "Feel free to look around the grounds as much as you like. But please respect the privacy of our residential quarters. You might enjoy the gardens or the telescope in the ramada on Observation Point. Just follow the garden path. It loops around right past it."

"Telescope, huh? Yeah, I'll have to check that out."

"You should be able to get a lovely view of the sunset. However, I wouldn't advise that you linger until it grows dark. The road down to the highway is not illuminated and it can be treacherous. Aside from that, the dragons become more active after dark."

"They do, huh? Are they dangerous?"

"They can be, but the greatest danger would be hitting one with your vehicle. You could become seriously injured. Your vehicle would certainly be damaged, and a rare creature would be killed."

"Oh. Well, I'll keep that in mind." He glanced at his watch. "I won't stay too long. Just long enough to enjoy the view. Don't often see country like this. Thanks again, Brother. You've been very helpful."

"Not much help at all, I fear."

"Well, look at it this way," Simko said. "At least we know one place where she's not." He shrugged. "It's a start. Thanks again for your time."

"You're very welcome."

As Simko left the office, he checked his watch again. It was after six in the evening, but he was not concerned about the time. It was not an ordinary watch. It was also a miniaturized T-scanner, so cutting edge and state-of-the-art that only a few government agencies had them. It was powered by thaumaturgically etched and animated chips, worth a small fortune and usually employed only in the most ad-

vanced AI computers. These had been specially designed and
enchanted to react to thaumaturgic trace emanations—to detect magic.

At the press of a button on the side of the watch, the function of the T-scanner was activated and if there was magic
present, the face of the watch would glow and the digital
display would give a reading based on a scale from 1 to 100.
The strength of the glow corresponded to the strength of the
emanations present. Simko wanted to double-check what he
had just seen in the office. The digital display showed 100
and was blinking on and off rapidly, indicating that the reading of the emanations present was higher than the scale
could indicate, and the glow of the watch face was strong
enough to read by in the dark.

"Gotcha," Simko murmured softly to himself.

*No, Mr. Simko,* a voice suddenly spoke inside his head.
*I've got you.*

The next thing Simko knew, he was somewhere else. It
was dark, pitch-black, and he felt something hard, uneven,
and unyielding against his back. He suddenly discovered
that he could not move. His arms were down by his sides,
spread out slightly, but they were immobile, pressed against
something hard. He felt cool stone beneath his palms.

A fire blazed up, and then another and another as tall,
heavy bronze braziers erupted into flame, one after another
in rapid succession, and for the first time, Simko could see
his surroundings.

He was in some sort of subterranean chamber, a cave or a
cavern, with massive stalactites hanging down from the ceiling. The walls were veined with crystal, which reflected the
glow of the flames and amplified it. A short distance away,
there was a large pool of water, fed by an underground
spring and bridged by a natural stone arch that led to what
looked like some sort of surreal church altar carved from
stone and surmounted by a massive crystalline formation
that resembled organ pipes in a cathedral.

"Is this what you really came looking for, Mr. Simko?" Brother Talon said, stepping into his field of view. Behind him was a tall, incredibly massive black man with a shaved head, a pencil mustache, and a neatly trimmed goatee. He wore jeans, black cowboy boots, and a torn white shirt. He looked like a bodybuilder, an ambulatory mass of improbable-looking muscle.

"That fascinating little watch of yours," said Talon. "May I see it?" He held out his hand.

Simko felt the metal bracelet snap and the watch flew to Talon's outstretched hand.

"Ingenious," said Talon, examining it. "What will they think of next?" He tossed it aside. "Really, Mr. Simko, did you think you could employ magic in the presence of a necromancer without his being aware of it?"

"Well, actually, yes, I did," said Simko. "Guess I was wrong, huh?"

"Who sent you?"

"The ITC," Simko replied.

Talon raised his eyebrows. "You surprise me with your candor. I expected you to lie, or bluster with manly recalcitrance."

"What would be the point?" asked Simko. "You could easily get the truth out of me."

"True," said Talon, nodding with approval. "I'm pleased to see that you're a sensible man. That should make things a great deal easier for both of us."

"I'm all for that."

"Good. Very good, indeed. So, you are in the employ of the International Thaumaturgical Commission." He said it with amusement. "How very grandiose. How did they find out about me?"

"Data banks, I should imagine," Simko replied. "Simple research. Well, maybe not exactly simple. These things are all relative, aren't they?"

"Yes, those wonderful computers you humans have developed. And now infused with magic. I never cease to marvel at how far you've come. And so tell me, are you here alone?"

"I came alone," said Simko.

"Just you? Against a necromancer?"

"I was only supposed to check you out. They don't know about you for sure, they only suspect. But if I don't report back in, they'll know then."

"I see," said Talon. The black man stood behind him silently, impassively. "A persuasive argument for keeping you alive, then, is that it?"

Simko tried to shrug, but found he couldn't. "Well . . ."

"What do you know about the avatars, the ones who bear the runestones?"

"They're working with the ITC. If I don't come back, they'll be coming after you next."

"Will they, indeed? How interesting. This is going very well. You're being most cooperative."

"Why make things difficult?"

"Why, indeed? But it strikes me that we could make things easier still. You could still be lying. Why waste time with all this conversation when I could simply take what I need to know directly from your mind?"

Simko shivered as he felt icy tendrils probing him, spreading slowly through his mind like the feeder roots of some rapidly growing parasitic vine, like little worms writhing in his brain. It felt *cold*, so very *cold*. . . . He clenched his teeth lightly, stiffening as he felt Talon entering his mind, feeling the cold numbness start spreading through him. He thought about the tanned, long-legged girls on the beach in their thong bikinis; the smooth stretches of gleaming white sand; the vivid, sparkling, sun-kissed blue of the Caribbean. . . .

He could feel Talon going deeper, merging with his mind. . . .

He thought of tall iced drinks of rum and fruit juice with

little pink and green and red umbrellas in them, slices of fruit garnishing the top, so smooth and inviting he could almost taste them. . . .

Come on, you bastard, he thought, come on in just a little more, a little more. . . .

He redoubled his concentration, pushing the thought aside lest it be detected. Warm wind gently blowing, palm trees bending, seagulls crying, steel drums playing in the distance. . . .

He felt Talon's amused chuckle in his mind as he found the place where he dreamed his reverie and shared it with him for a moment before rudely brushing it aside. . . .

Simko bit down hard on the cyanide capsule implanted in his tooth.

*Gotcha!* was his last lucid thought as he felt Talon's alarm at the poison rapidly permeating his body, and then both he and Talon became caught in the whirling vortex of the involuntary terror of life ebbing rapidly, awareness poisoned, the sudden flood of pain, the wash of white light—

Talon staggered back, recoiling from the contact as Simko's lifeless body, suddenly released, collapsed to the floor of the cavern like a sack. Doubled over, Talon held his hands up to his head, moaning, struggling to maintain his balance, retching with dry heaves.

For a moment, the control of the necromancer broken, Rafe came back to full awareness from the dim, conscious, yet anesthetized state he had been in and he blinked, shaking his head, then his gaze focused on Talon, bent over and retching, gagging, going down to one knee as his body spasmed. . . .

With a snarl, Rafe lunged for him.

*"No!"* Talon's shout reverberated through the cavern as he threw his arm out and Rafe felt himself suddenly hurled backward, flying through the air as if shot out of a cannon. He struck the cavern wall, fully thirty feet away, and the impact stunned him, driving the breath out of him as he struck

solid rock and fell to the cavern floor, bleeding and barely conscious.

Talon gulped for breath as he straightened, shaking off the death throes of the ITC agent. He stared at Simko's body with disbelief as the full realization of what had just happened hit him. The miserable cur had not only taken his own life, but he had tried to drag Talon down with him. Talon had almost completely extended his awareness into the unresisting human's mind. Another second and there would have been no escape.

The last thought that had flashed triumphantly through Simko's mind . . . *How could he have known?* Talon stood over the body, breathing heavily. No, he couldn't have known. He wasn't an adept, he could have known nothing about the principles of merging and projection, the risks involved, even to immortals. Somehow, intuitively, he had sensed it, sensed that he could pull Talon down into the void with him; Talon had felt Simko's consciousness grasping at him as it faded into oblivion. . . .

He kicked the body savagely.

He heard a deep moan and turned to see Rafe stirring slightly, trying to get up. "And you . . ." he said through tightly gritted teeth. "I see we have not quite learned who is the master yet. Well, we shall have to remedy that little failing, won't we?"

Rafe's scream echoed through the cavern.

This one she wasn't going to kill just yet. This was the one she had been working toward, the one who could help her fulfill her task, after which she would be free to leave Washington and return to Arizona's warmth and sunshine and wide-open spaces. Maybe she'd settle in Sedona. It was nice there and she could meet interesting people. She snuggled against the man lying in bed with her and smiled as she thought about it. She felt him nuzzling her neck and rolled her eyes.

"I can't believe I'm actually sleeping with a senator!" Maria said as she turned to face him.

He chuckled. "How is the experience shaping up for you?"

She kissed him. "Very nicely. But if they told me back in Tucson that something like this was going to happen, I'd have said they were crazy. I never even thought I'd ever get to meet a senator."

"How'd you like to meet the President?" he asked.

"The President?" She made her eyes wide. "Are you serious?"

"Umm-hmm." He fondled her breast. "What would your friends in Tucson say if you told them you had dinner at the White House?"

"My God. They wouldn't believe it!"

"Not even if you showed them a photograph of yourself with the President and the First Gentleman?"

"Is he really as good-looking as he looks on television?" she asked.

The senator grinned. "I wouldn't know. I don't really notice things like that. But I'll let you in on a little secret. He's got a bit of a wandering eye. I'm sure he'd notice you."

"But . . . I wouldn't have anything to wear to a dinner at the White House," Maria said, letting a note of disappointment creep into her voice.

"Well, I think we could fix that," the senator replied, letting his hand wander lower. "That dress you wore tonight would certainly get their attention, but it's not exactly the sort of thing you'd wear to a formal dinner. I'll have one of my aides take you shopping tomorrow and help you pick out something nice. My treat, for being so lovely."

"I don't know what to say!"

"You don't have to thank me by talking."

She smiled and slipped down under the covers. Makes no difference, she thought, rich or poor, senator or working-class stiff. When it comes right down to it, a john is a john.

\*       \*       \*

Makepeace sat in the hotel dining room, drinking his fifth cup of coffee and nervously glancing at his watch. Simko should have been back by now. They had been due to meet for dinner and discuss what he had learned before calling New York and making their report. He had wanted to call right away, but had let Simko talk him out of it.

"Look, we can't just call Wetterman and send up the balloon because the guy's got red hair and green eyes, for God's sake. We need to have something more solid."

"Such as what?" Makepeace had asked. "We already have more than enough to warrant taking this very seriously. What do you expect to learn up there?"

"I don't know yet. I want to have a look around the place. Meet the guy, see his face."

"Victor, you're taking a very big risk. And it's an unnecessary one."

"What risk?" Simko had said, downplaying it. "I'm a PI from New York, looking for a missing girl who's a druggie. I don't look like a cop. I'm too damn old to be a Bureau field agent, and I'm not exactly a newcomer at this game, Sebastian."

"You are at this one."

"Look, I can't take you with me and that's that. It would look suspicious, and besides, if there's a chance he could sense you as a fellow immortal, it would give the whole game away and then we'd really wind up in hot water. And I don't want to go giving any false alarms. Wetterman would have my ass in a sling and I could kiss my retirement plans good-bye. I want to see the place, get a feel for it, and for him, before we do anything else. We'll meet back here for dinner at about seven and we'll talk about it, okay?"

Makepeace glanced at his watch again. Seven-thirty. He shouldn't have let him go alone. But then, Victor was an old pro. He wouldn't do anything foolish. Would he? But what did he expect to learn? Did he think Talon would be so careless as to give himself away? He had a bed feeling about this. Maybe he should call New York, anyway.

"Mr. Makepeace?"

He looked up. "Yes?"

"Telephone call for you, sir."

He took the phone. "Where the bloody hell are you?" he said with exasperation.

"Makepeace?"

"Who is this?" Makepeace asked, momentarily disoriented.

"Wetterman. Who did you think it was?"

"Oh. I thought you were Victor."

"Isn't Simko with you?"

"No. He went to Dragon Park to check things out. I was supposed to meet him here about half an hour ago."

"He may not be showing up," Wetterman said tensely. "It's the real thing, Sebastian. We've got a fire. The team is already en route."

Makepeace shut his eyes. "I *knew* it! I never should have let him go up there alone."

"Maybe he's just running late," said Wetterman. "He's not a fool; he wouldn't have given himself away. He probably just went to get a reading for a confirmation."

"What do you mean, a reading?"

"He was issued a miniature T-scanner, disguised as a watch. Check the time, take a reading. Very unobtrusive."

"*What?*" said Makepeace. "Why the hell didn't you *tell* me? You idiot! Do you have any idea what you've done? You may as well have given him a neon sign!"

"You're overreacting. We tested it extensively with ninth-level adepts and up," said Wetterman. "Even twelfth-level sorcerers couldn't detect its emanations. They were much too subtle and—"

"Not for an immortal, you damn fool!" said Makepeace loudly, causing several heads to turn in his direction as he jumped up and sent his chair crashing to the floor. "You stupid, arrogant son of a bitch, you've killed him!"

He threw down the phone and sprinted from the dining room, leaving Wetterman repeating his name over and over on the other end.

# Chapter 8

The small military jet was being flown by a rotating team of pilot adepts. It was exhausting work. With all remaining fuel reserves used up in the last century, most ground and air transport operated on the principles of levitation and impulsion. Thaumaturgic batteries powered ground cars, save those operated for public transport, such as cabs, limousines, and buses, which were propelled by the spells of driver adepts. They were magic users, but of the lowest level. Trains operated on electricity generated at power plants maintained by sorcerer adepts, usually fourth-level or higher. Navigational adepts captained passenger ships and freighters. Air transport, however, was the most demanding and exacting of the transportational adept specialties.

Passenger planes were flown by a pilot and co-pilot adept, with usually at least one pilot adept in rotational reserve, enabling them to maintain a spell of levitation and impulsion that would propel the aircraft through the skies with stately silence, if at a considerably more leisurely pace than in the old pre-Collapse days. It was taxing work, maintaining the spells, which was why pilot adept was among the highest paid of magic use professions and pilots were legally required to spend time in recovery after each flight, with long paid vacations being an added bonus of the job. It was also why advanced-level adepts always flew for free, because another adept on board was always welcome.

For military and police purposes, however, speed was often of the essence and instead of levitation and impulsion, a different spell was used, one that worked directly on the engines in the place of fuel that was no longer available. Keeping the engines spinning at the required speeds was physically even more taxing and used up more energy the faster the aircraft was propelled. The small military jet aboard which Billy, Kira, Angelo, and Wyrdrune flew had been designed to seat twenty people—fifteen of whom were the flight crew.

From time to time, the door to the cockpit opened and a pilot adept came out, bathed in sweat, to collapse wearily into a seat and almost immediately fall into a deep sleep while another member of the flight crew went in to relieve him. By the time they reached their destination, Wyrdrune knew, the entire crew would be wrung out. They'd be picked up at the airport, taken to a hospital for observation, and then placed on recovery leave for at least a month before returning to active ground duty, unable to fly again until a thaumaturgically trained MD pronounced them fit.

Magic permeated every aspect of modern life, thought Wyrdrune, so much so that most people took it totally for granted. And it all started only three-quarters of a century ago, when Merlin awoke from his long slumber and single-handedly changed the world. Wyrdrune glanced at Billy, sitting in the seat across from him, next to Angelo. They had all come so far in what seemed like so short a time. Where would it all end?

Kira was sitting in the seat next to him, staring pensively out the window at the clouds and the patchwork of ground far below. She'd been very quiet after he'd told her about her transformation and what had happened while she had become Alira, one of the spirits of the runestone. She had recalled none of it. It was as if she'd blinked and missed it.

It was strange, thought Wyrdrune. While he had shared consciousness with Modred, it had been exactly that, *shar-*

*ing* consciousness. They were aware of each other at all times. He knew Modred's thoughts and felt his energy and Modred knew and felt Wyrdrune's. When he had occasionally metamorphosed into Modred, he had always been completely conscious of what was going on. The feeling had been similar in a way to astral projection, that peculiar sensation of floating up above your body, looking down at it, apart from it yet still connected. Except when Modred had manifested, it wasn't like looking down from the outside, but looking out from within.

Except Kira did not remember.

He tried to recall the times Billy had metamorphosed into Gorlois, before Gorlois had given up his individual life essence and fused it with Merlin's to save Billy's life, creating a new personality that was a manifestation of all three. Sometimes Billy had recalled what had occurred while Gorlois had manifested, sometimes he was foggy on the details.

But Kira did not remember.

He thought of Angelo, to whom Modred's runestone passed. It wasn't the same with Angelo as it had been with him. Modred seemed to have become subsumed into Angelo's personality, as if merging with him the way Gorlois and Merlin had merged with Billy. But Angelo came out of it with pieces of Modred's memory intact, and as time went on, he seemed to find more pieces and, with the help of ongoing therapy, incorporate them into who he was—or who he had become.

But Kira did not remember.

It worried him, but it worried her much more. Even since the whole thing started, Kira had been the one who was not only the most fascinated by the transformations they had gone through, but also the most frightened by them, because up till now, it had not happened to her.

They had all responded differently. Billy, to whom it had happened first when Merlin's spirit had possessed him, had thought he was losing his mind in the beginning, but after a time, he had accepted it—though it was a contentious sort of acceptance. One of his favorite pastimes had been going out and getting drunk and then "assigning" the hangover to Merlin. Then Merlin had started getting some of his own back. Just when they had reached a sort of uneasy *modus vivendi,* Gorlois came into the picture and Billy's psyche had, for a time, become a battleground between the father and the son. Now, Billy was integrated . . . and a different Billy altogether, while still being essentially the same. He seemed to have no trouble handling it, but then, Billy was Billy. An orphan who grew up abandoned on the streets of London and had packed a knife before he had even reached puberty could probably handle just about anything without flinching.

The same, perhaps, could have been said of Angelo, except that was not the case. Though he was a tough street cop who had seen more than his share of heavy situations, Angelo had been shaken up by the transformation induced by the ruby runestone that had passed to him. It had turned his world upside down and inside out, and for all his flip, Brooklyn macho, devil-may-care manner, John was having a tough time with it still. Most of the time, he acted as if the therapy were merely something that he had to go through, like a psychological evaluation after shooting someone in the line of duty, but he wasn't just going through the motions. It was important to him and it had helped enormously. The whole thing still unsettled him, but at least he was maintaining.

Which leaves me, Wyrdrune thought. For some reason, it had never bothered him. He had taken the merging with Modred as a matter of course, just another fascinating and bizarre experience that life had thrown at him. And a lot of it was fun. Especially the rather psychically kinky three-way relationship they had enjoyed with Kira, who had been both turned on and spooked by it at the same time. It just hadn't freaked him out at all. Well, maybe a little, right at first, but he soon accepted it, incorporated it into his worldview, and went on with taking care of business—which, in this case happened to be saving the world.

Was it all just a matter of perspective? Did the importance of their task so far overshadow any personal considerations that it just never really got to him? Or was there something strange about the way that he was wired that seemed to allow him to accept the most amazing, life-transforming things without getting too shook up about them? What was it?

For some reason, he suddenly thought of the incident that resulted in his scholarship being yanked and him being kicked out of school. It seemed like a lifetime ago now, though it had only been a couple of years.

He had taken a job doing special effects at a concert staged by the popular Boston band the Nazgul. He had needed the money, and besides, it was an opportunity to meet and work for his favorite band. There was, of course, the slight matter of its being illegal. They were looking for someone to handle special effects by magic and, as a graduate student of thaumaturgy, he still wasn't certified. But since he came cheap, compared to what industry effects adepts usually charged, the management of the band hadn't asked too many questions. They had told him what they wanted, then had him demonstrate in an empty warehouse by the waterfront some of the spells he planned to use. They seemed impressed and hired him. He never even got to meet the band.

The night of the concert, the hall was packed. The Nazgul were one of the hottest bands in the country and they were playing on their home turf, where they had started out ten years earlier, playing in small clubs. It was a triumphant homecoming from their recent national tour and their Boston fans had turned out in force for the occasion.

He had been ensconced next to the sound mixer, where he had brought up a fog that sparkled with electrical discharges, like tiny, jagged bolts of lightning dancing through it, and the audience went wild. It energized him and he thought, That's me, I'm doing that.

As the band launched into their opening number, "Riders of the Storm," a cover of an old pre-Collapse classic by a group known as the Doors, he had manifested a thunderstorm above them, complete with swirling black clouds and lightning, thunder that crashed throughout the hall at appropriate moments, and then rain, cascading down onto the band and moving out in sheets over the audience, drenching them until they were all soaked to the skin. The crowd absolutely loved it and they screamed themselves hoarse. He could still recall how James Darkstar, the lead singer, had looked right at him and given him a thumbs-up sign. Yeah, he had thought. *Yeah!*

He decided right then and there to make each succeeding effects spell even bigger than the one before it, deviating from the plan he had agreed on with the management, and between the Nazgul and himself, they whipped the crowd into an orgiastic frenzy until the band had reached the highlight of the show, their signature song, "Fire." As the guitars thrashed out a rapidly rising crescendo, Darkstar launched into his unearthly, screeching vocal:

> "Burn me with your cleansing fire,
> Feed the flame of my desire;
> Feel the heat between us rise,
> Sear me with your scorching eyes . . . Fiiiiire!"

As Darkstar screamed out the word, Wyrdrune cast the spell and pillars of flame, twenty feet tall and as thick as Doric columns, erupted from the stage. The audience went berserk. And the curtains caught fire. It spread rapidly, sheeting around the stage and licking up the walls, and at first the audience, as well as the band, thought it was all part of the show, but the heat was so intense, and it rose so quickly, it melted the sprinklers and within moments the concert hall was in flames. The audience panicked. The band members threw down their instruments and fled the stage, triggering a mass surge toward the exits. Fortunately, security was right on top of things and the doors were all quickly thrown open, allowing the crowd to spill out into the streets. Miraculously, no one was seriously hurt, although some people were taken to the hospital, suffering from minor injuries and smoke inhalation, but by the time the fire department had responded, the entire concert hall was engulfed in flame.

The aftermath was anticlimactic by comparison. He was arrested, arraigned, and thrown in jail. There wasn't anyone to bail him out, so he had time to sit and think about what he had done until the case came to trial. The band had a liability, as well, since they had knowingly hired an uncertified adept—and a mere student, at that—so their lawyers were brought into it and a deal was cut. He had been fined and the sentence was suspended. The Nazgul paid his fine in return for his agreement to indemnify them from any claims on his behalf arising from injuries or emotional distress or anything else anyone could think of and his written guarantee that he would not discuss any of it with the media, but it was the end of his career as an adept. The college pulled his scholarship and he was expelled. Everything that he had worked for had gone up, literally, in flames.

He couldn't blame anyone but himself. He knew he shouldn't have taken that job, had no business taking it, and he had known he was breaking the law. He also should have known that he was overreaching himself when he discarded his plan at the concert and allowed his emotions and his ego to run away with him. In one fell swoop, he had destroyed all his hopes and dreams just as thoroughly as he had destroyed that concert hall—except the concert hall would be rebuilt.

Perhaps, someday he'd be able to get back into a thaumaturgy school, but the odds of that weren't good, especially after what he'd done, which was a matter of public record. And even if he found a school that would accept him, how would he pay for it? Four years of college and two years of grad school down the drain. He wound up back in New York, living in a tiny railroad flat on Fourth Street, grateful that his mother hadn't lived to see how he had ruined his life.

But it had taught him at least one thing . . . life could change on you suddenly and drastically. You either learned to roll with the punches or it beat you down. The difference between an adult and a child was not necessarily a matter of chronology. When the shit came down, a child would throw a tantrum, whine, scream, and complain and not want to play anymore. An adult would just sigh heavily, shrug his shoulders, and say, "Well, here comes some more shit. Guess I'll just have to deal with it."

It was at that point, Wyrdrune realized, that his whole outlook on life had changed. The shit that came down, whatever it was, stopped getting to him. At least, it stopped getting to him in a way that would make him freak and freeze like a deer in the headlights.

But Kira did not remember.

Ever since he'd met her, Kira had been a control freak. She had lived life on her terms and her terms alone. They weren't very socially acceptable terms, but they were hers. And ever since he'd met her, when the runestones had brought them together, Kira had nothing resembling control. Being bonded with the runestone in her palm had frightened her right from the first. Being drafted into a war that had started at the dawn of time had changed her entire life. Being aware of the spirits of the runestone at the edges of her consciousness had always been a source of acute anxiety for her. And she had always worried about the transformations he and Billy had gone through. Would it happen to her? When? And how?

Now it had finally happened and it had thrown her for a loop. The more so because she could not remember. One of the runestone's spirit entities had taken control of her body, transmogrified it, used it, and she had no memory of it whatsoever. And that was what probably bothered her more than anything else.

"You okay?" he asked her quietly.

For a moment she did not respond. Then, without turning from the window, she said softly, "I don't know."

"Don't go falling apart on me now," he said. "We need you. We can't do this without you."

"Why don't you just have Alura or whatever her name is do it?"

"Alira," he corrected her.

"Whatever."

"Kira . . . just because you may not be completely in control of things doesn't mean you're not still you. None of us is completely in control. Of anything. And I don't just mean us; I mean everybody. You've just got to go with the flow, roll with the punches."

"I'm tired of rolling with the punches. Besides, wasn't it you I heard complaining about how he didn't have a life of his own anymore?"

"Yes, it was," he admitted. "I wish that we could have our old lives back. Well, maybe not exactly our old lives. I wouldn't want to go back to being broke and living on Fourth Street anymore. You've got to admit at least our lifestyle has improved considerably."

"Yeah, but is it *our* lifestyle or someone else's?"

"Think of it as a cooperative group effort," he replied, trying to inject some levity into the discussion, without very much success.

"I just want it to be over," she replied wearily. "However the hell it turns out, I just want the whole thing to be over."

"So do I," he said, "and so do John and Billy. And Sebastian. And Wetterman and Simko and McClellan and everybody else involved, including the President. But we're the only ones who can really do anything about it. You've got to pull it together and snap out of it. It's not just about us, you know. If we lose, everybody loses."

"I know," she said. "That's what really scares me. I never was all that hot on issues of responsibility. And suddenly I've got more of it than about ninety-nine point nine percent of the entire human race. Maybe it would be just as well if Alira came out again and just took over the whole thing for a while. I could sure use a vacation. Only trouble is, how do I know if I'd be coming back?"

He reached over and took her hand. "Don't worry. You're not going anywhere. I won't let you."

"Promise?"

"Promise."

"Okay."

The plane started to descend.

"Well, my old friends, it shall not be long now," Talon said as he stood before the massive crystalline formation surmounting the altar in the cavern. The incandescent glow flooded the entire cavern with brilliant light that reflected off the surface of the pool behind him and the veins of quartz and amethyst running through the walls. Inside the towering crystals, the figures of Beladon and the others were trapped like flies in amber, their features frozen into grimaces of horror. Alive, yet powerless, suspended in a limbo where they remained completely conscious, aware of one another, yet unable to communicate . . . but Talon heard their thoughts. And they heard his.

*They will kill you, Talon,* Beladon sent. *They will kill you without us.*

"But I have you," Talon replied with a smile. "I have all of you. I have all your power, without the added complications of your arrogance and your ambition and your condescension. I can depend on getting what I need from you without having to worry about trusting you, which I could no more do than you could trust me. Truly, it is the best of all possible arrangements. Maybe not for you, but it suits me admirably."

*And what if you should lose?* Adreia sent to him. *What will happen to us?*

"If I should lose, frankly, I don't care," Talon replied aloud. "But I doubt there is much chance that I shall lose. My acolytes channel more power to me every day. I can feel it flowing through me with each life that they snuff out. And you remain as my reserve. When the time comes, and it shall be soon now, the avatars shall face more power than they have ever encountered before. And we shall see if the Council can withstand it. For when they arrive, I shall unleash my acolytes in an unbridled killing frenzy, so that with each death my strength shall increase by the second, even as the avatars face me with all the power at their command. Doubtless, I shall lose many of my acolytes in the process, probably all of them, but there are many more where they came from. You see, my friends, that was your biggest mistake. You did not utilize the human resource. You saw only to exploit and consume it. But had you nurtured your acolytes instead of merely possessing them, had you empowered them without destroying their will, had you made them dependent upon you, sharing with them some of your strength and engendering within them a craving for the power that you so jealously hoarded, you could have sent them out to kill for you, and feed you, and protect you. You could have created predators to prey on their own kind with a hunger to match even yours. But you lacked the imagination. You were too superior, and too confident in your superiority, even to each other. That was why the Council had prevailed all those years ago. And that was why I prevailed now."

He received unarticulated thoughts of rage, loathing, and frustration. And he laughed.

"Yes, hate me!" he shouted at them. "Just as, for all those

years we were confined, I hated you! Hated you for your arrogant superiority, for your blind stupidity, for your shortsightedness which had brought me down along with you! But now the wheel has turned. And now you will know how I felt for all those centuries. And you will have all eternity to rage in helpless silence. That is, if you do not first go mad. It makes no difference to me. Sane or insane, your life force shall serve and sustain me. As it does even now."

He threw out his arms and shouted out the activating command of the spell. The crystals flared with blinding brightness and a concerted beam of energy came shooting out of each, uniting into one and bathing Talon where he stood, his head thrown back, his mouth open as he gulped in air, his body trembling as the life energy coursed through him. And as he felt their minds screaming in anguish, his laughter filled the cavern.

BOT Field Agent Peter Manly did not look like an adept. He was of average height, slim almost to the point of frailty, with graying hair, blue eyes, a handlebar mustache, and an alert, bright gaze that didn't miss a thing. He spoke in an easygoing, clipped, articulate manner and was very methodical and businesslike in his approach. Detective Marty Massoglia liked him and thought he'd make a good cop. Which, in a sense, is what he was, Massoglia realized. Except he was a very special sort of cop. A federal investigator who worked on major magic crime.

"Damn, there are enough T-emanations in this room to power an SR-71A Blackbird," Manly said as he looked around the murder scene.

"You guys can pick that up without a scanner?" asked Massoglia's partner, Detective Barry Bard. Around the precinct, the wits called them the BMs. They weren't wild about the appellation. Bard had no idea what an "SR-71A Blackbird" was, but he was not about to admit it. For all he knew, it could be some sort of airplane or maybe an exotic sports car.

"Most adepts beyond sixth level can sense T-emanations," said Manly. "You develop a sensitivity . . . it makes your brain itch."

"No kiddin'," said Bard. "So how do you scratch it?"

Manly gave him a look. "I was speaking metaphorically, Detective. Let's have a look at the body."

"Same ritual marks as all the others," Massoglia said, pulling back the bloody sheet on the bed.

"She's been a busy girl," Bard added.

"How do you know it's a she?" asked Manly.

"Well . . . they were obviously about to have sex. Or at least he thought so. Same MO as all the others."

Manly raised his eyebrows. "I repeat, how do you know it's a she?"

"We have a witness this time," said Massoglia. "Well, not an actual witness to the murder, but he saw her come and go. Places her on the scene at exactly the right time. It was the doorman. We took his statement before he went off shift. He didn't get a good look at her face, though."

"Well, what *did* he see?"

"He said she looked young, late teens to early twenties maybe, good legs, nice body, dark-complected, long black hair. She was sort of cradling her head on his shoulder as they came in, all lovey-dovey, and she had her coat collar up as she left. He said she seemed in no particular hurry. He called her a cab."

"And he just stood there while she waited for it and he didn't get a better look?"

"No, she called down to the lobby and asked for it, then he buzzed the apartment when it arrived. She had time to make herself a cup of coffee before she came down, got in, and took off."

"A cup of coffee?"

"We found a cup with a faint trace of lipstick on the rim.

She tired to wipe it, but missed a tiny smudge. No prints. Not even a partial. She must've been wearing gloves. Or else she handled the cup with a tissue or a paper towel or something. We sent it down to the lab anyway. We might be able to type the lipstick—that could give us something."

"So she kills the guy, then calmly calls down for a cab and just hangs around drinking coffee till it arrives," said Manly. "That's cold. And you say it's a similar pattern with the others?"

"The ritual marks, yeah," said Bard. "And killing 'em just as they thought they were about to get lucky. But it doesn't look as if she hung around with the others. She just stayed up here until the cab came because she didn't want the doorman getting a good look at her. Probably had the coffee to steady her nerves."

"Why not a drink?" said Manly. "There's plenty of booze in this place."

Bard shrugged. "Maybe she doesn't drink."

"Or maybe she just wasn't nervous," Manly said. "She had enough presence of mind not to get prints on the cup, and to wipe the lipstick off it. Or most of it, anyway." He shook his head. "I don't know. Most serial killers have been men. Female serial killers are pretty rare."

"You thinking it was a transvestite?" said Massoglia.

Manly wasn't sure what he was thinking yet. But what he'd been told during the briefing at HQ before he came on the case had him thinking that he had better not miss anything on this one.

"Well, if it's a drag queen, then it's a pretty good act," said Bard. "The doorman said she had great legs, a sexy voice, and a hell of a body. And the previous victims were all apparently heterosexual, so far as we can tell."

"That still doesn't mean they couldn't have been fooled," said Manly.

"I suppose it's possible," Massoglia replied. "But it seems like a stretch to me."

"The victims were all male, all upper income, right?" said Manly.

"A successful businessman, two attorneys, a lobbyist, a congressional aide," Bard said. "Young to middle-aged, all movers and shakers. Some single, some married. No pattern as far as physical appearance is concerned. Looks as if they were picked at random. Or maybe she let them do the picking. Like a black widow spider, sitting there and waiting to see who comes around. She mates and then she feeds. Except this one doesn't wait for the mating."

Manly grimaced. "It almost sounds as if she's working her way up the Washington social ladder."

"A social-climbing serial killer?" Massoglia said.

"Not just a serial killer, Detective, a necromancer," Manly said. "That's the worst kind of serial killer there is. You know anything about how this man died?"

"Killed by magic," said Massoglia. "The runes she cuts into 'em have something to do with a spell, right? She immobilizes 'em somehow, or puts 'em in a trance or something, then sets to work. Grisly business."

"A lot more grisly than you think," said Manly. "She doesn't really need the runes. It's more of a formal ritual. She uses black magic to drain off and consume the victims' life energy. Literally drinks their souls."

"Christ," said Bard.

"Christ has nothing to do with it," said Manly grimly. "Each time a necromancer kills this way, he—or she—becomes stronger, able to work more powerful magic. This isn't something just any adept can do; it requires highly advanced skills. This is the most dangerous kind of killer there is. You try to arrest a perpetrator like this, if they so much as blink or twitch their lip, you shoot first and worry about the investigation later. If you're wrong, you might do time, but at least you'll be alive."

Bard and Massoglia looked at one another. "Uh . . . the Bureau's taking over this case, right?" Bard said uneasily.

Manly smiled and gave a small snort. "Yeah, right," he said, nodding. "You give me everything you've got, and I mean *everything,* right down to your gut hunches, and then you're strictly investigative support. That means any more bodies like this turn up, you secure the scene and call me right away. Beyond that, you don't do *anything* without checking with me first. I mean that. I don't care if you come across a suspect matching the exact description and holding a bloody knife in her hands, with 'I did it' tattooed on her forehead. You stay the hell away and call me. Or you might wind up like this." He indicated the body. "Understood?"

"Understood," said Massoglia softly. Bard merely nodded.

"We're already way behind on this one," Manly said. "If you people hadn't dragged your heels—"

"Hey, look, we reported this as a magic crime from the word go," said Massoglia.

"Yeah, well, somebody in your goddamn department dropped the ball," said Manly, "and if I find out who it was, I'll hang him out to dry, and I don't care if it was the chief himself. This jurisdictional rivalry crap stops *now.* You don't play politics with murder. Especially this kind of murder."

But Massoglia wasn't through yet. "You'll get no argument from me. But I've got a question," he said.

"Shoot," said Manly.

"You're telling us a killing like this requires very advanced-level skills. I gather we're talking more than a mid-level sorcerer here. You Bureau guys are all at least level six, so I figure we're talking even more than that, right? How does that fit with the description we've got of the suspect being in her late teens to early twenties? You can't even get certified before you get out of grad school. To reach advanced sorcerer level, even if you're gifted, you've gotta be, what, late thirties to mid-forties, at least?"

Manly nodded. Massoglia was no slouch. Manly wasn't about to tell him everything he knew. The word from the

Commission was to keep information on a strict need-to-know basis. He answered guardedly, "That's true, but someone like that could probably use magic to alter her appearance for a limited time."

"Could a male appear female?" Bard asked.

"Possibly. It would use up a lot of energy, though. High spell cost. More likely, an older female would make herself look younger."

"So we can regard the physical description of the suspect as unreliable?" Massoglia asked.

"To a point," said Manly. "But she would have had to look that way when the victim met her, so that's what you go on for now. Find out where the victim was for the last twenty-four hours of his life. Find out where he connected with her. That may give us something."

"We're already on it," said Massoglia. "We've established prior whereabouts on all the previous victims. Chances are this one is similar. It looks like she's working the bars in the better restaurants in town. So far, never the same one twice, though."

"Okay, I want to see the full report," said Manly. "And all your notes. I've got a lot of catching up to do."

"This one's going to be a real bastard, isn't it?" said Bard.

"That, Detective, is probably the understatement of the year," said Manly.

# Chapter 9

Makepeace was halfway through filling out the paper-work for the rental car when he started to calm down and think twice about what he was doing. He went ahead and finished anyway, because it couldn't hurt to have another vehicle handy, especially since there was no telling what had happened to the car Simko had taken to Dragon Peak, but he realized that going after Victor would be a mistake. And Victor himself would probably agree. Assuming he was still alive, which was probably **not** a very safe assumption at this point.

He went out to the car and simply sat in it for a while. The hotel was just a couple of blocks away. He probably could have rented it through the registration desk and had it brought around instead of dashing to the lot on foot. He wasn't thinking clearly. He still felt tense, but what was needed now was caution and deliberation. Don't expend any thaumaturgic energy unless absolutely necessary. Save it for when it's really needed. The others would be arriving soon and they would want to know what he and Victor had learned before they took any action. And his going out there now would only compound the problem.

Talon had already been warned. Victor had done that, the poor fool. He had wanted one last shot at glory, and it had probably cost him his life. Talon would have no reason to keep him alive. He could easily turn him inside out, find out everything he knew, and then there would be no point to keeping him around. Victor was either dead, or else he was a mindless zombie. Most likely dead. If Talon had chosen to possess him, he would have had Simko make the dinner meeting and doubtless try to kill Makepeace. So then, why hadn't he done just that?

And the obvious answer immediately presented itself. Victor had suicided. One of those little cyanide capsules they issued, or whatever it was they used these days. That would be completely in character for Victor Simko. A pro right to the end. Poor Victor. He had so looked forward to those days of leisure on the beach, with his sun-bronzed girls and cool, tropical drinks. It was not to be. Makepeace found it strange and ironic that he was as affected as he was. He and Victor Simko were not exactly friends. They had not seen each other in years. They had not kept in contact until that day Simko had suddenly appeared in Lovecraft's. But in a way, it was sort of friendship, based on a mutual respect and past shared sins. The link between them had been Modred, back in the days when he was still caught between two worlds—the magical world that had receded into the mists of Avalon and the mundane world that he had always sought a place in and never really found.

Makepeace understood that all too well. Except he had been lucky. He had made his peace with the past—with all the several pasts that constituted his life—and found a place in the esoteric world of academia, which often provided a home for those who couldn't quite fit into the more mundane world, the world of nine-to-five and time clocks and business suits and corporate power plays and "Screw you, Jack, I've got mine." Which was not to say that the world of academia was free of its own political maneuverings and internecine conflicts, but there were ways to opt out of those games by simply doing your job and not being a threat to anyone. Gonzo had known how to do that, by staking out a territory that was uniquely his and not intruding on anyone else's turf. A popular professor whose classes always filled, a harmless and engaging eccentric who brought some cachet to his department and had no ambitions beyond simply being there the next semester. Do that for a few years, smile and be polite to the right people, give respect to those who crave it, whether deserved or not, avoid being too controversial—just enough to be colorful—keep your hands off the undergraduates, and, after a while, they grant you tenure and leave you pretty much alone.

And that was, Makepeace realized, exactly what he had done himself. He had played it safe. He had avoided rocking any boats—except the one of social convention, which was permissible as long as you did not go overboard—and he had settled nicely and comfortably into the fiction his life had become. And then, one day, it all changed.

In some ways, that change had been a long time coming, but at the same time, it had not come suddenly. It had gradually flowed over him, like a tide, and though he had tried to resist the undertow, it had steadily pulled him in. First there was Modred. They had first met during the dark days of the Collapse, in Europe. There had been a lot of work for Modred in those days. It was a violent time and Modred spoke the language of violence with an elegant eloquence.

They knew each other right away. Each of them had thought he was the last one left. They had no ties of blood, but it was like meeting family. And Makepeace had allowed himself to be pulled into Modred's world. Not fully, not all the way . . . just enough to have his hands soiled so that, like the lady of the Scottish play, he would never get them really clean again. Then came the awakening of Merlin and, with it, the gradual end of the Collapse. More work for Modred during the time of the transition from anarchy to order. That was when Morpheus, his *nom de guerre,* came to the attention of the people Victor Simko worked for, people who could not employ him openly, but who did not hesitate to work through intermediaries such as Simko and himself.

And then, the final touch . . . the runestones. And the knowledge that the Dark Ones were awake once more.

Even then, he had remained on the periphery. The runestones had not chosen him; he bore no real part of the risk entailed. He was a supporting player, nothing more. He had not even told Wyrdrune and Kira who and what he really was. But the runestones knew. He felt it. The spirits who animated the enchanted gems could not help but know. He wondered what they thought of him.

He started the car and pulled out of the lot. He felt awful. He never should have allowed Victor to go out there alone. So then, why had he? Why hadn't he stopped him? What had happened was his fault. He could have stopped him. He *should* have stopped him.

He tried desperately to recall if Simko had been wearing the watch before. He could not remember. Could he have kept it in a case hidden in his luggage and only taken it out and put it on when he left for Dragon Peak? If he had known Talon would be able to detect it, surely he would never have risked taking it. But perhaps he would have risked it. Victor had always worked close to the edge. Makepeace could not recall seeing the watch before. The thaumaturgically animated chips were small, the field weak, thought Makepeace; perhaps he could have failed to sense it. And then, suddenly it occurred to him that he had failed to sense the T-scanner in the elevator that took him to the penthouse at the ITC headquarters in New York.

The knowledge struck him so hard and so suddenly that he pulled over to the side of the road, just before the driveway leading into his hotel. That had never even occurred to him at the time. The emanations from that scanner in the elevator should have been stronger than what the watch put out, still too weak for a human adept to detect, but *he* had failed to detect it.

Why?

And then it hit him. He was sitting in a car powered by a

thaumaturgic battery. A battery that put out T-emanations. Relatively weak ones, but T-emanations just the same.

And he was getting nothing.

He pulled the car into the hotel driveway and parked it. He felt confused. What did it mean? As he got out of the car, several men in suits suddenly converged on him.

"Dr. Makepeace? Dr. Sebastian Makepeace?" A badge flashed quickly.

"Yes?"

"We have orders to place you under arrest, sir."

He blinked, glancing around at them. *"What?"* And then it hit him. Wetterman. He had left him hanging on the phone. Wetterman had probably panicked, thinking he was going out to Dragon Peak. Well, that was what he had almost done, so he could hardly blame him. "Could I see some identification, please?" he asked politely.

The badge was flashed again, held up this time so he could see it clearly. It was in one of those billfold things, badge on one side, ID on the other. Tucson Police Department. Not BOT.

"On what charge am I being detained, Detective Wiley?" Makepeace asked.

"Parking in a handicapped spot," the cop said with a perfectly straight face.

Makepeace raised his eyebrows. "But this isn't a handicapped parking space."

"Sure it is. See the sign?"

There was no sign. Makepeace shrugged. "Very well. Are you going to handcuff me or something?"

"No, I don't think we need to do that, sir. I'm going to read you your rights now. You have the right to kill about an hour or so in your hotel room, or in the bar, if you prefer. You have the right to enjoy our pleasant company and not give us a hard time about it, because we've been on our damn feet ever since the call came from the Bureau that something big was going down and a bunch of VIPs were flying in who had the authority to commandeer the whole damn department. We're all tired and hot and edgy and we could sure do with a couple beers, if it's all the same to you. You understand your rights as I've explained them to you?"

"Yes, I do, but I thought you weren't supposed to drink on duty," Makepeace said with a smile.

"We're not, but you're not going to see that, are you?"

"I didn't even see the sign," said Makepeace, raising his eyebrows.

The cop grinned. "Come on, I'll buy you a brew. And maybe you could tell me just what the hell is going on here."

They went inside and took a booth in the corner of the hotel bar. While they were waiting for their beers, Detective Wiley introduced the other plainclothes cops, Tyler, Glener, and Smith, and explained that they were part of a detail of combined Bureau and TPD personnel assigned to meet the plane at the airport. A call had come in from New York and the senior Bureau agent on the scene—the district chief, no less—had immediately sent them to the hotel with orders to find Makepeace and detain him, gently and with utmost courtesy, until the plane arrived. Unless he resisted, in which case they were supposed to swarm him like a bunch of linemen taking down a quarterback.

"I would've felt funny about that," said Wiley, "seeing as how they said you were in your sixties, but looking at you now, I can see you're a pretty tough old bird. I would've done it if I had to."

"Did they also happen to tell you I was an adept?" asked Makepeace.

"No, but I figured that, since this whole thing is an ITC case. They just gave us your name and a description." He smiled. "You weren't too hard to spot. And I didn't figure you'd go casting spells at a bunch of cops. We're supposed to be on the same team. I just don't know what game we're playing. I figure you were about to go off half-cocked on something and they wanted you chilled for a while till you could calm down. But you seem pretty calm to me."

"I am now," said Makepeace.

The others sat silent, content to let Wiley do the talking, but they were all watching and listening intently. "You suppose you could tell me what this is all about without violating security or something?" Wiley asked.

"How much do you know?" asked Makepeace.

"Well, I know it's magic crime, since the Bureau is involved, but if the ITC is calling the shots, it must be pretty major. I figure it's necromancy, since we had a bulletin about that a while back, but we haven't had any reported cases of that in Tucson, so my guess is it's a manhunt. The crime went down someplace else, but your suspect is here. Is that close?"

"Remarkably," said Makepeace. "What do you know about the Dragon Peak Enclave?"

"Drug rehab center and natural preserve run by a religious foundation," Wiley said. "They do pretty good work, by all reports. Well-connected in this town. Never been out there myself."

"You know somebody named Brother Talon?"

"Heard of him. He's supposed to be the chief honcho out there. Good reputation, but he doesn't get into town much, if at all. You saying he's the suspect?"

"There's no suspicion about it," Makepeace said. "Talon is the deadliest necromancer you could possibly imagine. My partner went out there. And I don't think he's coming back."

"I see," said Wiley, nodding. They all understood that. "So you were going after him. But you changed your mind. That car had rental plates and you were coming back to the hotel. Had time to count ten and decide to wait for backup, huh?"

Makepeace nodded. "That's about right. There's too much at stake for me to take the bit between my teeth."

"I can understand how you'd want to, though," said Wiley sympathetically. "It's tough when your partner's going down. How come he went out there alone?"

"Because he was a fool," said Makepeace bitterly. "And I was a greater fool to let him."

"So an ITC team is coming in and they're going out to Dragon Peak to make the bust," said Wiley. "And I guess we locals are supposed to provide backup and support, is that it?"

"Essentially," said Makepeace. He saw no point in telling them that there wasn't going to be any arrest. They probably wouldn't understand and he didn't feel like explaining it.

"Dragon Peak is technically out of our jurisdiction," Wiley said. "That's the Pima County Sheriff's Department."

"I imagine a lot of people are going to be involved," said Makepeace.

"You're expecting a lot of trouble, aren't you?"

"Yes, I'm afraid so."

Wiley sat silent for a moment. So did the others. "There's not going to be an arrest, is there?" he finally said, quietly.

Makepeace stared at him for a moment. The man was no fool, and these people were going to be putting their lives on the line, even as backup personnel. They had a right to know. He shook his head. "No. No arrest."

It was very quiet at the table for about a minute. The cops just looked into their beers. "Guess it would be kinda hard to hold a high-level adept in jail," Tyler said softly.

"Just how high are we talking about?" asked Wiley.

"Mage level," Makepeace said.

"You've gotta be kidding," Glener said. "There's like, what? Only four of those guys in the whole world!"

"I am most assuredly not kidding," Makepeace said.

"That's why this is ITC and not Bureau," Wiley said. "I was wondering about that. I figured there had to be an international angle, but I never counted on anything like this. No wonder they didn't tell us anything. A leak on something like this and it'll be all over the national media in a flash. It's gonna be hard enough keeping them out of it as it is."

"At the moment, that is the least of my concerns," said Makepeace. "When the plane lands—" He felt as if ants were suddenly crawling around in his brain. He glanced up and saw a large, muscular black man with a shaved head and a small goatee standing at the entrance to the bar, his eyes glowing with blue fire, like a sparking arc welder. *"Look out!"*

He threw himself out of the booth just as the bolt of thaumaturgic energy slammed into it. The table, the bench seats, and part of the wall, along with Tyler, Glener, and Smith, were vaporized instantly.

Trapped inside the booth, they couldn't have moved in time, but Wiley, who had been sitting on the outer edge, had thrown himself to the floor at the same time as Makepeace and had only caught part of the backwash. He was burning. Even as he screamed in pain, he pulled out his gun and emptied it at the black man. Makepeace thought he hit him at least twice before the man fled, staggering out of the bar, but he wasn't sure. The heat of the blast had singed him badly and he felt his hair burning. He slapped at it, then pulled his smoking coat up over his head, putting it out, then slipped out of the sleeves and threw the coat over Wiley, smothering the flames. He couldn't feel anything yet, but he knew he had suffered serious burns on his face and head. Wiley's condition, however, was much worse.

"Jesus . . . Jesus . . ." the detective kept saying, over and over, through teeth gritted against the pain.

"Hang on," said Makepeace.

There were screams as the bar emptied out. It had all happened so quickly that the black man was gone before the impact of what had occurred struck the patrons and they fled.

"Radio . . ." said Wiley, ". . . belt . . ."

Makepeace found the little radio clipped to his belt and

thumbed it on. "Help, somebody!" he said. "For God's sake, help!"

"Who is this?" a voice came through.

Makepeace quickly identified himself and told them there were officers down, then gave the name of the hotel and the street. He knew that would get a quick response. Then he tossed the radio aside and concentrated on Wiley, summoning up all his healing energy. He felt weak, but if he couldn't do something for Wiley now, he was going to lose him. He closed his eyes, summoning all his strength, placed his hands on the cop's chest, and concentrated, letting the energy flow through his hands and into the injured man. He kept it up until he passed out from the strain.

"Sebastian! Sebastian!"

His eyelids fluttered open. Kira and Wyrdrune were both bending over him, looking down anxiously. He was on his back, on the floor in the bar. He heard the noises of bustling activity all around him, the sound of radios, and saw, reflected on the ceiling, the flashes of police lights.

"Thank God," said Kira. "You're going to be okay."

"Wiley . . ." he murmured.

"The cop?" said Wyrdrune. "He's going to make it. You saved his life, Sebastian. They're taking him out to the ambulance now. They're coming right back for you."

"No . . ." He swallowed hard. "I'll be . . . all right. . . ." He tried to sit up and couldn't make it.

"Forget it, Professor," Angelo said, coming up behind Wyrdrune and Kira. "You're out of it. You're going to the hospital and you're going to stay there, like a good fairy."

"Up yours," said Makepeace.

"That's the spirit," Angelo replied with a grin. "You've got third-degree burns. Bad ones. You'll heal just fine, an old immortal like you, but you've got to get your strength back first."

"You're going to the hospital and you're going to *stay* there," Kira said. "Promise?"

"Acolyte . . ." Makepeace said. "Black man. . . ."

"We know," said Angelo. "There were a dozen witnesses. Billy's talking to some of them now."

"Promise me, Sebastian," Kira said. "You're going to stay in the hospital. *Promise* me!"

"All right . . . I promise."

The paramedics returned with the gurney and gently lifted him onto it.

"Simko . . . went out there. Think he's dead."

"I know," said Wyrdrune as they rolled the gurney out. "We'll get him for you, Sebastian. He's not getting away. Count on it."

They lifted the gurney into the ambulance, beside Wiley, who was unconscious. The doors were shut and a moment later, the ambulance rose up and whooshed away, siren blaring. The EMT bent over Makepeace.

"You're going to be okay," he said.

Makepeace glanced up at him. "How old are you?" he asked wearily.

"Twenty-four," the EMT replied, then smiled reassuringly. "Don't worry, Gramps, I'm old enough to know what I'm doing." He looked very fit.

"I need to borrow something from you," Makepeace said weakly.

"Borrow something?" The EMT frowned, then assumed Makepeace was delirious. "You just lie back and relax, Gramps. We'll have you at the hospital in no time. I'm going to give you something for the pain."

He held up a hypodermic.

"No . . ." said Makepeace. He reached out and took the EMT by the arm, murmuring a spell under his breath. The hypodermic fell from the man's grasp. "Just enough . . ." said Makepeace, closing his eyes as the strength of the

EMT's life force flowed through him. "Must take only . . . just enough. . . ."

Rafe sat slumped over the steering wheel of the car as it glided silently and swiftly down Valencia Boulevard. Valencia wound its way briefly through the hills at the edge of town, then it was a straight shot to where it T-boned into Ajo Way at Ryan Field, once a small private airport and now a suburban housing development. He turned left onto Ajo Way and headed out toward Dragon Peak.

He was getting blood on the seats. He had taken one bullet in the shoulder, the other high in his thick chest. It was his muscle density that saved him. The thick and massive slab of pectoral muscle had stopped the round before it reached his lung. A little lower and to the left and it might have struck his heart. Still, it hurt like a son of a bitch, but Rafe welcomed the pain. It was the pain that had snapped him out of it, severed the link with Talon.

That was the secret, he realized with a savage triumph. Make it hurt enough and it drives the motherfucker out, or else adrenaline kicks in and you snap out of it. It didn't matter either way. He knew how to beat him now. He couldn't beat his magic. He knew that. Talon could still blast him and turn him into nothing but a puff of smoke. But he just might catch the son of a bitch off guard, especially if Talon still thought he was under his spell. It was a risk, but Rafe didn't care. He had to take it. When he snapped out of it back there and realized what he had done, he knew it was all over.

Those were cops he'd snuffed. Talon had actually been the one to snuff them, but it didn't matter. Rafe was the one they'd seen. You don't kill cops and expect to walk away. Not in this town, he thought. And especially not if you were black. He was going to go down. All he cared about now was taking Talon with him. Getting his hands around that fucker's throat and squeezing the life right out of him. He welcomed the pain, cherished it, and hoped desperately he wouldn't lose so much blood he would pass out before he got there.

They were spread out all over the country, in twos and threes and fours. The largest group was in New York. They had lost several of their number, gunned down by Angelo with an expertise that came from skills and instincts acquired from Modred's centuries of hunting men. But there were still at least half a dozen left and they had spread out through the city at key points, where there would be crowds.

Each of them had already killed several times, bolstering their strength. Now they waited for the signal that they knew would soon be coming. Waited in the theater district and in the West Village, where café society would soon be filling up the bistros and the coffeehouses. Waited in Little Italy, where a street festival was in progress. Waited in Soho, where art galleries and trendy watering holes and restaurants would soon be filled with chic partygoers. Waited outside Madison Square Garden, where a crowd was lining up, choking the sidewalks as they waited for the doors to open and admit them to the first show of the Nazgul "Riding Out the Storm" tour.

They waited at similar places in Chicago and Detroit, in Denver and San Francisco and Salt Lake City, in Atlanta and Philadelphia and Miami, and in Phoenix, Dallas, and Los Angeles. Each of those cities had been plagued by a recent, sudden rush of necromantic serial killings. In each of those cities, the police were doing their best to hold the hungry media at bay, "no commenting" reporters who knew the authorities knew more than they were saying and worked every desperate angle they could think of to find someone, anyone, who would leak some information. To their utter amazement, no one did.

Some enterprising newshounds had already made the connection with similar rashes of killings in other cities, but without any details to report, they could only speculate.

Some restrained themselves, hoping to ferret out more facts, but they were in the distinct minority. Most speculated wildly about murder cults and organized crime warfare and terrorist plots. No one came close to the truth, for no one but the police knew that necromancy was involved, and the police—many of whom knew no more than the media did—weren't talking, under pain of having their badges melted down and poured into their nostrils.

Captain Rebecca Farrell of the LAPD was one of the very few who knew it all. Along with Commissioner Steve McGuire of the NYPD, on the opposite coast, she wasn't getting any sleep and had taken up chain-smoking. SWAT teams were standing by, not knowing yet what they were standing by for. Something was in the air. Something big and nasty.

And in the nation's capital, Senator Don Jones of Arizona, photogenic darling of the media and future presidential hopeful, was basking in the beauty of one of his constituents as she got into the limo, showing a nice expanse of leg in the indigo silk designer gown he'd paid for. She looks like a million bucks, he thought, never suspecting that just a month or so ago, she could have been had for a mere fraction of that sum. Wait'll the President's old man gets a load of her, he thought. The horny bastard will probably have a hard-on under the table all through dinner. Wouldn't be surprised if he puts the moves on her tonight. Probably be in her pants inside of a week. And then I'll put the screws to him, Jones thought. Yup, it was sure going to be an interesting evening at the White House.

# Chapter 10

They held the mission briefing in a hangar at Davis-Monthan Air Force Base before a combined force of Bureau and ITC agents, as well as U.S. Army rangers who had flown in, dressed for battle and armed to the teeth. Security was so tight, none of the military personnel had any idea what they were going up against until they arrived for the briefing. When they saw who would be conducting it, they were dubious at first. They were all called to attention as Wyrdrune, Kira, Angelo, and Billy came out to face them. A lot of curious looks were exchanged.

"As you were, or whatever," Wyrdrune said, speaking into a handheld mike that broadcast from a speaker in a truck bed. "In other words, sit down. Get comfortable, because I want you all to listen very carefully."

There was a lot of shuffling as they all sat where they stood in the hangar, on the floor, their curiosity mounting.

"As you are all aware by now," Wyrdrune continued, "this is not an exercise. This mission is for real and it's going to be a bitch. There's a damned good chance we're going to lose a lot of you, so don't kid yourselves. This is going to be dangerous and there won't be room for any mistakes."

He paused to make sure it had sunk in and he had their full attention, then continued. "This operation has been code-named 'Dragon Storm.' It is being conducted under the joint command of the U.S. Army, the ITC, and the Federal

Bureau of Thaumaturgy. You're probably all wondering who the hell we are and what we're doing here. I'd like to oblige with an explanation, but there isn't time and there are certain security issues involved. All you need to know is this: We are adepts, special operatives for the ITC, and we are in charge of this operation, by authority of the President of the United States. Take a good look at us, so you'll know who we are, and then stay the hell out of our way and do exactly as you're told. There are probably going to be civilian hostiles involved, and you may need to be able to tell us apart from them at a glance, so take a good long look. We don't want to be shot by mistake. Now, the object of this mission is to take Dragon Peak."

He saw many of them looking puzzled. "The Dragon Peak Enclave, located at the summit of the mountain, was once the Kitt Peak National Observatory. In recent years, it passed into private ownership and is now ostensibly a natural preserve and spiritual enclave, housing the Dragon Peak Drug Rehabilitation Center. In its latter capacity, the enclave has performed private and court-referred drug counseling, and in its former capacity it has functioned as a natural preserve for thaumagenetically engineered dragons, of which we estimate there are approximately seventy to one hundred on the mountain, roaming free behind the concrete walls surrounding the base. More on that in a moment.

"Behind its facade as a spiritual and counseling center and preserve, the enclave is in reality the headquarters of a cult of necromancers, led by a man calling himself Brother Talon."

Behind him, on a large screen, high-resolution satellite images of the enclave and its grounds were projected.

"There is no known photograph of Brother Talon. He is reported to be approximately six feet tall, slim, with green eyes and shoulder-length, fiery red hair. However, he is also capable of magically altering his appearance, so this description may be of little use to you. Talon is a highly dangerous adept of mage level, and he has been training a select cadre of necromancers drawn from the ranks of felons that were court-referred to the center. We do not know how many of his followers are among the population at the enclave, but our intelligence reports that among them are an undetermined number of innocent civilians who probably have no knowledge whatsoever of the cult's criminal activities.

"Talon is our responsibility. Yours is to secure the grounds of the enclave and make sure nobody gets out. Now . . . here's the tough part. The civilian population of the enclave can be regarded, for all intents and purposes, as hostages held by terrorists. The problem is, there isn't any surefire way to separate the terrorists from the hostages. And there is also a very real possibility that the hostages may be compelled by magic to attack you. If they do so, there is every reason to expect that it may come as a magical attack, where they may act as involuntary conduits for necromantic power. Possessed by black magic, in other words, and able to use it against you. Consequently, everyone within the enclave is to be regarded as a potential hostile, but we want to avoid, if possible, harming any innocent civilians. Under the circumstances, that's a hell of a tall order and there is only one way this task might be accomplished.

"Each unit commander, as well as each platoon and squad leader, has had a Bureau or ITC adept assigned to them. They will act as on-site advisers in the field. Listen to them. They are not there to take over your jobs, but to provide assistance. Remember, they're trained to deal with magic. You're not. If they give a direct order to use deadly force, instruct your personnel that they are to comply immediately. Their lives could be at stake.

"Now, certain units will be designated to set up a secure perimeter outside the walls of the enclave, at the summit, to make sure no one gets out. If you see anyone trying to get out past you, order them immediately to get facedown on the ground, hands clasped behind them. If they do not comply at once, fire warning shots. If they do not immediately comply at that point, open fire, especially if you see a blue glow emanating from their eyes."

He paused again to allow his words to sink in. The troops all sat perfectly still. There was not a sound inside the hangar.

"If we're lucky," Wyrdrune went on, "it won't come to that, because other units will be designated to storm the enclave and take down anyone they run across. Now in this case, 'take down' does not mean kill. Except in self-defense. All personnel will be issued strong, reinforced tape. The procedure will be as follows: hit the enclave hard and hit it fast. Anyone you encounter, immediately order them to lie facedown on the ground, hands clasped behind them. If they hesitate, *knock* them down. Secure their hands and tape over their mouths and eyes. Work fast. Speed is of the essence. Anyone who resists is to be shot. Yell, act mean, make a lot of noise. Intimidate them. Scare the crap out of them. And if they don't get scared . . . then shoot if you have to.

"Remember, it's possible that anyone you attempt to take prisoner could try to attack you magically. Do NOT let them speak, under any circumstances. Do NOT allow them to make any gestures or movements with their hands. *Watch their eyes.* Now, it's a normal human response to raise your hands when confronted with someone pointing a gun at you. Do not, repeat, do NOT allow them to do this. Yell at them to put their hands down and get down on the ground, *now.* Again, club them down if you have to. You will have to use overwhelming force and maximum intimidation to avoid getting yourselves killed. And, hopefully, to avoid getting them killed, too. You'll need to get in there fast and neutralize everybody as quickly as possible by immobilizing them. Once you have their eyes and mouths taped up and their hands restrained behind them, just leave them lying on the ground and move on quickly. Secure the grounds, go through all the buildings. Don't waste any time. Once the grounds are secure, gather all the prisoners in the central courtyard, here. . . ." He indicated the spot on the screen with a pointer. "Just pick them up and dump them all together on the ground, gently, then set up a perimeter around them and watch yourselves. Be ready for anything. A long whistle blast, repeated three times, will sound the all-clear. When you hear that, stand by for further instructions.

"Now . . . about the dragons. They could be dangerous. We don't know how they will respond. They may flee; they may attack. If you encounter them, fire warning shots to scare them off. However, don't let them get close if you can help it. They *are* dangerous. And carnivorous. If warning shots won't work, then drop them. They're officially an endangered species, but then under these circumstances, so are we. And human lives come first. Remember, your primary responsibility is to immobilize and neutralize everyone on the enclave grounds, male or female, without lethal force, if possible. The key words are, *'if possible.'*

"Chances are we're going to have casualties. I don't know if there's any way we can avoid that. We'll do our part to try to minimize that possibility. Talon will be the greatest threat, the one most likely to use the hostages as conduits for his power. However, he's not your concern. Talon is our responsibility. We're going to do our damnedest to make sure he's too busy with us to worry about what you're doing. But if you should encounter any resistance, don't hesitate to shoot. A magical attack can take place faster than you could believe.

"Now, we don't want you to get trigger happy, but then we don't want you to take any unnecessary chances, either. I realize that doesn't sound very reassuring, but you've got one thing working in your favor. You're not going up against trained troops or seasoned terrorists. These people are civilians. That means they'll scare a lot more easily. We *want* you to scare them. We don't want anybody being nice to any of the hostages. We want you to scare them so badly, they won't have time to think; they'll just blindly do exactly as they're told. We can apologize to them later, after we've saved their lives. All right, at this point, I'll turn you over to your mission commander for the final details of the briefing. Good luck to all of you."

It was to be a two-pronged assault. The main part of the force would be choppered in directly to the summit while the remainder would be dropped at the base of the mountain to help the police block the highway and secure the road up to the enclave, making sure nobody got in or out. Wyrdrune, Kira, Angelo, and Billy rode in the lead chopper with the ranger colonel, who would command the military part of the mission while the Bureau and ITC agents, likewise dressed in battle fatigues, only with white helmets and white armbands to identify them, would function as individual advisers to the various units.

As the sun went down behind the mountains, flooding the sky with the brilliant colors that had made Arizona sunsets famous the world over, Operation Dragon Storm was launched. First, various ground units stationed near the area were contacted and ordered to move in to surround the mountain, then the choppers lifted off and flew in formation toward Dragon Peak.

They left the city far behind and flew over the rural areas of the Sonora Desert, dotted with clusters of homes scattered throughout the Altar Valley. If anyone on the ground looked up and saw the helicopter squadron, they would probably think nothing of it. Military aircraft from the base routinely conducted exercises over the desert and no one would give it a second thought.

"I'm not thrilled about you people being out of uniform," Colonel Foster said, as they sat in the lead chopper. The commander of the ranger unit was in his early forties, but he easily looked ten years younger. He was stocky, extremely fit, and no-nonsense army all the way. "I'd be happier if you at least wore helmets and armbands to identify yourselves.

The men all saw you, but once things get under way, they're still liable to confuse you with the people of the enclave, you being in civilian clothes."

"There's little chance of that," Kira replied. "The members of the enclave all dress in white robes, according to our information."

"Besides," said Wyrdrune, "we're not going to look like this once things get really started."

The colonel gave him a sharp look. It was clear he wasn't wild about their appearance to begin with, Wyrdrune's and Billy's in particular, with their long hair. "What the hell is that supposed to mean?" he said.

"Our physical appearance is liable to change," said Angelo.

Foster frowned. "To *what*?"

"To tell you the truth, we're not quite sure," said Wyrdrune. "But it's liable to be pure energy."

Foster stared at him. "Are you putting me on?"

"No, sir, not at all," said Wyrdrune. He took off his headband. The colonel stared openmouthed at the emerald runestone in his forehead. It was glowing, getting brighter by the moment. "This magic stuff can be a little unpredictable sometimes."

"Shit," said Foster.

Kira took off her glove. Her sapphire runestone was giving off a bright blue glow. Angelo unbuttoned his shirt. The ruby set into the skin over his heart flared brightly.

"What the hell?" said Foster.

"Just be ready for anything, Colonel," Billy said. "These three are going to change. But don't worry, I'll still be me old lovable, handsome self."

The pilot of the chopper came on over the colonel's headset. "Colonel, you better get up here and take a look at this."

Foster hurried forward. They were rapidly approaching Dragon Peak. As he looked out through the cockpit bubble, his eyes grew wide at what he saw. *"Ho-ly shit!"* he said.

As the chopper squadron approached, shapes were rising up to meet them from all over the mountain. Large, dark shapes . . . with huge, batlike wings.

"We were told there were two patients coming in," said the emergency room nurse, as Wiley's gurney was wheeled in. "Where's the second one?"

The ambulance driver just stared at him, shaking his head. He was supporting the other EMT with an arm around his shoulder. The man looked dazed, exhausted to the point of collapse.

"What's the matter with him?" the nurse asked.

"I don't know," the driver said. "I think he's sick."

"But where the hell's the other patient?"

The driver moistened his lips. "I was paying attention to the road."

"What? I asked you where the other patient was. Come on, snap out of it! What the hell is wrong with you?"

The driver shook his head again. "All I know is I heard the doors open in back and when I looked in the rearview mirror, I saw the gurney go flying out. I almost swerved right off the road."

"Good God!" the nurse said. "Are you telling me the patient fell out into the *road*? And you didn't *stop*?"

"You don't understand," the driver said. "The gurney *flew* out. It didn't slide out; it didn't fall; it fucking *flew.*"

"What the hell are you talking about?"

"It *flew,* I tell you! It just flew *away!* Floated out the back doors and went zooming off into the sky."

*"What?"*

The driver pantomimed with his hand, palm down, fingers together and extended, rising up and out in an arcing motion. *"Whoosh!* Like that."

"Are you stoned or something?"

"Look, I know what I saw."

"Christ, I don't have time for this. . . ."

"*Whoosh!* Just like that. . . ."

Rafe saw it, but he could barely believe it. As he drove up the road leading to the enclave, a dragon stepped out in front of him, about thirty, forty yards away. The creature shuddered, then threw back its head and roared as the wings on its back unfolded and started to grow rapidly right before Rafe's eyes. They extended and kept on extending, growing larger and larger with astonishing speed, spreading into huge, leathery, batlike wings that dwarfed the roaring creature as it shuddered and spasmed. Then the dragon lowered its head and made convulsive motions with its throat that made Rafe think of a cat about to spit up a hairball.

Only instead of a hairball, the dragon spat out a gout of flame.

"Damn!" Rafe said. As he watched through the windshield, the beast flapped its huge, newly sprouted wings and took off like a gigantic hawk. And as he followed its flight, he saw others rising toward a squadron of rapidly approaching helicopters. In the distance, flashing lights were coming down the highway, moving fast. A lot of flashing lights. He grinned savagely, then winced with pain. His shirt was red with blood. It looked as if Talon was about to have his hands full. And that was liable to distract him just a bit.

"Works for me," said Rafe through gritted teeth. And he continued driving up the road.

Should've canceled the damned dinner, Manly thought. That would have been the prudent thing to do. But the President had disagreed. The lady had guts, he had to give her that. He still couldn't believe he'd gotten through to her as quickly as he had, but when she found out what it was all about, she got on the phone herself and told him to come right over. Sure, he remembered thinking after he hung up the phone, come right over. To the White House. Just like that.

After the Secret Service checked him out, he was conducted directly to the Oval Office, at which point he had seriously started to worry. What if he was wrong about this? This was the *President,* for God's sake. And he was coming to her with nothing but a hunch. Pete, he thought, you're going to have your ass handed to you on a platter if you're wrong about this. They'll transfer you to Nome, Alaska. Or maybe Guam. Someplace very far away, where he'd have plenty of time to think about what an asshole he had been.

The President had listened carefully as he laid it all out, her chief of staff standing off to one side, not missing a word. Manly had tried hard to sound as if he knew what he was talking about, like he was sure. But in the end, he knew he'd blown it when the chief of staff said, "That's it? That's all you've *got?* And you came to the President with *this?*"

"Hold on a minute, Dan," the President said. "Agent Manly, let me be sure I understand you correctly. You believe that I am going to be this killer's next intended victim?"

"Yes, ma'am."

The chief of staff rolled his eyes.

"And you believe this because the killer, a necromancer, has systematically killed a businessman, two well-respected Washington attorneys, a lobbyist, and a congressional aide?"

"Yes, ma'am."

"And you believe this constitutes a . . . ladder of sorts . . . which the killer is trying to climb in order to reach me?"

"That's right, ma'am."

"Because you think the killer has followed a chain of well-connected individuals that would lead to someone—a congressman or a senator, perhaps—who would have access to me?"

"Yes, ma'am."

"But you have no real proof of this. You're basically just following a hunch?"

Manly saw his entire career spinning away into an abyss. He took a deep breath. What the hell. "Yes, ma'am, that's correct."

"Jesus H. Christ," said the chief of staff, shaking his head.

"Okay," the President said, nodding. "That's good enough for me."

*"What?"* said the chief of staff, staring at her with disbelief.

"It took a lot of nerve for him to come here with just a hunch, Dan," President O'Connor said. "It took someone who has a lot of faith in his instincts." She nodded again. "I respect that. And *my* instinct tells me to go with it. So, Agent Manly, how do you propose to handle this?"

He had been enormously relieved that things had gone his way, but at the same time, he kept hoping he was wrong, even while knowing that being wrong could cost him his career. He had been inserted into the White House Secret Service detail, as personal guard to the President of the United Sates. He had also learned, to his relief, that a number of adepts had been added to the detail. Still, if he was wrong about this, he was going to be finished. Nevertheless, he kept hoping he was wrong.

Now he was staring straight at her.

He knew it was her. He knew it beyond the slightest shadow of a doubt. He could *feel* it.

Her emanations were so strong, it felt as if bees were buzzing in his brain. But at the same time, she didn't seem to be sensing him. Of course, any T-emanations he would project would be infinitesimal compared to hers, unless he was casting a spell. But she was putting them out steadily, all the time. Which fit with something else that had occurred to him. She was much too young to have that kind of power. So it wasn't really hers. Someone was using her, working through her. She herself probably couldn't sense anything at all.

She came on the arm of Senator Jones. And she matched the rough description they had from the doorman. Young, Hispanic, dark, great legs, dynamite body. . . . But he wouldn't have needed the description, sketchy as it was. He would have known her anywhere. Those emanations were like a signature he'd seen before. And he had.

She was dressed to the nines in a chic designer original and wore a small and very tasteful diamond necklace with matching earrings and tennis bracelet. Still, for all the elegance of her apparel, Manly thought, she looked like a cheap slut. She simply had no class. She oozed a trashy sort of sexuality, crude and blatant. He saw the other women notice it at once. They greeted her politely, but their body language was unmistakable. He just managed to overhear a soft, woman-to-woman aside from Senator Dane to Congresswoman Gemetta. "My God, where did he find *her*? She looks like a hooker!"

Manly caught the eye of one of the Secret Service adepts and gave him a slight nod, indicating the woman with his gaze. The agent caught it at once and gave a barely perceptible nod in return. He whispered softly into his mike. The woman was gushing all over the President's husband, making heavy eye contact and practically sticking her breasts into his face. Subtle she certainly wasn't.

Manly acted to make his move. Only he couldn't. Not until everyone was clear. It was maddening. He *knew* she was the one, *knew* she was a killer, and yet, he could not act on that knowledge without endangering the others.

There was a tense, hollow feeling in the pit of his stomach. He held his breath. Some of the most powerful people in the country were in this room, including the President of the United States, who was at that very moment being approached by Senator Jones, to introduce his date for the

evening. Manly felt as if time were slowing down as the
adrenaline triphammered through his system.

"Madame President," Senator Jones was saying, "allow
me to present Ms. Maria Santoro, of Tucson, Arizona."

"Dragons!" said Colonel Foster. "Hell, nobody said the
goddamn things could *fly*!"

"They're coming awfully fast, sir," said the pilot uneasily.

"Well, so much for the element of surprise," Foster said.
He glanced back over his shoulder. "Hey, did you—*Jesus!*"

The cabin of the chopper was filled with brilliant, blinding light. He couldn't even make out the people sitting back
there. All he saw were incandescent beams crisscrossing like
a latticework of lasers, red to green, green to blue, blue to
red, growing brighter and brighter until he had to cover his
eyes. The light formed a swirling vortex in the cabin and
shifted, moving out the open helicopter bay doors and into
the sky.

"What the hell is going *on* back there?" the pilot shouted.

Foster blinked several times and shook his head. Only
Billy Slade remained. The others had all disappeared.

"It's your show now, Colonel," Billy said, coming up beside him. "Give 'em what for."

"Sir . . . the dragons . . ." said the pilot.

"Well, what the hell are you waiting for?" the colonel
shouted. "*Shoot* the sons of bitches! All units open fire!" he
spoke into his headset.

The helicopters opened up on the dragons with machine
guns and air-to-air missiles. A number of the creatures were
hit at once and those struck by machine gun fire plummeted
to the earth like rocks while those hit by the missiles exploded into flaming bursts of blood and viscera. But there
were about ten times as many dragons as there were choppers, and as they closed, more dragons were destroyed, but
some of them got through.

Billy saw one chopper explode into a ball of flame as a

dragon belched fire and then smashed into it like a kamikaze Zero, killing itself and everyone aboard. So much for trying to do this quick and easy, he thought. If they couldn't get rid of these dragons, they'd never make it to the ground. He ran to the open bay doors and secured himself with a safety line, then concentrated, braced himself, and started throwing bolts of thaumaturgic force at the creatures as they flocked around the choppers like huge and obscene birds.

"Get us down!" he yelled to the colonel. "*Now* or we'll never make it!"

"Keep your shorts on, kid," Foster yelled back. "These things catch us on the ground, we've had it! They're breathing fire, for chrissake!"

"*Bloody hell!*" Billy swore. He knew that Wyrdrune, Kira, and Angelo would be no help now. That would be just what Talon wanted. He meant the tactic to delay them and make them use up energy against the dragons. But they had already formed the Living Triangle and they would be going after Talon, who was by far the greater threat. The choppers were on their own. As was he.

Suddenly he blinked, shook his head, and blinked again to make sure he was seeing what he thought he was seeing. It came swooping past the open helicopter doors, banking sharply, sheets flapping in the wind, and the figure seated aboard was unmistakable.

"Christ, what the hell was *that?*" the pilot shouted.

One of the other pilots came through on his headset. "Am I losing my damn mind or did Santa Claus just fly by on a hospital gurney?"

"Who the hell cares?" Foster replied, raising his voice to be heard over the noise. "Whatever it is, it's on our side."

"Sebastian, you are a bloody marvel!" Billy said, grinning as he watched Makepeace dart among the dragons like an angry hornet. He came in close, so close he risked being burned by their fiery breath, but he flew so quickly that the creatures could not react to him in time. He buzzed around them like a horsefly, swooping at their heads and then swerving away at the last possible second, narrowly avoiding their snapping jaws, distracting those who had come closest to the choppers long enough to allow the gunners time to bring their weapons to bear the fire the moment he darted away.

"I see it, but I don't believe it," yelled Foster, shaking his head with amazement. "Who the hell *is* that guy?"

"Would you believe he's an English teacher?" Billy yelled back from the open bay.

"At this point, I'd believe just about any damn thing," Foster called back as the chopper fired its air-to-air missiles. "I'm in aerial combat with a bunch of overgrown, fire-breathing lizards, for cryin' out loud! And if I live through this, I'll probably have to take on the damn Sierra Club!"

The dragons were dropping like very large flies as the weapons systems did their work, but one chopper had already been lost. The creatures were like huge flying flame-throwers and they hurled themselves at the choppers the way bugs smashed themselves against lighted windows. One chopper narrowly avoided a collision, its pilot doing a superb bit of flying as he spun the craft away from an on-rushing dragon and his gunner poured machine-gun fire into the screaming creature's flank. The formation was totally disrupted as the choppers spread out to give themselves maneuvering room and minimize the danger of getting caught in their own crossfire. And both the pilots and their gunners had their hands full keeping the dragons at bay.

But they were not all successful. Through the open bay door, Billy saw a dragon come swooping down upon a chopper like a bird of prey and he threw a bolt of energy at the creature, but not before it had time to breathe a huge gout of flame at its intended target. The energy bolt he threw struck home and the dragon screeched like an express train as it was wreathed in an incandescent blue aura, but even as it died, the helicopter it attacked spun wildly, its pilot blinded by the flame, and was struck broadside by another dragon that hurled itself against the chopper like a charging rhino. The fireball from the resulting explosion made Billy flinch and cover his eyes.

"Jesus, look at 'em all," he heard the pilot say over the headset. "We're never gonna make it."

"They're just big flying lizards, Lieutenant," he heard Foster reply. "All you gotta do is shoot 'em down."

"Right. Well, we just fired our last missile. We've only got the guns now."

"So *use* 'em, dammit!"

Billy knew the beasts had to be controlled to keep on attacking in such a suicidal manner. And they had no natural ability to fly or breathe fire. That meant Talon had to be expending tremendous amounts of energy to do all this. The bastard had to be incredibly strong. He was drawing on an enormous amount of life force energy. He had to have been storing up a great deal of it, at a cost of who knew how many lives. But how much more could he have left?

The answer came a moment later. As Billy watched the swirling, sparkling vortex that was the Living Triangle swoop down upon the mountain like a comet, he saw that magical control abruptly relinquished as Talon responded to their approach. The spirits of the runestones had done exactly the right thing and it had been their only chance. Talon knew that they were coming for him and he released the dragons to concentrate his full power on the greater threat. The remaining dragons suddenly plummeted to earth like stones as their wings started to shrink. If there was anybody down below, thought Billy, he hoped they had time to get out of the way. It had been a close call, but now the choppers had a clear flight path to the summit.

"Take 'em in!" the colonel shouted, and the helicopters started to descend.

\*     \*     \*

Rafe's car smashed through the gates of the enclave as the helicopters came in low over the compound. As he lurched from the car, out of the corner of his eye he saw one of the choppers come in low, just beyond the walls, and disgorge a platoon of army rangers. There was pandemonium on the grounds of the enclave. People were screaming and running around in a panic. They had seen the dragons take flight and watched the fantastic aerial battle with disbelief and horror. Now, as the choppers came swooping in, they were scattering in all directions, some running for the gates, some to take shelter in the buildings, some simply running around aimlessly.

"Oh, my God, you're bleeding!" a girl shouted as Rafe stumbled inside the mission.

He brushed her aside and staggered down the aisle, heading toward the side door leading out into the courtyard. He knew where Talon would be. He just needed to reach him before he passed out. As he staggered out into the courtyard, a huge blinding light suddenly descended on the adobe house, a sparkling, swirling, incandescent cloud so bright that he recoiled from it.

As Rafe shielded his eyes, there was a tremendous explosion and he was thrown to the ground. Debris rained down all around him and when he raised his head, he saw that the entire house had been blown open, as if smashed in by a gigantic wrecking ball. The roof was gone and the walls were cracked and buckled. The entire wall in front of him had collapsed. The bright light that had descended had disappeared, but there was now a gaping hole in the center of the house, right in the floor where the tunnel led down to the cavern.

Rafe had no idea what it was. A missile? Some new kind of energy weapon? He tried to struggle to his feet, but he had no more strength left. He was too weak from loss of blood. He collapsed back to the ground, cursing through the pain. His vision swam. Not yet, goddamn it, he thought, not yet!

Somewhere beyond the courtyard walls, he heard the

sounds of gunfire and men shouting, people screaming. He tried to stand again, but could only manage to get up to his knees. Everything around him was blurred. With a mounting fury, he realized he wasn't going to make it. He was going to die right here, so close, and yet too far away to take that bastard Talon with him. He screamed with rage, pain, and frustration.

And then he saw something coming down in front of him. He couldn't quite make out what it was. It was too small to be a chopper. He saw someone moving toward him, reaching out. . . .

"Good Lord," a voice said, "it's you!"

As the face came closer, Rafe tried to focus on it. He could make out only blurred features, a rotund face framed by long, shaggy white hair. "Help me. . . ." he said. "Gotta get that fucker, Talon . . . get him 'fore I die."

He felt a hand on him, steadying him. "All right, hang on. I'll try to help. I don't know if I have enough strength left for a healing. . . ."

Rafe felt a rapidly increasing warmth rushing through him, passing into him from the hand that touched him, permeating his entire body. He thought of the terrifying, numbing cold that had spread throughout him when Talon had possessed him, but this was different. It was warm, soothing, and comforting. He trembled involuntarily as he felt it reach his wounds and his vision started to clear.

He could feel his strength returning. Something shifted inside him and he winced with pain as he felt the bullets in his chest and shoulder start to worm their way out through his flesh. It hurt like hell, but he could feel the ruined muscle knitting as the bullets worked their way back up to the surface. A moment later, they dropped to the red brick of the courtyard and he stared at the misshapen little lumps of jacketed lead that had mushroomed as they plowed their way through his tissue when he was shot. But the wounds were already healing rapidly, even as the bullets fell out onto the ground.

He stared up at Makepeace and at first he didn't recognize him. He saw a large, heavily built white man with a thick shock of white hair, but hair that had been singed badly on one side. The white man had been burned recently. Very recently. He looked terrible, as if he could barely stand. And then Rafe suddenly remembered where he had seen him before.

"I . . . I tried to kill you," he said, mystified at why this man had helped him.

Makepeace shook his head. "It wasn't you," he said. "I know. It wasn't . . . your fault. . . ." He staggered and fell against Rafe.

"Here, man . . . take it easy," Rafe said, easing him down onto the bench beneath the tree.

Makepeace was breathing heavily. "I'm afraid . . . I don't have anything left," he said wearily. "No more strength."

"You just rest here, old man," said Rafe. "I owe you. And I'm comin' back for you. I promise. If I make it."

He moved off toward the gaping hole in the ground where the house once stood.


"We've *got* to get her away from the President," Manly whispered tensely into his mike. *"Now!"*

"Hang tight," came the reply through his earpiece. "We're on it."

One of the Secret Service agents approached Senator Jones. "Excuse me, Senator," he said, "there's a telephone call for you, sir."

Jones glanced around irately. "Who the hell is it?"

"I don't know, sir, I wasn't told. But your office said it was urgent."

Jones sighed. "Oh, very well." He made his excuses to the President, then the agent escorted him out of the room.

Unobtrusively, the circle of agents around the President

had tightened. None of the guests seemed to notice. They were all too intent on chitchat, on working the room, on playing that most time-honored of Washington games. It was, ostensibly, a social evening, but no gathering in the nation's capital was ever entirely social, especially at this level. The guests had their own agenda with which they were preoccupied and everyone was vying for the President's attention.

Manly noted with satisfaction that the President's husband was taking advantage of Senator Jones's brief absence to steer the woman away from his wife, where he could talk to her alone. He almost laughed out loud with nervous tension when he heard one of the Secret Service agents whisper to himself over the earpiece, *"That's it, you horny bastard, make your move. Get her the hell out of here."*

It was a remarkable lapse, all the more indicative of the tension among them. Can't risk anything going down here, thought Manly. Screw the legalities of the situation, it would be far too dangerous. Some of the most important and powerful people in the country were in this room, about to sit down to dinner. He wanted to have it over with before they did that. And so far, the woman seemed to be cooperating. She was moving off with the President's husband, going into another room . . . and then it suddenly hit him.

As they ambled out of the room in a seemingly casual way, Manly caught a glimpse of the First Gentleman's face. The woman seemed to be talking to him, leaning on his arm with her head close to his ear, but he wasn't saying anything in reply. The President's husband was glassy-eyed, his features slack, his mouth open slightly, as if he were in a trance. And Manly realized that they weren't having a conversation. The woman was casting a spell.

He'd been wrong. It wasn't the President that she was after. It was the man who was closest to her. If the necromancer who controlled her could also control the President's husband . . .

"Jesus Christ," said Manly in a shocked whisper. He was already moving rapidly across the room. Out of the corner of his eye, he saw several Secret Service agents following him, while others remained with the President and her guests. He ducked into the next room and looked around frantically. There was no sign of them. They must have gone out the other door into the hall.

"Where did they go?" asked one of the Secret Service agents, coming up behind him.

"Spread out and find them!" Manly said. "And take her the hell *down*! Now! *Move*!"


"DOWN! GET DOWN! Facedown, on the ground! Hands behind your back! NOW! MOVE!"

Small bursts of automatic weapons fire into the air punctuated the shouted commands as the rangers moved quickly through the compound, ordering people to the ground, throwing down those who hesitated even for a second, clubbing anyone who attempted to protest, but there weren't many of those. The grim, intimidating manner of the soldiers, coupled with the staccato sounds of the chopper blades and the crackle of automatic weapons fire, did its work. Most people immediately dropped wherever they stood. While one soldier covered them, another would quickly truss them up, first the tape around the mouth and eyes, then around the hands. The men moved quickly, fanning out across the grounds, and within moments, dozens of immobilized robed figures, lying facedown, dotted the courtyards.

Already panicked by the aerial battle between the dragons and the choppers, the residents of the enclave were too shocked, frightened, and disoriented to offer any sort of resistance. Those whom Talon had made his acolytes were no longer among them, having been sent out on their deadly missions, and the remainder had no idea what was going on or why.

The violent battle in the air they had just witnessed gave them dramatic proof that this wasn't some sort of exercise and that the soldiers meant business. When the rangers stormed the enclave, yelling at them to get down and firing their weapons into the air, most of them simply dropped to the ground and covered their heads without a moment's hesitation. Those inside the buildings had all been drawn out by the spectacle of the aerial battle and most of the residents had simply congregated in the courtyard, following some ancient herd instinct. When the chopper came in, they had scattered, running around aimlessly in terror as the gunners raked the area just beyond the walls with machine gun fire, "walking" it right up to the gates to drive everybody back.

The soldiers either heard or saw the explosion when the house next to the mission was destroyed, but they could spare no time for that. With all the gunfire, for all they knew, return fire had come from the house and one of the choppers had leveled it with a missile. Either way, it wasn't their concern. Their orders were explicit. Immobilize and neutralize everyone within the enclave first and do it *fast*.

"Sir?" said one of the rangers, glancing up from the prone form of one of the enclave members.

"Come on, mister, that one's done. Move it!"

"Sir, I think this one's dead."

"Damn. You sure? Okay, leave her. Move on."

"Sir?" another soldier called. "This one's dead, too."

The lieutenant ran over to the body, accompanied by the ITC agent assigned to his platoon. There was another one a bit farther off. And another. And another.

"What the hell?" the lieutenant said.

They were all dead. The ones they had already immobilized, the ones they had ordered down to the ground and hadn't gotten to yet, even those who had been running and had apparently dropped to the ground in obedience to the shouted commands of the soldiers, all were dead. Every one of them.

"Heads up!" the lieutenant shouted, remembering the warning from the briefing—*be ready for anything.*

The soldiers all stood with their weapons at the ready, glancing nervously all around them. The enclave had suddenly fallen eerily silent. No one moved. Only the staccato beating of the chopper blades as they circled the area broke the stillness on the mountaintop.

"They've all been drained of life force," said Billy, as he straightened up from one body, then bent over another one. "This one, too. Bloody hell, every single one of them's been drained."

"What does that mean?" asked Foster.

"It means the shit's about to hit the fan," said Billy grimly.

And then they heard a distant rumble and the ground below their feet started to shake.

Talon stood atop the stone altar surmounted by the glowing crystalline formation that held his immortal captives. Beams of thaumaturgic force lanced down from the massive crystals, bathing him in swirling light that funneled around him like a vortex, whipping his robes and hair and raising a wind that moaned inside the vast cavern as it whistled through the rock formations, howling as it picked up speed.

Things had not worked out quite the way he'd planned, but that made little difference now. He was prepared for this contingency. He had planned for a long time. His acolytes had failed in their mission against the avatars in New York, but he had anticipated that. It had still been worth the risk. Even if he had only managed to kill one of them, the power of the Living Triangle could have been broken, diminished to the point where the spell of the Council could no longer attain its full potency. Unfortunately, that had not happened, so he had shifted smoothly to the next phase of his plan.

His acolytes had embarked upon their murderous spree throughout the country, yet even that had failed to distract the avatars. They had left his acolytes to the human authorities to cope with and had instead concentrated their full attention upon him. Again, he had anticipated that possibility. Beladon and the others had always underestimated the humans. Talon had not done that. The avatars remained his first concern, so the acolytes were all expendable.

All save one.

The dragons had slowed the attack by the human forces, even if they had failed to stop the avatars, and that had bought him enough time to initiate the spell he had already prepared in anticipation of this moment. Confronted with the spell of the Living Triangle at full force, he knew he would need all the power he could possibly command, so he had called up the spell to drain all the members of the enclave, absorbing all their strength and life essence into himself, even as the soldiers stormed the grounds. Then he bolstered it with infusions of concentrated life force from his fellow necromancers held captive in the crystals.

He could feel the power surging through him, more power than he had ever felt before. It sang through every fiber of his being, jolting him, energizing him, filling him with an almost sexual ecstasy as he trembled violently from the sheer force of it.

He had prepared his spells painstakingly and now they cycled continuously, energy expended fed by energy absorbed as he reached out to his acolytes through the psychic link he'd forged with them and gave the command for the slaughter to begin.

They were unable to resist. Already primed with lust for power and slaved to his will by the link between them, which had grown stronger with each transferral of life energy, they all went on a wild killing rampage the moment he gave the psychic command. In New York and Chicago, Boston and Philadelphia, Denver and Detroit, Los Angeles, and San Francisco, everywhere they had dispersed to pursue their predatory hunt for victims, they all suddenly began to kill indiscriminately, like blood-crazed sharks in a feeding frenzy.

In Los Angeles, Captain Rebecca Farrell responded to a call that an adept had gone berserk in the Hollywood Bowl and had started killing people. Moments later, even as she was en route, a second call came over her radio that another adept had run amok on Sunset Boulevard, followed by a report of still another one in Westwood, and yet another at the Galleria.

My God, it's started, she thought, as she quickly dispatched SWAT teams to the sites and hoped like hell that Wyrdrune and the others were on top of it. If they weren't, it was going to be the worst case of mass murder in the history of the country.

As her car shot around the corner, skimming several feet above the surface of the street, lights flashing and siren wailing as her driver adept banked around the turn like an aerial stunt pilot, she could see the pandemonium in the streets outside the Bowl. People were streaming out of the popular concert venue like stampeding cattle, running straight out into traffic. Horns blaring, people screaming, and over it all, the sound of gunfire.

"This is Farrell, talk to me!" she spoke into the mike. "What's happening?"

"We got him, Captain," came the reply. "He's down."

"Casualties?"

"At least a dozen dead, three officers down. He didn't even try to get away. Bastard just kept comin' till we dropped him."

"Christ," said Rebecca, exhaling heavily. "Farrell to all units. Report on what's happening in Westwood, the Galleria, and the Strip."

The units responded quickly, identifying themselves and then reporting briefly. The killer on Sunset had been brought down by the first unit arriving on the scene; nine civilians dead, no police personnel injured. They took him out with

two shotgun blasts at close range. They got the one in Westwood, too, but not before at least a dozen people had been
killed. They still didn't have an exact count. Two police officers down, both dead. The one in the Galleria was the
worst. The popular shopping mall was crowded and even
though she had thought to station units on the scene in anticipation of possible trouble there, the necromancer had
killed at least fifteen or twenty people and four officers before the SWAT team arrived on the scene. She waited
tensely in her car, listening to it unfold, and then breathed a
sigh of relief when the report came in that they got him. She
checked with dispatch. No other reports of adepts running
amok had come in. Apparently, it was over . . . at least as far
as her jurisdiction was concerned.

Bad as it was, it could have been much worse, she
thought. The whole thing couldn't have taken longer than
ten minutes. Ten minutes, and over thirty people had been
killed. If they hadn't been forewarned, if they hadn't had
every available cop out on the street, and if they hadn't
moved as quickly as they did . . . she didn't want to think
how bad it might have been. She bit her lower lip, wondering what was going down in other cities.

Steve McGuire didn't reach the first murder scene until
the smoke had cleared. By then, it was over, all across the
city. Special units had been standing by, organized into
highly mobile and heavily armed flying squads, prepared to
be dispatched to any area of the city at a moment's notice.
Every cop on the street had been alerted, extra units had
been detailed to potential trouble spots. They knew something would be coming. They just did not know exactly
where or when. Still, it was their preparedness that kept the
death counts lower than they would otherwise have been.
And when he saw how quickly and how savagely the killers
had struck, McGuire shuddered at the thought of what might
have happened if they had not been ready for it.

In Soho, the city's fashionable art district, thirty people

had died before police sharpshooters arrived and brought the killer down. In the theater district, there were nine deaths before a patrolman who had been nearby put a bullet through the perpetrator's skull. He had only been half a block away when he had heard the screams and it couldn't have taken him longer than thirty seconds to arrive on the scene. Yet, in that brief time, nine people on the street had lost their lives.

At Madison Square Garden, a disaster of cataclysmic proportions was narrowly avoided. McGuire had rightly guessed that the Nazgul concert would draw the biggest crowds in the city on that night and had detailed extra police for security duty as well as calling up all the available police reservists and sprinkling them throughout the crowd. The department's finest sharpshooters had been stationed up where the lights had been set up and it was one of them who had scored the extremely risky direct hit, but not until some people had been killed and others injured in the panic that broke out. Miraculously, no innocent bystanders had been shot in their attempts to drop the necromancer, but it was still too early to tell how many had been killed or injured in the pandemonium that broke out when people started dying.

It was the same in cities all over the country. Talon's human necromancers, stationed in crowded areas, went off like a pack of firecrackers and started on their murderous rampage, funneling life force energy back to their master with each killing. From the moment Talon triggered them, they became automatons with no will of their own, like living machines that killed with no thought to their own self-preservation. Talon didn't care if they all died. He expected that they would.

In a few cases, the authorities lucked out. In San Francisco, an alert police detective dropped a necromancer who went berserk in Ghiradelli Square. He just happened to be about twenty feet away when the killer struck at his first victim. And in Denver's Mile High Stadium, a necromancer who started killing people in the stands during a game was overwhelmed by angry Broncos fans and beaten to death in moments. But in other areas of the country, the death toll mounted steadily until, one by one, the necromancers were brought down by the authorities. And then only one remained. . . .

Talon felt it as each of their lives was snuffed out, but it caused him slight concern. He even conceded a grudging admiration for the human authorities, who had been prepared to move so quickly to counter the attack. He had anticipated that his acolytes would die as the police and thaumaturgic agencies responded, but he had hoped for more time in which to absorb the energies of those they killed. Within a fairly short time, all of them were dead, except the one, his final contingency plan, and he had still managed to increase his store of power, though not as greatly as he'd hoped. And when he heard the explosion up above and felt its tremors all the way down inside the cavern, then heard the howling rush of wind sweeping down through the tunnel passageway, he knew that they were coming and he was ready for them.

*Talon!* he sensed Beladon's anguished cry within his mind. *Talon, for pity's sake, release us! Don't be a fool! You cannot take them on alone!*

"But I am not taking them on alone," Talon replied calmly, as the swirling vortex of light around him flashed and sparkled, reflecting off the veins of crystal in the cavern walls and flooding the darkness with light and dancing shadows. "I have you, my friends. And I have you where you cannot desert me to save your own miserable skins. I now command more power than any necromancer ever has before. One way or another, it ends here, and it ends *now*."

The noise of rushing wind increased to a shrieking pitch and the cavern exploded in a brilliant wash of light as the swirling vortex that was the Living Triangle came hurtling through the tunnel, the spirits of immortal mages and three human avatars embodied in a cloud of living, pulsating, pure energy.

"Welcome, my old friends," said Talon from within his funnel cloud of spinning light. "I have been waiting for you."

He stretched forth his hand and a wash of cobalt blue light leaped like burning plasma from his outspread fingers and struck the cloud of living energy full force.

Like a mirror shattered by a hammer, the cloud of swirling, sparkling light that was the Living Triangle burst apart into dozens of light shards, like pulsating globules of liquid mercury, shifting in the color spectrum to a duller hue, then rushing back together once again, flaring brightly and swooping down upon the vortex within which Talon stood, fed by beams of thaumaturgic force emanating from the massive crystals. The two energy fields met, sparked, ignited in a wash of white flame and set off jagged bolts of blue lightning that danced throughout the cavern.

As the Living Triangle rebounded off the funnel cloud of energy within which Talon stood, it floated up near the ceiling of the cavern, its form becoming more distinct, a triangle revolving rapidly, crackling and humming with energy, looking like a spinning star as it shifted colors through the spectrum, recovering from the earthshaking contact.

Talon laughed. "Is that the best that you can do?" he shouted.

In answer, a bolt of concentrated thaumaturgic force came lancing out of the spinning energy triangle, but Talon met it with a force bolt of his own and the two blasts collided in midair, setting off an explosion that rocked the cavern and brought debris raining down from the ceiling. Several times they hurled force bolts at one another, shaking the entire cavern and causing the earth to rumble, but neither was able to break through.

*"Show yourselves!"* yelled Talon. "I want to see your

faces! Manifest! Look your last upon the one who will destroy you!"

The spinning triangle flared several times, its deep, oscillating hum rising and falling metronomically, and then it slowly settled to the cavern floor and split apart, one smaller triangle spinning off from the central mass, glowing with a bright blue light, another revolving off to the right, flaring with a bright green hue, and the third pulsating, with brilliant, bright red light. Within each of the spinning forms, the indistinct outlines of oval-shaped figures started to appear, glowing with light to match the spinning forms around them until the triangular auras gradually faded and only the glowing, pulsating oval figures remained.

Talon hurled incandescent bolts of force at them, but before they struck, the three glowing figures fragmented, dividing like cells, each splitting apart into four brightly pulsating shapes like human silhouettes. Those shapes continued to move outward, all twelve of them, hovering above the cavern floor, floating rapidly to different points throughout the subterranean chamber, surrounding the necromancer.

Talon extended his awareness through the crystals towering over him, using his captives within to "see" the sorcerers materializing all around him, registering their shapes within his mind as they were reflected in the facets of the crystals overhead.

"Expend more energy that you cannot replenish!" he shouted at them. "Divide your strength, you fools! It will not save you. It will only draw out the inevitable. You grow weaker, while I grow ever stronger!"

The glowing forms resolved into white-robed, hooded figures standing on ledges and atop rocky outcroppings in the cavern, each one wreathed in a protective, transparent, glowing aura: the Council of the White, made manifest once more after centuries of existing in only spirit form, contained within three enchanted runestones that were keys to lock a spell meant to have remained unbroken till the end of time. As they surrounded him, the mages hurled bolts of thaumaturgic force at the swirling light funnel that enshrouded him, but Talon sent his power through the crystals, calling upon the life forces of the Dark Ones trapped within, and beams of energy lanced out from them in all directions, striking the sorcerers who stood around him.

Over and over, the tumultuous exchange continued, blasts of energy hurled back and forth, rocking the cavern, splitting stone and sending stalactites crashing to the ground. The cavern became a webwork of force beams shooting back and forth, striking one another, some breaking through and hitting the auras surrounding the necromancer and the sorcerers, and as each one struck, the protective auras flickered and grew weaker until their force was replenished by the life energy of the adept maintaining them.

Talon saw one of the auras weakening and poured forth a long stream of thaumaturgic force. The aura flickered like a guttering candle and winked out, the adept within discorporating, immortal spirit snuffed out once and for all. With a cry of triumph, Talon redoubled his efforts and the cavern shook with the force of the energy, being thrown back and forth. More debris rained down, fissures opened in the walls, and another spirit member of the Council used up his last reserves of energy and was vaporized by a bolt of energy he was unable to counter.

The others continued to pour forth everything they had at Talon and he inevitably felt the power drain. He could not keep this up much longer. Two were gone, but ten more remained, though several of those were weakening visibly as their protective auras flickered. They were all that stood between him and all he ever wanted, all that he waited for over the centuries that he been confined. It was all or nothing now.

*Talon!* he heard Beladon shout within his mind, as he sensed what Talon was about to do. *No!* The others all cried out in desperation with him.

"Sorry, my friends," said Talon, gritting his teeth with concentration. "I have no other choice."

And as the minds of his captives in the crystals shrieked in agony, he drained them of every last bit of life force they possessed. As they died, one by one, the massive crystals shattered with loud reports into thousands of shards that went spinning off across the cavern, refracting light from the latticework or energy bolts the antagonists hurled at one another. Talon felt renewed strength fill him as he poured even more energy into his attack and another Council spirit was struck down, winking out forever, then another. . . .

"You've lost!" he shouted triumphantly. "I am stronger! I can feel you weakening! You have nothing left!"

Another spirit mage was vaporized, his aura winking out as Talon concentrated his energies upon those that remained. And he could sense them growing weaker now, feel less force in the spells they threw at him, see their protective auras fading as they used up what little strength they still had left.

But even with the remaining life force he had drained from his captives, Talon felt his own strength ebbing quickly. The spirits of the Council were growing steadily weaker, but he was expending much more energy than they were now and he had drained Beladon and the others more than he had thought before he consumed their remaining life force. The renewed rush of strength he felt when he took what little they had left was ebbing quickly now and, as another Council spirit was struck down, the remainder joined their forces in one last push against him. It took almost all the strength that he had left to withstand their concerted assault and he realized that it would not end here, after all.

If they continued, there was a chance they might destroy one another and he knew that was a price the white mages would pay if they could bring him down. But he was not willing to give his all to win. Not after he had come this far. It would be pointless if he failed to survive.

He had still prevailed, however. He had destroyed enough
of them to weaken the power of the Living Triangle to the
point where they would never again be able to call upon the
spell. It was forever broken. It would take the survivors
years to recover from this battle, and in that time, he would
redouble his strength to the point where they could never
threaten him again. For now, however, retreat was the prudent thing to do. And he had prepared for that.

They would think that they had beaten him, that he was
destroyed. But they would succeed in killing just his body.
And they would never suspect that his spirit had survived, or
where it had escaped to. With the last bit of strength that he
had left, he poured his remaining power into the swirling
light shield that enveloped him and reached out with his
mind. . . .

It was perfect, thought Maria, as she led the First Gentleman out of the room. She had known what was on his mind
and it hadn't taken any magic to see it. It was going to be
even easier than she had expected. He was attracted to her
and he clearly hoped that something might eventually develop, but it was going to happen much more quickly than
he thought. And it would turn out very differently from what
he had in mind.

When she made contact with him, looked into his eyes
and spoke the spell, he had succumbed to it immediately.
Not much will there to break down. And he was already
halfway there. The love spell took hold instantly and over-
came him with uncontrollable desire.

He had brought her into one of the bedrooms—she could
not recall which President it had been named after; he had
told her, but then he could control himself no longer and his
hands were all over her as he seized her and started kissing
her passionately. She was making merely token protests as
she prepared to take him—and then she stiffened as a numbing cold started to spread rapidly throughout her mind.

"Talon?" she mumbled.

"Sssh, honey, come on, now, let's get over to the bed. . . ."

Talon was taking her over once again and as she felt herself receding, panic filled her. He had never possessed her so quickly or completely before; he was flooding her with his essence, forcing her out of her own mind and body. She wanted to scream, but couldn't. She couldn't move. It felt as if she were growing smaller and smaller within herself, falling away into a dark and frightening cold abyss. . . .

The door burst open and Manly rushed into the room. *"Get away from her!"* he shouted.

The President's husband looked up sharply as, involuntarily and guiltily, he jerked back, stepping away from her, his eyes trying to focus. "What the hell?"

Manly saw the blue glow sparking in Maria's eyes and emptied his entire pistol magazine in rapid fire, pumping all fifteen rounds into her as she fell back onto the bed.

Talon recoiled from the contact, his consciousness snapping back into his own body as he doubled over, still feeling the burning pain of the bullets slamming into Maria as he was in the act of transferring his spirit into her. For a moment he was disoriented and the swirling shield around him flickered and sparked out. Instantly, he realized his vulnerability, but before he could throw the energy shield back up, a large, dark figure rose up behind him and he felt powerful fingers close around his throat.

"Hey, muthafucker, remember me?" said Rafe.

Gasping for breath as he felt his larynx being crushed, Talon concentrated fiercely, with his last ounce of will, his eyes flaring with a bright blue glow.

"I—don't—fucking—think—so," Rafe said, as he jerked the necromancer's head around, stepped forward quickly, then came down hard, bending Talon over backward sharply and snapping his spine over his knee with a sharp crack. Talon's cry was cut off abruptly, then he collapsed to the cavern floor as Rafe released him, stood up, and kicked the body. "End of story," he said.

And then the roof of the cavern started to cave in.

The last thing Rafe remembered was a bunch of swirling lights enveloping him, so blindingly bright he couldn't see, and he thought, This is it, man, this is what happens when you die.

Except he didn't die. He came to inside a helicopter. He heard the sound of the blades whirring overhead. Several soldiers were crouching over him, one of them apparently a medic.

"I think he's going to be okay," the medic said.

"Are you all right, mister?" A female voice. Rafe moved his head and saw a dark-haired young girl looking down at him with concern.

He blinked. "Don't know," he said. "What the fuck happened?"

A young man with long, curly blond hair leaned over him. "What's your name, friend?" he asked.

"Rafe. Who's askin'?"

"The name's Wyrdrune. And you just saved the world, Rafe."

"No shit?"

Wyrdrune grinned. "No shit."

"Well, damn. You be sure to tell my parole officer."

The soldiers laughed.

"You've got my guarantee, Rafe," Wyrdrune said.

"Works for me," said Rafe. And then he closed his eyes and went to sleep.

# Epilogue

"**A**mazing," said McClellan as he listened to the story. "The most powerful threat humanity ever faced and an ex-con thug takes him out."

Wetterman shook his head. "The President wants to give him a medal. I can just see this guy at a ceremony in the rose garden."

"Oh, I think he'll be okay," said Makepeace. "He knows how close he came to dying in that cave-in. He figures he's got himself a new lease on life, a chance to start all over. He wants to go back to school and finish his education, then train to become a paramedic. I'm all in favor of that. I think the least we can do is help him out."

"This is the same guy who tried to kill you," said McClellan.

"*Talon* tried to kill me," Makepeace corrected him. "Rafe was just his instrument. He had no will of his own. Besides, he's been cooperating fully. Can you imagine the money he could make from selling his story? He'd be world famous. We're asking him to turn down quite a lot. And he knows it."

"Well, I'm sure that little account you established in his name was an incentive," Wetterman said dryly. "He'll be the world's only paramedic millionaire."

"The man has simple tastes," said Makepeace with a shrug. "And he just wants to be useful."

"The media's going crazy over this whole thing," Mc-

Clellan said, shaking his head. "What the hell are we supposed to tell them?"

"A shaded version of the truth," said Wetterman. "Cult of necromancers, renegade adepts, terrorist ransom demands, the need for more controls and more thorough screening in adept certification. . . . There's going to be a lot of backlash from this, but we'll get through it. And we'll be able to use it to push through some stricter legislation. We'll just all keep our mouths shut about immortals. I don't think the public's quite ready for headlines right now. Scandal always plays better than murder. Fortunately for us."

"Are you quite sure Talon was the last of them?" McClellan asked.

"Yeah," Wyrdrune replied. "It's over. Finally."

McClellan heaved a sigh of relief. "Well, thank God for that. I haven't had a decent night's sleep since all this started. But I'm still not really clear about what happened to the runestones."

Wyrdrune's hand went to his forehead, feeling the spot where the emerald runestone was once bonded to his flesh. It was gone now, just as Kira's sapphire had disappeared from her palm and Angelo's ruby had vanished from his chest. "To tell you the truth, I don't really know," he said. None of us do. The last thing we remember was battling Talon in that cavern. But we weren't really there. That is, we were, in a manner of speaking, but we had been transformed into energy . . . pure life force, out of which the spirits of the Council manifested."

"But you said a number of them died," said McClellan. "Or their spirits died. I don't know, I'm still confused about that part. What exactly happened?"

"We couldn't tell you, exactly," Kira replied. "After all, we're dealing with levels of enchantment no human truly understands. Or may ever understand."

"The best way I can figure it is that old story about cats having nine lives," said Angelo. "We each had one. The spirits of the runestones were the other eight. Only in our case, we each had four of them. Some of those lives were lost. But the runestones lost them, we didn't. Otherwise, we wouldn't be here, would we?"

"That's assuming you're still you," McClellan said.

Wetterman glanced at him, uneasily.

"I feel like me," said Angelo with a shrug.

McClellan grunted. "Yes, well . . . we may never know."

"You could always run a T-scan on us," Wyrdrune said. "If we're actually immortal mages, it should read off the scale." He smiled. "But then, you've already done that, haven't you?"

McClellan glanced at Wetterman, then smiled. "Yes, as a matter of fact, we have."

"And?" said Kira.

"You all read perfectly normal. For high-level adepts, that is. Nothing quite so dramatic as Sebastian's reading, which *is* right off the scale. I guess the runestones gave you all a boost before they went to wherever the hell it was they disappeared to."

"When Gorlois merged with me, his runestone shattered," Billy said. He shrugged. "Whatever's left of the other three is probably still down in that cavern, buried under tons of rock."

"But what became of the surviving spirits of the Council?" asked McClellan.

"What becomes of anybody's spirit?" Makepeace replied. "Where does the soul go when its time on earth is done?"

"Are you telling me you know?" McClellan asked.

Makepeace raised his eyebrows. "No. Do you?"

McClellan grimaced. "So that's it, huh? That's all you're going to tell me?"

"What more is there to tell?" asked Makepeace.

"Why do I have the feeling there *is* more and you're just not telling me?"

"Because, my dear Mr. McClellan, you are at heart and

you will always be a government bureaucrat," said Make-peace. "No answer will ever satisfy you fully. You will always think there's more. But I'm afraid you will have to search for those answers in books about philosophy and religion. And all you will succeed in finding is more questions."

"Thanks," McClellan said. "You've been loads of help. So . . . what happens now?"

"I dunno about the rest of you," said Billy, "but I'm going back to England. I spent a lot of years just scraping by, living on the streets, and now I've got some money—more than I ever thought I'd have, thanks to old Modred's bank accounts, which we're all splitting up between us—so I think I'll buy me a mansion in the country where I can live like a proper gentleman and throw some of the biggest parties the London social set has ever seen. 'Cept I won't be inviting any o' that lot. Just working-class sorts like meself. And then maybe I'll start a band or something. Always wanted to do that."

"You're a mage-level adept and you're going to become a *musician*?" Wetterman said with disbelief.

Billy shrugged. "Why not?"

"Because the ITC could use you, that's why not."

"Nothing personal, but you've already used me," Billy said. "I figure I've done my part. Now I'm going to kick back and have some fun, if it's all the same with you."

"Well, you're certainly entitled," Wetterman replied. He glanced at the others. "What about the rest of you?"

"Once a cop, always a cop," said Angelo. "Commissioner McGuire's arranged to transfer me to the Bureau. I want to do fieldwork. The streets were always what I knew best. And I like catching the bad guys, though of course this last act is going to be a little tough to follow."

"And you two?" asked McClellan, glancing at Wyrdrune and Kira. "Got any immediate plans?"

"I've offered them both jobs," said Wetterman, "but

they've turned me down flat. Of course, it's not as if they need the money."

Wyrdrune and Kira glanced at one another and smiled. "We haven't made any long-term plans," said Kira, "but we think a vacation is definitely in order."

"We've made some good friends along the way," said Wyrdrune. "We just might spend some time visiting with them without having to worry about people trying to kill us for a change. After that, we'll see."

"And what about you, Sebastian?" asked McClellan. "Going back to teaching? Might seem a little tame after all this."

"You haven't seen the current crop of freshmen," Makepeace said wryly.

"We could use you in Washington, you know."

Makepeace looked scandalized. "Perish the thought! I have a reputation to consider."

McClellan grinned. "Okay, well, I tried. Oh, by the way, the President has invited you all to the White House for dinner next week. It will be a strictly private affair, no press, no VIPs. I trust you will all accept?"

"We'll be there," Wyrdrune said. "But after that, we're gone."

"Well, if you ever need anything from Washington, you know whom to call," McClellan said, getting up. "I'll see you at the White House next week. I'll be in touch about the arrangements. Transportation and everything else will be on the U.S. government. I figure it's the very least that we can do. The whole world owes you a debt of gratitude. Too bad most of them will never know about it."

"That suits us just fine," said Wyrdrune. "We've had about all the attention we can handle for a while. All I want to do now is take a nice long cruise on a slow boat going nowhere in particular."

"So, when are we leaving?" Broom said as it swept into the room, wearing a navy blue yachting blazer and a captain's cap atop its handle. "I've always wanted to go on a cruise. Dancing, entertainment, shuffleboard, aerobics . . . and it's about time somebody waited on *me* for a change."

They all burst out laughing.

Agent Manly turned off the television set and leaned back in his chair, opening a beer. They were handling the media pretty well, all things considered. After the story first broke, there was the predictable outcry over stricter controls on magic and demands for further investigations and the usual groups came out in opposition of "unnatural forces," but it all blew over fairly quickly after new, stricter legislation governing magic use was introduced in Congress and other sensational events crowded the "necromancy cult" off the evening news and onto the back pages of the tabloids.

The story that got the biggest play was the President's divorce. There was a scandal, charges of numerous "indiscretions" on the part of the First Gentleman, but the truth about the straw that broke the camel's back had been very neatly hushed up. Which was just fine with Manly. He was glad it was all over. And the President was better off, as far as he was concerned. The public sympathy was with her. She was a hell of a woman, Manly thought, and she certainly deserved much better. Recent reports had her linked with her chief of staff, who had revised his original opinion of Manly considerably after that night and offered his apologies. They had gotten to know each other better since then and occasionally played tennis at his club. Dan was a stand-up guy, thought Manly. He was okay, once he loosened up.

The phone rang and he picked it up. "Manly," he said.

"O'Connor," came the distinctly feminine reply, in slightly mocking kind.

"I beg your pardon?" Manly said.

"Katherine O'Connor? Remember me?"

Manly sat up suddenly, almost spilling his beer. *"Madame President?"*

"Ah, I see you do remember. I'm so glad. I was beginning to think I hadn't made a very strong impression."

Manly cleared his throat. "I'm sorry, ma'am. I, uh, was hardly expecting the President to call. How may I be of service?"

"Well, if you're not busy this Friday night, I'm having an intimate little dinner at my place and I seem to be without an escort at the moment. I suppose I could ask Dan, but you know how the gossip is in this town. They'd have us shacking up and then I'd have to marry him. So, what do you think?"

Manly cleared his throat. "Excuse me, ma'am?"

"Kathy," said the President. "I'm asking you out, Pete. How about it?"

"You mean, like . . . for a *date*?"

"Well, unless you have other plans, of course. I've taken the liberty of checking and I know you're not involved with anyone at present. So what do you say? Dinner at my place Friday?"

"At the White House?"

"That is where I live, yes."

"Well, uh . . . I'd be honored, ma'am."

"Kathy."

"It would be my pleasure . . . Kathy."

"Good. I'll be entertaining some very special guests I'm sure you would enjoy meeting. Cocktails at six sharp. Black tie."

"I'll be there."

"Great, I'm looking forward to it. Good night, Pete."

"Good night, Madame Pres . . . uh . . . Kathy."

She chuckled and hung up the phone.

Manly sat there just staring at the receiver. "Damn," he said. "I'd better get my suit pressed."

\*     \*     \*

They sat at their usual table in the back of Lovecraft's, pitchers of dark Guinness stout before them. Morrison Gonzago looked down at the table mournfully.

"So that's it, then?" he said. "You're just going to disappear and I'm never going to hear from you again?"

"Oh, I didn't say that," Makepeace replied. "You're my best friend, Gonzo. You may hear from me, in time. But I shall have to be discreet. And it really would be for the best if you did not know where I was. Or who I was, in my new identity."

"Won't be the same around here without you," said Gonzago, shaking his head. "When are you leaving?"

"Tonight."

"Already? What about that dinner at the White House?"

"I fear that you shall have to communicate my regrets to the President," Makepeace said. "But I think it would be for the best if I made myself scarce as quickly as possible. I'm the last immortal now. For the moment, they may feel gratitude toward me, but it won't be very long before that wears off and they start to worry about me, because I have more power than any of their registered adepts. And I will always be different. People tend to mistrust those who are different. Especially when they're only part human. Who knows, perhaps there are others like me somewhere, half-breed fairy survivors, hiding among human society. And if there are any of us left, besides myself, I'd like to try and seek them out."

"I'll miss you, my friend."

"I'll miss you, too, Gonzo. But I'll get in touch someday, if I can. Meanwhile, here's something to remember me by."

Makepeace placed a small leather pouch on the table between them. Gonzago picked it up, opened the drawstrings, and shook out three gems into his palm—a sapphire, an emerald, and a ruby.

"So . . . the famous runestones," he said, gazing down at them. "They look so ordinary."

"They are now," Makepeace replied. "The magic's gone. They're just ordinary precious stones. But I thought you might like to have them."

"What happened to them?" asked Gonzago, looking up at him. "Where did they all go? The ones who survived, I mean."

"Here," said Makepeace, touching his heart.

"In *you?*"

"Their energy replenished me," said Makepeace. "They were hurt and severely weakened. And I was dying. I thought I had a lot more time, but I was wrong. My sensitivity had begun to fade. That was the first sign. I should have noticed it, but what with everything else that was happening, I suppose I just didn't pay very close attention. And then, toward the end, I became injured and I used up about all the life force I had left in the battle with the dragons. Healing Rafe pretty much finished me. I was already dying when the surviving spirits of the Council brought Rafe and the others up out of the cavern. Between what little fading life force I had left and theirs, we had just about enough to effect a merging."

"So then . . . does that mean you're a true immortal now?"

Makepeace shrugged. "Perhaps, but I'm not really sure. All I know is that I'm different. I always was, and I always will be. I'm a fairy," he added with a smile, "and the world has grown much too mundane for fairies."

Gonzago sighed. "I wish you didn't have to go."

"I'm afraid I must."

"You know, I don't even know your real name."

"It's Puck."

Gonzago stared at him. "*Puck?* You're kidding."

"Nope. That's my true name."

"Like in Shakespeare?"

"It was his idea, actually, to use my name for that character. I thought it amusing at the time, and could not think of a better one, so I used it. Will liked to feel that he was making a contribution every now and then, since his name was on the plays. And I didn't really mind. He was a drunken Elizabethan actor who was charming company, but not terribly literate."

Gonzago's jaw dropped. "Aw, no! You mean to tell me it was *you*?"

"There are more things in Heaven and Earth, my dear Gonzo, than are dreamt of in your philosophy," said Makepeace. "Including fairies."

Gonzago stared down into his glass morosely and shook his head. "All these years and you never told me. How the hell am I supposed to teach that course now?"

Makepeace got up and placed his hand on his friend's shoulder. "The same way you've always taught it. From the heart. The author doesn't matter. The stories are what count."

"Even if they're fairy tales?" Gonzago said with a snort.

"Clap your hands if you believe." The reply came like an echo.

Gonzago looked up.

Makepeace was gone.

"I'll be damned," Gonzago said. And then everyone in the bar turned to stare at him as he started to applaud.

## ABOUT THE AUTHOR

Simon Hawke became a full-time writer in 1978 and has over sixty novels to his credit. He received a BA in Communications from Hofstra University and an MA in English from Western New Mexico University. He teaches writing at Pima College in Tucson, Arizona.

Hawke lives alone in a secluded Santa Fe-style home in the Sonoran desert about thirty-five miles west of Tucson, near Kitt Peak and the Tohono O'odham Indian Reservation. He is a motorcyclist, and his other interests include history, metaphysics, gardening, and collecting fantasy art.

# Welcome to a Fantastic World of Danger and Intrigue!

Simon Hawke takes you where you've never dreamed . . . into a fantasy universe of wizards, wonder and terrifying excitement.

**THE NINE LIVES OF CATSEYE GOMEZ**
☐ (0-446-36-241-7, $4.99, USA) ($5.99 Can.)

**THE RELUCTANT SORCERER**
☐ (0-446-36-260-3, $4.99, USA) ($5.99 Can.)

**THE SAMURAI WIZARD**
☐ (0-446-36-132-1, $4.99, USA) ($5.99 Can.)

**THE WHIMS OF CREATION**
☐ (0-446-36-518-1, $5.50, USA) ($6.99 Can.)

**THE WIZARD OF CAMELOT**
☐ (0-446-36-242-5, $4.99, USA) ($5.99 Can.)

**THE WIZARD OF 4TH STREET**
☐ (0-445-20-842-2, $5.99, USA) ($6.99 Can.)

**THE WIZARD OF LOVECRAFT'S CAFE**
☐ (0-446-36-517-3, $4.99, USA) ($5.99 Can.)

**THE WIZARD OF SUNSET STRIP**
☐ (0-446-20-702-7, $3.95, USA, $5 Can.)

**THE WIZARD OF WHITECHAPEL**
☐ (0-446-20-304-8, $4.99, USA) ($ an.)

**THE AMBIVALENT MAGICIAN**
☐ (0-446-36-521-1, $5.99, USA) ($6.99 Can.)

Available at a bookstore near you from
Warner Books.

ALSO BY SIMON HAWKE

*The Nine Lives of Catseye Gomez*
*The Reluctant Sorcerer*
*The Samurai Wizard*
*The Whims of Creation*
*The Wizard of Camelot*
*The Wizard of 4th Street*
*The Wizard of Lovecraft's Cafe*
*The Wizard of Sunset Strip*
*The Wizard of Whitechapel*
*The Ambivalent Magician*

Published by
WARNER BOOKS

# "CHOOSE TO BE STRONG, MARIA. TAKE HIS POWER AND MAKE IT YOURS."

**S**he murmured a spell under her breath and her eyes began to glow.

"Maria!" Joey shouted. "*Don't!*"

Joey Medina's body went limp and then collapsed to the cavern floor as the glow faded from Maria's eyes. Talon watched her as she breathed heavily through parted lips, her chest heaving as she trembled with the delirious sensation of the life force coursing through her. It was like no high she had ever experienced before.

"*God* . . ." she whispered, as she closed her eyes in ecstasy.

Talon smiled. There would be a very different sort of hunger for Maria from now on. She would be hooked on necromancy as no drug had ever addicted her before. She was the perfect predator.

"Go and rest now," he told her. "For a time, everything will feel strange to you. Your perceptions shall be clearer, sharper; your senses shall be more acute. You will need time to become accustomed to your new strength."

As she left, Talon walked around to the other side of the stalagmite where Rafe was held immobile. The others were all dead, their life energies consumed by acolytes Talon had selected, the first of his new necromancers . . .